"There is no friend as loyal as a book."
– Ernest Hemingway

Christmas in

Sugar Land

~ Collection One ~

By

Karen Sue Burns

~Four romantic and heartwarming Christmas themed stories featuring fictional residents of Sugar Land, Texas~

With Enriched Content

Copyright

ISBN 978-0-98960-273-0

<u>Credits</u>

Editors — Lori Leger (Cajunflair Publishing) and Rae Renzi

Cover — The Killion Group

Cover Photo — "SugarLandTXCityHall" by WhisperToMe - Own work. Licensed under Public domain via Wikimedia Commons.

Christmas themed graphics – Purchased from www.123rf.com, credit for profiles in order: dimdimich/yurkina/nenovbrothers/piep600/dimdimich.

<u>Notes</u>

"The Christmas Star" was previously published in 2012 by Cajunflair Publishing under this book: *Seasons of Love – Book 1*. It has been updated for this collection.

"Christmas by Candlelight" was previously published in 2013 by Cajunflair Publishing under this book/story title: *Seasons of Love – Book 4 – "A Heart Awakens."* It has been updated for this collection.

For Mom, who was my biggest fan, and never failed to say a kind word about my writing, even when it sucked.

Welcome!

Thank you for purchasing my first collection of romantic Christmas stories centered in Sugar Land, Texas. The text of this book has additional "Enriched Content" that includes pictures, recipes, and author notes all related to one of the four stories.

When this additional material is relevant to the action in a story, I've included the page number in brackets—[*See EC on page XX*]—for the location of the related matter in the Enriched Content section at the back of this book. An outline of all the Enriched Content is provided on page 263.

Of course, you have the option to proceed through the story without checking out the Enriched Content while reading. The choice is yours.

I'd appreciate hearing from you as to your opinion about this type of content and the notation of it throughout the text of each story. Please use the contact page on my website to email me: www.karensueburns.com.

Again, thank you, and I hope you enjoy ***Christmas in Sugar Land.***

Table of Contents

THE CHRISTMAS STAR

The Perfect Tree

A cloudless sky shimmered over Sugar Land, Texas and set the perfect mood for Christmas tree shopping. Buying a fresh tree, as opposed to one out of a box, was a ritual for Meg Wilson and her seven year-old daughter, Emma. Meg had money in her pocket that she'd saved all year for their holiday decorations, and the time had arrived to spend it.

She parked along the street, close to the nursery's entrance. "Come on, let's go shopping."

"Okay, Mama." Emma scampered out of their SUV and took her mother's hand. "I'm so excited I can hardly breathe."

Meg squeezed her daughter's hand as they entered the tree lot. At first glance it seemed like a chaotic mess. As they walked down the rows, Meg realized the nursery was organized into varieties of trees and then sizes. She didn't know one type from another, but she did know what she liked—a very green tree with full branches that stood about six feet high.

Two weeks before Christmas Eve, Meg and Emma hunted for their holiday tree with the intensity of a Houston Texans quarterback, focused and determined to make the right play to win the game, or in this case, light up their family room.

Emma pulled her mother down one row and then another. "Mama, I like every tree. How will we ever decide on just one?"

"I think we'll know when we find it."

They turned down another row, and Emma stopped walking. She pointed to a beautiful tree.

"That's the one."

Meg studied the tree, it did look good. But she didn't want to make a mistake. They had to find the perfect tree to make up for last Christmas when Meg had been an emotional wreck.

"You may be right. Let's check a few more to be one-hundred percent sure."

Five minutes later, they were back at the same spot. A man and a young girl were looking at their tree.

"You can't have that one, it's ours," Emma shouted.

"Emma," Meg said. "That is impolite. Apologize."

The man had an understanding look in his hazel eyes as he looked from Emma to Meg. "Not to worry. We understand how a tree can speak to you. We actually found one around the corner and we're making sure it's the right one."

"Oh, we were doing the same thing. But Emma, you still need to say you're sorry."

Emma looked at the ground, one tennis shoe clad foot scraping at the dirt. She looked up, a single tear rolling down her cheek. "I'm sorry, mister. It's just that, uh . . . I really want that tree for our house." She tugged on her mother's sleeve. "Please, Mama, that's the tree to take home."

The man leaned over and spoke directly to Emma. "Then that's the tree you need for your house. Right, Kasey?"

"Yep, I agree. When you find the right tree you have to take it home." Kasey grabbed his arm and shook it. "Come on Dad, we need get *our* tree before someone else buys it."

He let his daughter pull him away, then looked back over his shoulder and shot Meg a wink. "Merry Christmas, ladies."

Meg and Emma waved them off with a jovial "Merry Christmas!" After their departure, Meg bent down low in front of Emma. "Sweetie, you know what you said was rude, right?"

Emma nodded, her chin tipped against her chest. "I'm sorry."

Meg let out a sigh of relief. She worried night and day that the lack of a father would have a negative impact on Emma's upbringing, no matter how hard she tried to function as both parents.

Meg gave her a quick hug, then stood. "Okay, we need

to get this tree bought and on top of the car."

The drive home was filled with laughter and songs, *Jingle Bells* being a favorite.

"I have a Christmas joke for you," Emma said. "Would you like to hear it?"

"Absolutely," Meg said as the SUV turned onto their street.

"Alton Bodeene told me at recess. What is red and white and round all over?"

"Hmm, that's a tough one." Meg grinned. "I'll say . . . Santa Claus."

Emma burst out laughing. "Noooooo, it's a red apple with a white ribbon around it."

"Oh." Meg groaned silently. "That's a good one." She pulled in their driveway, parked next to her mother's red sedan, and honked the horn. "Granny's here."

"Whoopee." Emma ran to the front door as her grandmother stepped onto the porch.

"Looks like you got your tree, Emma Bug." Ellen Wilson hugged her granddaughter and walked with her to the driveway.

Meg had untied the ropes holding the tree. "Glad you're here, Mom. I can use your help."

"I figured you might need some extra muscle."

"I can help, too," Emma said, jumping up and down.

Meg easily pulled the tree from the roof so it stood straight up, leaning against the back of the vehicle.

"This is the plan. Mom, you take the top of the tree, and I'll take the bottom. Emma, you keep the front door open, and we'll carry it straight to the family room."

Ellen nodded and Emma ran to the porch.

"I don't think this will be too heavy for us," Meg said. "You ready?"

"Let's do it."

And they did. Within a minute, the tree rested on the family room rug with three Wilson women staring at it.

"Getting it upright in the holder is the hardest part," Ellen said.

"I have a new holder this year. A super-duper one as the guy at the hardware store told me."

"A super-duper holder," Emma repeated and danced next to the tree. "I can help. Please let me help."

"You may," Ellen said with a wide grin, her blue eyes twinkling. "Let's get this tree decorated. I brought cookies and hot chocolate for the after-the-tree-is-up party."

One hour later, with minimal drama, the tree was up, watered, and had lights strung around its branches. Meg plugged in the twinkly lights.

"Wow, that is beautiful." Emma eyed the tree with the critique of a holiday designer.

"I agree, baby girl," Ellen said. "How about a cookie before we tackle the ornaments?"

"Yes, please."

"We do deserve a break," Meg said, "Cookies for everyone."

~~*

On Monday morning, Meg arrived at work ten minutes early and decided to treat herself to a mocha coffee to take to her office. The best features of her high-rise office building were the specialty coffee shop and the first-rate deli next to it.

She worked as an accounting supervisor for a mega

commercial real estate company. She counted her blessings each and every day for having a fantastic job with a great boss. She'd passed the CPA exam over a year ago and hoped it would lead to being promoted to manager within the upcoming year.

The coffee shop had a long line queuing to the order window, and she stepped to its end. Almost every table was filled with customers either reading a newspaper or hunched over a laptop computer. How did people have so much time in the morning to read or surf the web? She tapped a foot, now concerned she'd be late. Thankfully, the line moved quickly.

"Hello."

Meg turned at the sound of a male voice. The man behind her looked vaguely familiar. "Hi."

"Did you get your Christmas tree decorated?"

She then recognized him from the tree lot on Saturday—dirty blond hair and broad shoulders. "Sure did. I'm sorry my daughter was over the top about it."

"Like I said, not to worry." He smiled, displaying perfect white teeth and a sexy curve to his lips. "I'm Ben Abbott, by the way. You come here often?"

"Every once in a while. I'm Meg Wilson. I work on the eighth floor."

"Really?" he said. "My office is on the fourteenth floor—Jones, Smith, and Abbott at your service."

"You're an attorney."

"Guilty as charged. The Abbott in the name is my father. He's not ready to add another Abbott to the letterhead."

"Oh, that's too bad." Meg moved forward as the line

shortened.

"Nah, part of the game with my father. Must pay my dues. I'd do the same with my own son."

"You have a son in addition to your daughter?"

He shook his head. "No, Kasey is my only child."

"Maybe you should talk with your wife about having a son." She caught her breath as something resembling pain, or regret, flashed across his face.

"No wife. She died when Kasey was born."

Meg wanted to disappear. "I'm so sorry." Thankfully, she'd reached the counter—saved from making another foolish comment. She placed her order and reached for her wallet.

Ben leaned around her. "Add a tall black coffee." He handed the clerk a bill.

Meg turned toward him. "Thank you." Ben's kindness after her remark about a son had her so flustered she dropped her wallet. Ben retrieved it for her. She soon had her coffee and once again turned to him, holding up the cup. "Thanks. Maybe I'll see you again, and I can return the favor. I must get to work. Have a good day."

She hurried to the elevator, praying she could get on before Ben had time to get there. He made her nervous, plain and simple. And why did she say she'd return the favor? Obviously, she'd lost her mind.

For the next two days, Meg managed to avoid Ben coming and going from the building and the parking garage. She'd never seen him before, but now she was vigilant of everyone in an elevator. Avoiding him would keep her from making another stupid comment.

No such luck on Wednesday. She was leaving the deli

with a salad and a soft drink and nearly collided with him as he entered.

"Meg, good to see you again." Ben's lips curved in a sexy grin.

"Nice to see you, too."

"You come here often?"

"Only when I forget to bring my lunch, it's too expensive every day."

He pointed to her left hand. "Your ring, it's beautiful."

She looked at her hand. "That's my grandmother's ring. It doesn't fit any other finger."

"Oh, you're not married then."

Meg nodded as a man behind Ben slapped his hand on the door jam and loudly cleared his throat. "Hey man, you gonna block the entrance all day?"

Ben moved aside.

"I better get going. Nice seeing you again." She once again hurried to the elevators. She didn't look back. It was too weird seeing him twice in three days.

She knew exactly why he made her so nervous, easy answer to that. She punched the Up button and the doors opened. On the way to her office, she thought about Ben. He was the kind of man she'd always thought she'd marry—good looking, likes kids, and with a good job.

Entering her tidy office, she shook her head. Her childish thoughts about the right man for her were just that, juvenile. She had no business thinking about Ben in the first place. Giving Emma a fantastic Christmas was her only priority.

She'd messed up so badly last year after John had broken their engagement the day before Christmas. You'd think that after two years of dating and being engaged for a year, she would have known him better. But no, he'd surprised her and she'd launched into an emotional tailspin that had left Emma wondering why her mother cried so much and Ellen shaking her head in dismay as Meg ruined the holiday for all three of them.

She sat at her desk with resolve and determination. She would make this Christmas the best one ever with no emotion and no tears over a broken engagement. She'd think long and hard before getting involved in another relationship. Right then, her heart needed protection.

The Right Decision

"M-o-o-o-m, we're going to be late." Emma rushed to her mother.

"I'm ready. I had to fix the halo for your costume." Meg rose from the dining room table and wrapped the halo in white tissue paper and carefully stowed it in a tote bag. She then draped the white angel robe over her arm. "Come on, we'll be late if we don't leave now."

Meg poked her head in the kitchen. Ellen was drinking coffee. "Mom, time to get this show on the road."

They piled into the SUV and made it to Highlands Elementary in less than ten minutes. The parking lot was full of parents and students rushing into the school. The annual Christmas pageant was scheduled to start in fifteen minutes and it looked as though more people were late than not.

Inside the school, Ellen went to secure seats while Meg

hustled Emma to the teacher's lounge. They found Mrs. Rogers, Emma's second grade teacher, marking names off of a list.

"Emma, good, you're here," she said in a soft voice. "Mrs. Wilson, would you mind helping her put on the costume? The wings are on the chair behind you. I need to find our three Wise Men."

"Will do," Meg said. "Let's get you dressed."

Once her coat was off, Meg slid the white angel robe over Emma's head. She found the wings made of wire, chiffon, and sequins. Ribbon straps fit over Emma's shoulders, crossed over her chest, and tied in back.

Emma turned around to face her mother. "How do I look?"

"Oh, sweetie, you look like the prettiest angel ever, of all time, in the whole-wide world." Meg's heart welled at the picture of her little daughter with shining blue eyes, spaghetti straight brown hair, and sweet smile.

"Really? I do?"

"Yes, you do. Let's add the halo." Meg unwrapped the gold halo and placed it on Emma's head. "Now, you are the complete angel." She dug her phone out of her purse and snapped a few pictures as Emma posed.

Mrs. Rogers clapped her hands. "Okay angels, I need you to line up behind me."

"Show time, Emma," Meg said. "I'll go find Granny. We'll see you after the pageant." She kissed her daughter's cheek. "Get in line and have fun."

"I will, Mama." Emma walked carefully, with one hand on the halo, and lined up behind Mrs. Rogers.

Meg gave her a quick wave then made her way to the

cafeteria to find her mother.

Ellen had found excellent seats in the fourth row of folding chairs.

"Is she nervous?" Ellen asked.

"I don't think so." Meg glanced around the cafeteria. It buzzed with excitement as parents and grandparents anticipated the show's opening.

Meg prayed that Emma would remember her one line and where to stand on stage. Surely the butterflies in her stomach would go away once the show began.

The lights flashed, signaling everyone to be seated. A minute later, the lights dimmed and the principal walked on stage in front of the red curtain.

"Welcome to Highlands Elementary annual Christmas pageant. Our teachers and students have worked hard over the past month to bring you a fantastic evening. I'm sure you'll enjoy it. Now, on with the show." She walked a few steps, and then turned back to the audience. "I forgot to mention that recordings and photos are perfectly acceptable." *[See EC on page 264]*

The crowd clapped as the curtain opened. The pageant began with the school choir singing *Joy to the World*. Meg settled back in her chair to enjoy the show. She knew it would be at least ten minutes before Emma came on stage.

An hour later, the pageant was over and the crowd enthusiastically clapped as the teachers and students crowded onto the stage after the entire room sang *Jingle Bells*. Meg couldn't have been prouder of Emma, who'd 'on-staged' with precision and clearly recited her single line.

"What a wonderful pageant," Ellen whispered in Meg's

ear. "Emma was the prettiest angel on stage."

Meg nodded. "I think so, too."

"The little girl who sang *Silent Night* has a beautiful voice."

"I agree and she's cute, too." Meg thought she looked familiar but couldn't remember where she'd seen her. Maybe it was at one of the birthday parties Emma had attended.

The curtain closed and the lights came on in the cafeteria. "It'll take us a few minutes to get out of here," Meg said. "We're supposed to meet Emma at her classroom."

They fell in line and slowly made their way through the crowded hallway. At last they reached the classroom and found twenty students drinking juice, nibbling cookies, and talking non-stop. Emma had taken off her costume and dumped it on her desk. She was gesturing with her hands and laughing with another student when they found her.

"Emma Bug, you were wonderful." Ellen hugged her granddaughter.

"Thanks, Granny. Mrs. Rogers said we were the best second grade class she's ever had."

Meg hugged Emma next. "You were a fantastic angel. You said your line just the way you practiced, good job."

"I remembered that you said to have fun. If you're having fun you don't have time to be nervous."

Meg exchanged smiles with her mother. Emma seemed to have wisdom beyond her years.

"Put your coat on." Meg pulled it from the tote and added the discarded costume. "Let's go home. I promised you popcorn and a movie after the pageant."

Emma clapped her hands. "Yes, you did."

Back in the hallway, they had an easier time getting to the school's front entrance.

Near the door, Emma called out "Kasey," and ran over to another student. Meg followed her and bumped into Ben.

"What are you doing here?" Meg asked, surprised to see Ben at Emma's school.

"My daughter goes to school here."

Meg stared at Kasey as recognition dawned. "So she's the child who sang *Silent Night*. I knew I'd seen that face somewhere." She smiled at Ben. "Her voice is beautiful."

"I think so, too. She gets it from her mother."

"Not you?"

"No way, I can't even sing in the shower."

"Same with me, can't carry a tune."

"Listen," Ben said moving closer to her. "If you're not busy tomorrow night, would you like to have dinner with me?"

"Dinner?" Meg's hand flew to her chest. Ben had asked her to dinner . . . on a date, a real date.

"Yes." He smiled at her. "Will the day work for you?"

"Sure, I guess so." She could have kicked herself for sounding blasé and tried again. "I'd love to have dinner with you."

"Great, I can pick you up at seven."

"I'll meet you at the restaurant. That will be easier for me." Driving herself would give her the leeway to leave if Ben was a dud as a dinner companion.

"Great. I'll meet you at Charley's in Sugar Land at seven tomorrow evening."

"It's a date." She motioned to her daughter with one

hand. "Emma, we need to get on home."

Emma trotted over to her mother and waved at Kasey as Meg flashed a parting smile at Ben. They rejoined Ellen, who stared curiously after Ben.

"Who was that?"

Meg hustled Emma toward their car. "He works in my building."

"Really?"

"Uh-huh. By the way, can Emma stay with you tomorrow night?"

"Sure, you have a hot date?"

Meg grinned. "Something like that."

~~*

In the last twenty-four hours, Meg's attitude had transitioned from trying to avoid Ben, to excitement at the prospect of dining with him. For one, she was hungry and had heard good things about Charley's. Then, there was the fact that it had been over a year since she'd been on a date. That explained why she'd tried on ten different outfits in the past hour since Ellen had picked up Emma.

She finally decided on a black pantsuit that nipped in at the waist, a red V-neck sweater, and chunky heels. Since Ben was tall, high heels weren't a problem for the usual man-woman-height dilemma.

She spritzed her favorite perfume in the air and walked through it. A quick glance at her watch told her she had enough time to get to the restaurant and order a glass of wine before Ben arrived. She wanted to be totally relaxed before he made an appearance.

~~*

Ben stuffed the valet ticket in the pocket of his navy sports jacket and entered Charley's. He went straight to the bar for a glass of wine before Meg arrived. Once he'd ordered a cabernet, he looked at himself in the mirror behind the bar and smoothed back his hair. He'd changed his shirt five times, which was silly, and finally settled on a white one.

He couldn't remember his last date. His mother harped on him at least once a month but his top priority had always been Kasey, not dating. Although, he did miss—

"Ben! You're early, too."

He'd been so lost in his thoughts he didn't realize Meg had slipped onto the bar stool next to him.

"Sorry, I didn't see you walk in." Ben liked what he saw. She was beautiful—dark hair that curled around her face, bright blue eyes, and lips that . . . well, he wouldn't start thinking in that direction, just yet.

"Traffic was lighter than I expected. Would you like something to drink?"

She pointed to his glass. "I'll have one of those."

Ben ordered another glass of wine before turning back to her. "How was your day?"

"The usual, including Saturday chores."

"Same here, grocery shopping and laundry."

"Oh, you do laundry?'

Ben loved that teasing tone of Meg's—the way she tilted her head, causing a lock of hair to fall against her cheek. He reached up, using one finger to gently brush the hair back from her face. The bartender placed her glass of wine on the counter, and Ben smiled at the hint of a blush on her cheeks as she reached for it.

He tapped his glass against hers, somewhat surprised there was a woman alive who still blushed. "Here's to a good evening."

"Cheers." She sipped the wine. "Very nice."

"Did your daughter have fun at the pageant last night?"

"She did. I thought she was the cutest angel on stage."

"I agree. She takes after her mom."

"Thank you. Kasey was the hit of the show though. She sang beautifully."

A hostess tapped Ben on the shoulder. "Mr. Abbott, your table is ready. Bring your wine, we'll transfer the tab."

Meg and Ben rose and followed the hostess to the blue and gold dining room. Most of the tables were occupied, yet the noise level was subdued. They were seated in a cozy corner, at a table with a small poinsettia in the middle. Red and green plaid placemats over a red tablecloth added to the holiday decor.

Meg placed her wine glass on the table before she sat in the chair Ben pulled out for her. "Thank you."

Once he was seated, the hostess handed each of them a menu with a blue dolphin on the dark leather cover. "Enjoy your evening." She smiled and disappeared to the front of the restaurant.

Meg sipped her wine and glanced at Ben from above the top of her menu. "I've never been here before. What's good?"

"Everything on the menu is excellent. What's your favorite? Chicken, beef or seafood?"

"How about a salad?"

"That comes with the chicken, beef or seafood."

"I see." Meg grinned. He didn't care what she ate so long as she wasn't one of those women who picked at her food.

"I'm a beef man myself," he said with a slight nod.

"In that case, I think I'll have seafood."

"You will, will you?"

~~*

Meg loved Ben's sense of humor. "Yes, I will. I'll have grilled shrimp and a Caesar salad."

Ben chuckled. "Good choice."

After placing their orders, she sat in silence, trying to come up with an opening line to a non-intrusive conversation. She was dying to ask why he hadn't remarried after the death of his wife. Maybe he didn't think another woman could replace her. That made sense.

"Do you date much?" he asked.

And *she* worried about being too nosy.

"Not much lately," she replied. "Busy at work and taking care of Emma. You know how it goes, not enough hours in the day."

"Yes, I do. May I ask you a personal question?"

"Sure, doesn't mean I'll answer though."

"Fair enough. Where's Emma's father?"

"I figured that question would come around." Meg wondered how much she should share. Could she trust Ben with such a private story? She didn't know. She hardly knew him. On the other hand he was an attorney and paid to keep a confidence.

"Emma's father died in Iraq."

"I'm sorry to hear that. How long were you married?"

"We weren't married. I got pregnant my senior year of college and graduated before I gave birth. It wasn't a love affair. Just good friends celebrating too much and not taking precautions."

"Was he a father to her?"

"He saw her a few times." Meg sipped her wine and gathered her thoughts. "He sent me money when he could. I didn't hassle him. He joined the Marines right after we graduated. Always said he'd make it up to Emma once his last tour was over."

"I'm really sorry. It can't be easy for you."

"My mother has been fantastic." Meg said a prayer of thanks every day that her mother lived close by and loved spending time with Emma. "You're a single parent, too. Raising Kasey alone must be trying at times."

"You're right." Ben nodded with a slight curve to his mouth. "Single parenting isn't the ideal situation. I've done my best and so far, so good."

"Same here. I'm not looking forward to the teenage years. I hear those can be rough."

"We were both teenagers, and we turned out okay."

"That we did." Meg liked Ben. He was smart and a good father. Two qualities she admired.

The conversation turned to more mundane topics after their dinner was served. Meg tasted her salad then bit into a shrimp. She closed her eyes, savoring the perfect combination of spices and grilled crustacean.

"My gosh, this is delicious," she said.

"Told you so."

Meg laughed. "Are you always right?"

"I try to do the right thing. Uphold the law and all that."

"That must be complicated. Being an attorney, I mean."

"Probably just as complicated as being a CPA."

"I'm not official yet," she explained, wondering when she'd told him she was an accountant. "I have another year before I can apply for my license. But yes, we have rules that are the law to us. What type of law do you practice?"

"The firm does criminal, personal injury, family, and corporate. I tend to do more family law like wills, estates and trusts, and wealth planning."

"So . . . if I were to win the lottery, I should talk to you before I pick up my winnings?"

"Absolutely. The funds going to a trust helps with the tax issues."

"That's what I've heard." She loved his straightforward response. "Guess I should start buying tickets."

"Yep, that would be the first step." Ben grinned, a flash of humor crossing his face. "What do you do for fun?"

"Fun? Good question. My time is devoted to my job, my daughter, and keeping up my house. I don't do much without Emma."

"Surely you and Emma do things that are fun."

"Of course we do," Meg said. "What *do you do* for fun?"

"To be honest, I'm like you. The most fun I have without Kasey is going to the gym."

"Sounds like we're both in a work-home-work-home rut." Meg hadn't considered that a single father would have the same issues as she did.

"You're right. Maybe we can work at changing that."

"How? I have only twenty-four hours in my day and they're already full."

"Cut out sleeping?" Ben teased.

"I'd be a zombie in no time. How would you add more fun to your life?"

"Ask you out for a second date."

Heat from yet another blush spread across Meg's face. She did her best to ignore it. "Yes, you could do that. What would we do for the fun part of the date?"

"The fun factor is a relative thing," Ben said lightly. "This is the season of gifts under the Christmas tree so how about some shopping and then a bite to eat afterward?"

Meg considered the suggestion for two seconds. "That sounds great. I do have more shopping to do. When?"

"Are you free Tuesday after work? I can meet you at the First Colony Mall."

"That works for me." Meg nearly melted with joy, her heart opening a sliver. He wanted to see her again. But wait, this was only date number two, no reason to get giddy. She could finish her shopping and have fun, too—a win-win on all sides.

"Great. I could use your advice on a gift for Kasey."

The conversation turned to the perfect Christmas presents for grade school daughters. Meg enjoyed hearing a man's point of view. He was very tuned into his daughter's personality, which translated to "good father" in Meg's world.

~~*

Ben walked beside Meg out of the restaurant, wondering when he'd last had such a fantastic Saturday evening. She was cute as hell, serious, funny, and focused. They arrived at the valet stand just outside the entrance and Ben asked for her ticket.

She retrieved it from a pocket and Ben handed it and

his ticket to the valet. He hardly had time to make small talk before her vehicle arrived. He walked her to the driver's door to say good-bye, trying to decide if he should kiss her.

She smiled at him and he made his decision. He leaned forward and kissed her lips. "Drive carefully. Send me a text so I know you arrived home safely."

Meg looked at him with wide eyes and the hint of a smile. Good, he'd made the right decision. She climbed in the SUV and drove off, waving at him. Yep, he'd definitely made the right decision.

Cinnamon and Sugar Plums

On Sunday morning, Meg knocked on her mother's front door before letting herself inside.

"Mom, it's me."

"In the kitchen."

Meg found her mother at the stove. "Wow, you're cooking?"

Ellen turned with a spatula in her hand. "Yes, I do cook sometimes. I'm making pancakes for Emma."

"Where is she?"

"In the shower, she slept late."

"Is that because she stayed up late last night?" Meg already knew the answer.

"Maybe, but it's the weekend. She needs to live a little."

Meg poured a cup of coffee. "You're right. She was good for you?"

"Always."

"Could you watch her on Tuesday evening? I'm going to finish my Christmas shopping and have dinner with Ben."

"Sure . . . wait, I may need to change a date. But that's not a problem."

"Mom, don't change your plans for me."

"It's no big deal, he'll understand."

"Is that a date with your mystery man?" Meg had been miffed for months that her mother kept him away from her and Emma.

"Meg, don't be childish."

"Childish? How can you say that? Is it wrong for a daughter to want to meet the man her fifty-something year-old mother has been dating for a year? Promise me you won't elope."

"That's silly." Ellen rolled her eyes.

"Not any sillier than leaving your daughter and grand-daughter out of your life. Don't you trust us?"

Ellen stacked pancakes on a plate and set them on the counter in front of Meg. "I truly don't understand you. Why would you think I don't trust you?"

"You've been dating a man for a year and haven't introduced him to your family." Meg folded paper napkins as she talked. "You're still young and could get married again. You'd do that without me knowing my new step-father?"

Ellen put her hand up. "Stop right there. I am not getting married so erase that thought from your head."

"Then what are you doing?"

"I'm feeling my way, that's all. I don't want to subject

you to someone who's here today and gone tomorrow."
Ellen's mouth quivered.

"After a year? Seems to me you're the one who's unsure of how you feel about this man."

"Please, try to understand my position."

"Whatever. I'm going to check on Emma."

Meg found her brushing her hair in the bedroom.

"Hey, sweetie, did you have fun with Granny?"

She ran to Meg and hugged her. "Mama, we had so much fun. She showed me how to make sloppy Joes and then we watched two movies."

Meg picked up Emma's pink duffle bag and ruffled her hair. "Come on, Granny made pancakes for you."

Emma skipped to the kitchen with Meg behind her. "Yay, I love pancakes. Granny, what kind did you make?"

"What's your favorite?" Ellen asked, pouring orange juice.

"Chocolate chip," Emma said.

"Then you're in luck. Sit at the counter and I'll get your breakfast." Ellen placed pancakes and bacon on Emma's favorite pink plate. "Here you go. Bon appétit."

"I know what that means. Julia somebody said it at the end of her TV show," Emma said.

"Where in the world did you see that?" Meg asked.

"Kasey and I are friends now, and she told me at lunch. She said she and her dad have a DVD to learn how to cook. She said one of the shows was on how to cook fish, and it was gross."

Ellen winked at Meg. "Hmm, a man who likes to cook, I like that."

Meg sipped her coffee in silence.

~~*

On Monday evening, Meg shut the door to Emma's room after the nightly bath ritual and a goodnight kiss. She hummed to herself as she put a load of whites into the washing machine. It had been a good day.

Her office had enjoyed the annual potluck Christmas lunch with a variety of dishes. Meg took stuffed mushrooms that everyone seemed to like. It was a new recipe, and she'd added it to her stockpile of go-to recipes.

The highlight had been the delivery of flowers as the luncheon ended. Her co-workers teased her mercilessly about a new beau. Once the yellow roses were in her office, she opened the card: "Enjoyed our dinner, looking forward to shopping with you—Best, Ben."

The flowers sat on the corner of her desk, reminding her of Ben's kindness. She'd glanced at them all afternoon. She rarely received flowers and was flattered Ben had thought to send them.

She'd brought one of the roses home and set it in a bud vase on the kitchen counter. The right thing to do was to call Ben and personally thank him for the flowers. Was that too forward? No, it was being polite. She pulled her cell phone out of her purse and found Ben's number in her contacts.

"Hello." Ben sounded out of breath.

"It's Meg. Is this a bad time?"

"No, I was doing pushups and ran downstairs."

"I thought you went to the gym."

"I do. This is my nightly ritual."

"Oh." Meg tried not to imagine how he looked, wanting to stay on script. "I called to thank you for the flowers."

"You're welcome. I hope you're not allergic to roses."

"Nope, they're one of my favorites."

"Good. I made a guess. My mother says every woman likes roses."

"She's right. Does she have any other words of wisdom?" Meg nestled into the sofa, curling her legs under her.

"Words of wisdom? My mother has an opinion on everything. Name a topic and she has a view on it."

"I think I'd like your mom. Not enough women speak up." Meg realized she knew little about his family.

"Oh, yeah, she has no problem keeping my father in line." Ben laughed. "Poor dad hasn't figured out she rules the family."

"She sounds like a strong person, like her son."

"I guess so. The Abbotts have a tendency to speak up, especially when we watch football together."

"What's your favorite team?" Meg loved football.

"The Houston Texans, of course."

"Of course. Emma watches the games with me. We make snacks and have an indoor tailgating party."

"I bet Emma enjoys that. Have you been to a game?"

"No, we watch on TV." Meg felt so comfortable talking to Ben. "What else do you like besides football?"

"I play golf, but not very good. My brother Jack is the golfer. He's on the team at USC and hopes to make it a career."

"Hmm, you have a talented family."

"Right, I guess," Ben said. "Then there's my older sister who refused to go to college, eloped at nineteen, and has four kids now. She has a blog for mothers and loves dishing out wisdom on motherhood."

"I wish I had extra hours to read blogs like that." Meg cringed at her words—she'd complained again about not having enough time.

"I can send you the link. It's funny."

"I'd like that. Maybe I should write a blog on single working mothers and juggling all the things in my life."

"I bet you'd find an audience for it." Ben sounded sincere.

"Maybe so, but where could I squeeze it into an already full schedule?" Meg's hand went to her mouth. Complaining on overdrive.

"I get a feeling that having free time is an issue for you."

She laughed at the irony in his words. "It's just the way my life is . . . busy."

"I understand. Being a single parent isn't easy. You make every decision about your child by yourself, no input from another parent." Ben made such good sense and it mirrored Meg's thoughts. "I'm not complaining, just stating reality," he said.

"My mother always says you have to play the cards dealt to you."

"She's right. May I ask you a question?"

"Sure." Meg was curious about the subjects Ben had an interest in.

"Have you considered getting married?" Ben hesitated before continuing, "If you found the right person?"

Taken a little off-guard by his directness, she decided to answer anyway. "I had considered it once, but it didn't work out. I don't date often, so my chances of coming across the right person are slim."

"You never know, it might happen."

"I suppose you're right, but I'm not holding my breath." Meg brushed a hand through her hair. "I don't think many men would be interested in becoming a step-father to a seven-year-old."

"You might be surprised."

~~*

Ben walked into the main entrance of First Colony Mall on Tuesday evening with a shopping list in his shirt pocket and a smile on his face.

He found Meg sitting on a bench not far from the entrance. She looked fantastic. Light from the overhead chandelier made her dark hair shine like bronze. She turned her head, recognized him, and stood like a goddess rising from a lake of still water.

"Are you ready to shop until you drop?" she teased.

"I'll do my best." He wanted to kiss her but held back. "What stores are on your list?"

"I figure we could begin with the main department stores and then work our way through the mall."

"Good idea. Let's go."

They threaded their way through the mall's main walkway filled with shoppers laden with packages and hurrying from one store to the next. Christmas songs blared in the background as a Santa rang a sleigh bell outside an electronics store, encouraging shoppers to enter.

As he suspected, even a mundane shopping trip to the mall proved to be enjoyable with Meg. Much better than the typical single person method, which he'd struggled with during the last eight years. They soon reached a department store and stopped at the first display of specialty chocolate.

"This would be great for Emma's stocking," Meg said. She picked up a bar of cheesecake chocolate.

"Good idea." Ben picked up two bars, thinking he could give them to Kasey and his housekeeper. "Where do you want to shop?"

"I think we'll be more efficient if you do your shopping and I do mine. How about we meet up here in an hour?"

That wasn't exactly what Ben had envisioned, but he recognized the practicality of her suggestion. "Sounds like a plan. I'll see you in an hour. Call my cell if you need more time."

Meg nodded, turned away from him, and walked down the aisle between make up and sportswear. He paused for a moment to admire the view, and then shook it off. Gathering his wits, he pulled out his shopping list, ready to finish the chore and get back to a more important matter named Meg Wilson.

~~*

Meg's heart pounded as she walked away from Ben, wondering if he was watching her. Her reaction to sharing such a normal setting with him was a complete surprise. The simple nearness of the man had her breathing heavy, and *damn*, he looked good in that dark suit with his blue tie slightly off center. The man should be a New York model. She'd thought her heart would explode with longing . . . her fingers itched to trace the planes of his face. But she wouldn't. It was too risky.

She hurried to the escalator for the children's department upstairs. Emma needed pajamas and a new coat. Ellen had hinted she needed a new robe, something blue or yellow, so that was on the list as well.

Almost an hour later, Meg stepped on the down escalator. She saw Ben waiting for her as she reached the first floor. Her heart skittered at the smile he sent her direction.

His gaze landed on the large shopping bag she carried. "Looks like you knocked some items off your list."

"I'm nearly done," Meg said. "I've got to hit the perfume counter—my mother is out of her favorite scent."

"Great idea."

Once at the counter, Meg quickly made her purchase while Ben busied himself smelling samples. He picked up a square shaped bottle.

"Meg, do you like this brand?" Before she could answer, he'd taken her hand to lightly spray her wrist. He lifted it to his nose and closed his eyes. "Mm, delicious," he said, pausing to place a gentle kiss on her opened palm.

Meg fought to keep her knees from buckling at the tenderness of his actions. She'd never experienced such a truly romantic gesture in her life, let alone in the middle of a department store.

"Thanks," she said, slowly withdrawing her hand from his, ending the contact that was sure to make her putty in his hands. "Uh, I need to go over to shoes . . . it won't take but a couple of minutes."

He nodded, and she hurried off for a few minutes to catch her breath. Once she turned a corner, she stopped and smelled her wrist, not sure it smelled delicious, but it was nice. She made her way to the shoe department, ambling around for several minutes before going back to Ben.

As she caught sight of him, she paused to study the casual way he leaned against the counter to wait for her, cell phone in hand and his face a study of concentration.

"I'm back," she said, walking up beside him.

He gaze switched from the screen to her and he put the phone in his pocket. "That was quick. You ready to get back to shopping?"

"Absolutely. I need to stop at the game store we passed."

"Let's go."

The mall traffic had picked up in the last hour. People hurried from one shop to the next, carrying their lists, and smiling. Something must be in the air to make the shoppers happy when it was so crowded. But then again, Christmas always seemed magical to Meg.

The game store was full of teenagers and a few adults. Meg walked straight to a prominent display of the newest handheld gaming device. She picked up the box and looked at the price. Ouch, but she had a twenty percent off coupon, so she could handle it.

"You're getting that for Emma?" Ben asked as he picked up a box.

"This is the first item on her list."

"Same for Kasey." Ben chuckled. "The big decision is the color."

"I have that on the list, too—pink."

"I'll get Kasey lime-green, then."

"Good choice." Meg replaced the box and found a pink one. "The difficult part is choosing a couple of games she'll like that won't break the bank."

Ben led Meg to a wall of assorted games. Meg found

two for Emma, one car racing and the other basketball, knowing she didn't want any "girly" games, even though she was far from being a tomboy.

Ben did the same for Kasey and they took their place in line to check out.

Once outside the store, he looked at his watch. "Are you ready to get some dinner? There's a decent restaurant near the food court."

"Do you mind if I check the Christmas store? I think it's on the way and I promised Emma I'd find the perfect tree topper to replace our broken angel."

They walked slowly, in step with the rest of the shoppers, taking time to comment on the spectacular window displays. Red and gold ribbon intertwined with multicolored, oversized ornaments scattered among clothing, shoes, house wares, and computers. The mall was a veritable Mecca of Christmas shopping.

Ben took her hand and squeezed it. "Thanks for shopping with me. I usually do this alone and don't enjoy it nearly as much."

"My pleasure," she said, smiling at him. "I like shopping with you, too."

~~*

Ben performed a mental fist-pump, thinking their chance meeting was beginning to look more like a blessing from heaven, either that or a gift from the tree gods.

They reached the Christmas store and entered a magical wonderland of trees, angels, and Santa's elves. *Deck the Halls* played as they strolled around the display tables and shelves laden with over-the-top decorations.

"I want a tree topper on the simple side. I'll know it

when I see it," Meg said.

After searching the entire store, she looked at Ben and shrugged. "It's not here, I'll keep looking."

"Okay, let's eat."

Their second meal together was even better than the first. The more he learned about Meg, the more he liked her. She was the real deal—a woman with a good sense of integrity and work ethics, as well as an excellent mother. Those qualities made her even more beautiful to him. He recited a silent prayer of thanks. No doubt about it, meeting her at that tree lot had been his good fortune.

After a cup of coffee, they made their way back through the mall to the entrance.

Meg pointed to the right. "I'm parked over there, not far from the door."

"I'll walk you to your car." Ben placed one hand on the small of her back and held the door open with the other.

She veered to the right once they exited the mall and continued down a row of vehicles. "I'm right here." She stopped at the back of a white SUV.

Ben helped her load her packages and shut the tailgate before escorting her to the driver's door. She turned and gazed at him, gracing him with a smile.

Ben basked in her presence, wishing the evening didn't have to end. He reined in his thoughts, not wanting to scare her off. "Thanks for shopping with me, Meg."

"I enjoyed it."

"Me, too." He meant that. He'd never shopped for Christmas presents with a woman other than his mother, not even his wife. This had been a special night.

"I better get going," Meg said, glancing at her watch.

"I know." Ben couldn't help but focus on Meg's gorgeous face and her full lips. Lips made for kissing.

He stroked a finger across her cheek and inched his face slowly toward hers. He smiled as she licked her lower lip in anticipation. To his great delight, her mouth was a perfect fit to his, and for some reason, she tasted like cinnamon and sugarplums. What? He brushed his lips lightly across hers before increasing the pressure, suppressing a groan of pleasure as Meg's arms looped around his neck.

After one of the best minutes of his recent life, he finally pulled back, attempting some semblance of self-control. He grinned at Meg, whose flushed face let him know he wasn't the only one affected. "I know you're busy with Christmas the next few days, but would you have time to get together after that?"

"I think so. What are you and Kasey doing for Christmas?"

"Christmas Eve together and then to my sister's house for dinner on Christmas Day, the usual."

She nodded. "It's about the same for me, but yeah, give me a call afterwards." She gave him a quick peck on the cheek, and quickly entered the SUV and waved as she drove away.

Ben stood for a moment staring at her vehicle as it turned out of the parking lot. He felt like he'd entered an alternate universe where cupids and rainbows ruled the day. He shook his head and walked to his car. It was official—he was seriously *in like* with Meg.

~~*

Meg hummed as she drove home. It had been so much fun

shopping with Ben. She could get used to doing ordinary things with him. Normal things that were good for her.

Whoops. Where did *that* come from? She shouldn't be thinking like that after only two dates. Sure, he was a great guy, but two dates did not make a relationship. Of course, he had asked about a third one after Christmas. She shook her head and smiled. Maybe meeting Ben was some of that Christmas luck her grandmother used to talk about.

Nana Wilson swore that special things happened to people as they waited for Santa to arrive on Christmas Eve—women with no hope of having children discovered they were pregnant and long-standing family feuds resolved with hugs and kisses. Meg had always suspected she made up all of her stories. They made for good entertainment around the Christmas dinner table, but who in their right mind would believe them?

Nevertheless, Meg continued to hum the rest of the way home. She pulled in her driveway and hit the clicker to open the garage door. Emma should be in bed, so she'd have no problem hiding her gifts. She sighed, three more days until Christmas Eve, and so much still to do.

Christmas Magic

Meg had intended to spend Wednesday's lunch hour looking for the tree topper but wasn't able to get out of the office. That meant Thursday was the day since she'd promised Emma she would bring it home that evening.

She headed to a specialty gift boutique that carried decorations. It was on a newly revived street in Sugar Land with antique and specialty stores of all kinds. She slipped her SUV into a parking spot in front of a tie shop and paused to look in the store's window. A tie would make the perfect gift for Ben. She could give it to him on their next date, whenever that might be. Once inside, she had an easy task of picking out the tie, sophisticated yet whimsical, per the salesman. She asked for it to be gift-wrapped and was quickly on her way to the boutique.

Once again, she stopped to look in the window. The ornaments and decorations were artfully displayed, but she didn't see anything that shouted, "Take me home."

As she pulled the door open, bells jingled. The sound seemed to swirl around her as she took a step forward. A man appeared in front of her, from where, she didn't know.

"Good afternoon, young lady," he said. "How may I help you?"

Meg loved the deep, rich bass of his voice. An image of Santa Claus flitted through her mind. But the man looked nothing like Santa—tall, thin, thick dark hair, clean-shaven, and sparkling blue eyes. Maybe he was a cousin. She realized she was staring at him and stepped to the side.

"Hello, I'm looking for a topper for my Christmas tree."

"I see. What do you have in mind?"

"I'm not sure. I haven't found anything that speaks to me, er, seems just right."

"I have something you might like. Please follow me." He moved without seeming to walk toward the back of the store.

Meg's head whipped from side to side as she followed him. She'd never before seen such unique gifts. She didn't have time to browse but would definitely return next month for Ellen's birthday present.

She nearly bumped into the man as he stopped suddenly and turned around to her.

"These might be what you're looking for." He pointed to several miniature Christmas trees scattered across a dark oak sideboard, each topped with a three-dimensional star. A phone rang. "I must get that." He hurried to the front of the store.

Meg studied the stars. They were different colors and sizes, some plain, others decorated with sequins and glitter, and all of them shining brightly. They were beautiful. How could she select the one Emma would like?

She closed her eyes and pictured their tree at home with a shining star at the top. Yes, a star was perfect. She raised her hand and held out a finger toward the stars. Her eyes opened to view where she pointed.

Three stars were within the line of her finger. Which one? She simply couldn't decide. Then a strange thing happened. The star in the middle, with gold glitter outlining its edges, began to flash. She stepped closer for a better view.

The center glowed, and a picture emerged. She blinked, and the picture was clearer—Emma and Meg stood in front of their tree at home, smiling, and dressed in matching Santa sweaters. What in the world? She blinked again, and the picture was gone. What?

The salesman came back and stood next to her, smiling. "Have you made your decision?"

The smell of peppermint, cinnamon, and sugar cookies floated to Meg, reminding her of the kitchen when her mother baked Christmas cookies.

"Yes, I have." She pointed to the star that had glowed. "That's *the perfect topper* for our tree."

"Excellent choice. I'll wrap it for you with the utmost care." He gingerly took it off the small tree. "I have a feeling this star is a good omen for you and your daughter."

She didn't know about that, but it was pretty. She followed him to the cash register to pay. "Do you take credit cards?"

"Of course," he said. "Santa understands the needs of the modern parent."

He retrieved a red box from under the counter along with several pieces of green tissue. He carefully wrapped the star in the paper then lined the box with layers of gold tissue. He nestled the star in the box and added its top. Lastly, he cut a length of gold ribbon, draped it around the box, and tied a pert bow on top.

"You're good at wrapping," she said, handing him a credit card.

"Years and years of practice." He quickly produced a charge slip for her to sign then placed the box in a red and green striped paper bag.

Meg signed the slip and accepted the bag from him. "Thanks so much for your help. I'm really happy with the star."

"As you should be. I'm certain you and Emma will have a wonderful holiday." He smiled, and then winked at her. "Merry Christmas, Meg."

"Merry Christmas," she said as she walked toward the door, wondering how the man had known her name. She felt a little silly once she remembered she'd used her credit card. Of course he knew. She frowned, trying to remember when she'd mentioned Emma's name to him. She couldn't. And not only that, but she couldn't remember telling him she had a child. The entire incident was a little eerie.

Nana would say it was Christmas magic. Meg liked that explanation better than thinking he was a strange old gentleman.

~~*

Meg arrived home to find her mother and Emma in the middle of a heated competition with Uno, Emma's favorite card game. She set the bag with the star on the kitchen counter.

Emma jumped off the couch. "Mama, what did you get? Can I see?"

Meg kissed the top of Emma's head. She smelled like fresh rain. "Yes, you may. This is our topper for the Christmas tree."

Ellen joined them. "Good. A tree doesn't look finished until you have the topper."

Meg extracted the red box and placed it on the counter.

"Can I open it?" Emma asked.

"Yes, just be careful."

"That is a gorgeous box," Ellen said, surveying it. "Where did you get it?"

"At a gift boutique store on Chestnut Street." Meg could tell Emma was itching to untie the ribbon and take off the lid. "Go ahead," she said.

Emma did so, and pulled back the gold paper. She looked at her mother. "I'm afraid I'll break it. You do it."

Meg smiled at her practical daughter. "You take it out of the box, and I'll unwrap it."

Within five minutes, the star was plugged in and graced the top of the tree. It glowed, and the tree itself seemed brighter and happier.

"I need to get going. I have a couple of errands to run this evening." Ellen put on her coat and gave Emma a big hug then kissed Meg on the cheek. "I'll see y'all at ten tomorrow morning to make our cookies for Christmas Eve. I'm glad you have the day off."

Emma grinned. "We'll be there, Granny. Right, Mama?"

"You bet. Don't forget we're bringing all the sprinkles and candy decorations."

Emma clapped her hands excitedly. "I almost forgot about that. Granny, we're the cookie decorators, the uh, official decorators."

"Right you are, Emma Bug."

After her bath, Emma sat on the sofa near the Christmas tree. "Mama, the star is so beautiful. It's just like the star over baby Jesus. Please tell me the story again."

Meg brought Emma a mug of hot chocolate, expecting a request for the story. "I think this is the perfect time." She tucked Emma's pink blanket around her legs. "It's so cold outside, we must stay warm."

"Mama, the story."

Meg settled on the sofa and sipped a glass of white wine. "Okay, here goes," she said as Emma snuggled into her blanket.

"Mary was the mother of Jesus and Joseph was her husband. Baby Jesus was born in Bethlehem in the time of King Herod. Remember?"

Emma nodded enthusiastically and sipped her hot

chocolate.

"The three kings, known as the Three Wise Men, went to Jerusalem and asked King Herod 'Where is the child who is to be king of the Jews?' They had seen the rising Star of Bethlehem in the east and wanted to pay their respects to the child. King Herod was disturbed by this and called together all the smartest people he knew. They all told him the Messiah was to be born in Bethlehem."

Meg stopped to sip her wine. She patted Emma's leg. "Okay, sweetie?"

"Yes, Mama, I love this story. What happens next?"

"The King asked the Wise Men, also called the Magi, to go to Bethlehem and search for the baby. As soon as they found him they were to report back to the King so he could also worship the child. Do you remember what guided them on their search?"

"The star that rose in the east." Emma pointed to the shining ornament topping their Christmas tree. "Just like our star."

"That's right. They saw the star rising on the eastern horizon and followed it to Bethlehem. The star was their guide as it stopped over the manger where baby Jesus lay with his mother."

"Donkeys were there, too, right?"

Meg nodded. "The Wise Men brought gifts for baby Jesus, and then they left and went back to their own homes, rather than going back to King Herod."

"Wow, that was one smart star showing them the way to baby Jesus. Do you think our star is smart, too?"

Meg smiled. "Probably not. I think there is only one Star of Bethlehem."

Emma sipped her chocolate then licked her lips. "Ya know, I think you're right. We only get one star that has special powers."

"Special powers?"

"Like Superman or Spiderman, they have powers you and I don't have."

Meg laughed and hugged Emma. "You're right. We don't have those kinds of super powers. It's bedtime so go brush your teeth and I'll meet you in your bedroom."

Emma scampered off the sofa and handed her mother the mug. "I'll see you in five."

Once Emma was tucked in and said her nightly prayer, Meg went back to the kitchen to clean up and start the dishwasher.

She flopped on the sofa, stretched out her legs, and flipped through the television channels until she found an old Christmas movie. She'd seen it a dozen times but good movies were like good books, the great stories never got old.

She watched the movie for several minutes then dozed off. Her eyes fluttered open a short time later and her gaze swung to the Christmas tree. The star glowed much brighter than before. She sat up. The center of it swirled with flashes of red and gold. Curious, she rose and walked to their beautiful tree.

They had done such a great job decorating the tree with colorful glass balls, Emma's handmade ornaments, and white twinkly lights. Wide gold ribbon draped across the branches like garland. The star made everything else on the tree more beautiful. *[See EC on page 265]*

She stared at the star, and it began to blink. She moved

closer and saw a picture just like she had at the store. But this one was different, very different. Meg stood next to Ben with his arm over her shoulder. They were both smiling and standing close to each other.

Meg stepped back so quickly she almost tripped over the edge of the rug. She looked at the star again, and the picture was gone, the glow had lessened, and it was no longer blinking.

What did this mean? The picture on the star had to signify something. Things like that didn't happen every day, and certainly not in Meg's orderly life. Well, duh, obviously it had something to do with her, Ben and Christmas. Or was her mind playing tricks?

She decided it was simply a matter of wishful thinking, and her thoughts turned to the dinner for Christmas Eve. She mentally went through her shopping list of last minute items needed for tomorrow and went to the kitchen for pen and paper.

As she started the list, the image of Ben and her standing in front of the tree flashed in her mind, and it finally clicked. The star—or something—was prodding her to invite Ben and Kasey to Christmas Eve dinner. It made perfect sense. She picked up her cell, clicked on Ben's name, and began to pace a steady route from kitchen to family room and back again.

He picked up on the third ring.

"Meg, what's up?"

"I'd like to invite you and Kasey to my house for dinner on Christmas Eve."

"Really?"

"Yes. I hope you can come. We'd love to have you join

us." She didn't wait long for his answer.

"We'd be honored."

"Great." Meg did a little jig before controlling herself. "How about coming over around five?"

"We'll be there. What can I bring to add to the dinner?"

"Hmm, how about an appetizer?"

"I can handle that. We'll see you on Saturday."

Meg tossed her phone on the sofa and looked at the star. Now it was blinking again as though winking at her. She shook her head and blew it a kiss.

"Superman has nothing on that star," she muttered as she turned out the living room and kitchen lights. She'd finish the grocery list in the morning.

~~*

The next two days flew by. As usual, Meg was busy and barely had a chance to sit down. But it was all worth it. Her house looked and smelled like Christmas. Standing in the kitchen, she gazed around the family room and the homey holiday scene she'd created for Emma. Scented candles burned on the mantle over the fireplace, a reindeer afghan was tossed over the back of the sofa, and the twinkling tree lit up the room.

She had wanted to make this year a thousand percent better than last year and so far, she'd succeeded. Pride in her accomplishment heightened her anticipation of seeing Ben again.

"Mama, I'm ready."

Meg gazed at her daughter dressed in a red sweater and green jeans. "My goodness, you look like one of Santa's elves."

"Good. When will Granny get here? I want to show her

the napkin rings we made."

The doorbell rang right on cue.

"I bet that's her. Go answer it, please."

Emma ran to the front door while Meg continued to work on their dinner. She finished tearing the lettuce into her large wooden salad bowl and put it back in the refrigerator to stay crisp. Next, a mountain of cheddar cheese had to be grated.

"Mama, Granny's here, and she brought a friend."

"What friend?" Meg washed her hands, dried them on a dishtowel, and headed to the front door. Standing next to her mother was a man. Hmm, could this be the *mystery* man?

She reached her hand out to him. "Hi and welcome, I'm Meg, Ellen's daughter. I guess you already met my daughter, Emma."

The man was gray haired with animated brown eyes, and a firm handshake. "Nice to meet you, I'm Gary Taylor, Ellen's friend." He winked at Meg then raised a shopping bag in the other hand. "Where should I put this?"

"I'll take it. Mom, show Gary where to put his coat. Y'all make yourselves comfortable."

Ellen and Gary went toward the bedrooms with Emma while Meg set the bag on the back counter. She had cheese to grate. A few minutes later the trio returned to kitchen.

"Gary has graciously agreed to play a video game with Emma," Ellen said, her eyes twinkling. "I'll help with dinner."

"Come on, Mr. Gary." Emma pulled at his hand and led him to the sofa.

"Emma, you be easy on Gary. Remember he's a guest."

"Don't worry, Mama, I'll be nice . . . I may even let him win," Emma said, with a good dose of glee.

Gary and Emma set up their game on the television while Meg whispered to her mother. "What made you decide to bring Gary? I'm so happy you did."

"I listened to what you said last week, and you were right. It's time for me to acknowledge life goes on, even after a divorce."

"Yay, Mom." Meg high-fived Ellen. "Did you bring the salad dressing?"

"I did, along with our cookies and a special dessert."

Meg started to grate the cheese. "Special, huh? Can't wait."

"It's Gary's favorite. Do you want me to cut the soft cheese?"

"Yes, please."

Meg and Ellen worked silently getting all the ingredients ready for the cheese-potato soup. As Meg began to thicken the milk, the doorbell rang. "Mom, would you get that. I don't want the milk to burn." *[See EC on page 267]*

Ellen headed to the front door. Within moments, Ben and Kasey entered the family room. Ellen introduced them to Gary then Kasey ran to the sofa to join the game.

Ben rounded the corner to the kitchen holding a dish and grinning at Meg. "I brought an appetizer."

"Great. I could use a bite, I'm starved."

"May I heat it in the microwave?" Ben displayed the dish in front of his chest.

"Mom, can you help? I have to keep stirring."

"I bet Ben knows how to work a microwave," Ellen

said impishly as she walked away. "I'll help Gary with the game."

"Go for it." Meg smiled at Ben, adding cheese to the milk. "My kitchen is your kitchen."

"I like the sound of that."

A moment later, Meg chewed on a mini beef kabob, the perfect accompaniment to her meatless dinner. She continued to stir the soup. Ben stood next to her looking at the pot.

"That looks good. What can I do to help?" Ben threw a dishtowel over his shoulder, ready for action.

Meg pointed out that the garlic bread should go in the oven and then five minutes later, the salad could be put together.

"You always time everything so carefully?"

Meg nodded. "I like everything done at the same time."

"You're a good planner."

"No, just a control freak." Meg smiled at Ben and really looked at him—red shirt, black jeans, and cowboy boots—he looked almost too good. God bless that contemporary cowboy look. "I'm glad you came."

"Thanks for inviting us." He kissed her cheek and displayed a crooked grin. "I'll get right to the bread."

Ben and Meg finished preparing their first Christmas Eve dinner together. They served it buffet style then everyone gathered at the dining table. The group fell silent as Ellen said the blessing over the meal, then Emma and Kasey started to talk and didn't stop. With much animation, they explained every twist and point made in the game with Gary, and then Ellen. The adults laughed at their antics and they consumed the dinner in an atmosphere of merriment and good cheer. Meg's soup was quite the hit. Ben praised it and had a second helping.

After they finished eating and clearing the table, Meg gathered everyone around the Christmas tree. It was their tradition that Ellen read *The Night Before Christmas* prior to dessert. Meg noticed the star glowed brighter as Ellen settled in the chair by the fireplace. *[See EC on page 268]*

"Are y'all comfortable? This is a special treat for my granddaughter every Christmas Eve. Sit back and enjoy." Ellen opened a book with a tattered cover. The lights from the tree gave her face a special radiance. She began to read. "Twas the night before Christmas, and all through the house . . ."

Meg leaned back against the sofa and allowed the words to flow over her. She loved her mother for this Christmas Eve tradition. The girls seemed entranced with Ellen's soft, lyrical voice. Ben's arm was slung around Kasey and he patted her shoulder. Gary had a wide smile on his face. Meg liked that.

Ellen's voice rose and she pumped her left arm as Santa shouted out the names of the reindeer. Emma and Kasey sat up straighter on the sofa and locked hands. It amazed Meg how quickly they had become friends, and it pleased her. She snuck a glance at Ben's handsome face and then at the Christmas tree. Meeting the two of them had started with the tree. No matter the future course of her relationship with Ben, she would always be thankful for this very special Christmas Eve and the hours they had shared as family and good friends.

Meg stopped her musings and listened to her mother

read the final line of the poem. "Happy Christmas to all, and to all a good-night!"

Ellen slowly closed the book. No one said a word.

Snuggled back against her father, Kasey broke the silence. "I love that story."

"Me, too," Emma added then looked at her mother. "Mama, can I show Kasey my room?"

"Yes, you may. We'll have dessert in a few minutes."

The girls ran down the hall giggling while Meg and Ellen rose.

"We'll start the coffee," Ellen said. "You guys, uh, play a game or something."

Once in the kitchen, Meg turned to Ellen. "I like him," they said in unison, then hugged each other through mutual laughter.

"Mom, I'm so glad you brought Gary with you. He's a good guy."

"I like Ben as well." Ellen spooned coffee into the pot. "Check out the dessert, Gary made it."

Meg peeked at the dish and licked her lips.

After chocolate cheesecake and cookies, Ellen and Gary said their good-byes.

"I'll see you tomorrow, Emma Bug, and we'll open our gifts." Ellen gave kisses to all, Gary shook everyone's hand, and they left.

Once the door closed, Emma cornered her mother in the kitchen. "Please, can Kasey and I watch a Christmas movie before she has to leave?" She pointed her index finger straight up. "Just one, I promise."

Ben agreed and the girls settled on the sofa under the afghan to watch *A Charlie Brown Christmas,* one of

Emma's favorites. Meg turned down the floor lamp. The tree provided just the right ambience for the two little girls to enjoy their movie.

Meg led Ben to the kitchen for some adult time.

"Would you like a glass of wine?" Meg kept her voice low. "I have chardonnay and cabernet."

"Hmm, I'll have white."

Meg poured the wine and suggested they sit at the island counter, with a good view of the girls on the sofa.

"Did you have enough to eat?" Meg said. "Your beef kabobs were delicious by the way."

"Thanks. My claim to fame is grilling." Ben sipped the wine and nodded his approval. "How about you and Emma come over next week and I'll cook dinner. It won't be too cold to grill."

His suggestion had Meg's head spinning. Her thinking hadn't progressed past Christmas and creating a spectacular holiday for Emma. Now Ben had asked her on another date, one with Emma this time. She looked at Ben's smiling face and the goodness and the integrity so handsomely displayed. She'd be a fool to decline.

"Mr. Abbott, we would love to have dinner at your home." She leaned forward and kissed him, right on the lips. Her heart fluttered and then soared. This relationship with Ben felt so right . . . *was* right for her.

He rubbed his thumb lightly over her lips. "Let's see, that will be date number four."

"You're counting?"

"You bet, after date number ten, we're going steady."

Meg laughed and glanced at the family room. The tree twinkled over Emma and Kasey as they watched their movie, side by side on the sofa. Meg's heart filled at the image of the two little girls, happy and secure, snuggled against each other.

"Meg, look." Ben pointed to the Christmas tree. "The star is blinking. Is there a short in the wiring?"

"No, it's talking to us."

"What?"

"Go look at it and tell me what you see."

Ben rose and went to the tree, and gazed at the star. After a few moments, he walked back to her, shaking his head.

"I don't believe it." He rubbed a hand over his face, and then finally smiled at her. "I get it now."

"You get what?"

He hugged Meg tightly, stroking a hand over her back as he spoke in a low whisper. "When I find the right person, I'm not letting her go."

Meg nodded and understood exactly what he meant. The glowing star had super powers that even Superman would envy. Christmas magic, indeed!

* * * * *

A HOLIDAY SURPRISE

December 1, Monday

After exiting her little red convertible, Avery Burke glanced at the solemn gray sky and frowned, then wrapped her jeans jacket around her middle. The North Pole had descended on Texas. She had a hunch this would not be a typical December. Slipping the strap of her favorite tote bag over her shoulder, she strode through the parking lot to the door of the Sugar Land Starbucks closest to her home.

It was a few minutes after nine a.m. and the early going-to-work crowd had thinned out. She walked to the line hugging along the counter and waited only a couple of minutes for her turn.

Being a Monday morning regular, Avery knew every barista in the shop. "Hey, Jimmy, how's it going today?"

"How you doing, Miss Burke? It sure is cold today." Jimmy smiled like a birthday balloon that refused to pop. "What can I get for you?"

"My usual." Avery didn't hesitate with her reply. She liked what she liked and had favorites at every coffee shop or restaurant she visited. "And yes, it's cold, stupid winter." She handed him a credit card.

Jimmy laughed. "Not winter yet but I agree it's too cold, too soon." He returned the card and opened a glass case for a sticky bun with walnuts. He handed the bun to her. "Good seeing you again, Miss Burke. Hope your writing goes good."

"Thanks, I appreciate that." She moved to the end of the counter and waited for her Café Mocha minus the whipped cream. She made use of the wait time by mulling over her current novel. For some reason, the plot twist wouldn't gel. It shouldn't be this difficult. If writing a cozy mystery equated to brain surgery, her every move would leave a trail of dead bodies.

After a minute or two, she carried her coffee to a corner table, out of the way and with a good view of the door, her two requisites in any restaurant since witnessing an attempted burglary at an Italian bistro a few years ago. It had been a scary experience.

She sat down and pulled her laptop out of the tote. Once it displayed her work-in-progress, she sipped the coffee and plucked off a bite of the sticky bun with her fingers. The coffee and the bun were her weekly indulgence to signify the start of another week of writing. She'd kept the same work schedule as when she'd been director of financial aid at Houston Cullen University. It kept her on target for meeting her deadlines and her books rolling off bookstore shelves or loading on an e-reader.

She closed her eyes for a moment, enjoying the sweetness of the sticky bun.

"Avery, what are you doing in Sugar Land?" Her eyes blinked open at the deep base of her ex-husband's voice. Fifteen years since their divorce and she still recognized his voice. Damn it.

Avery kept her tone cool and calm. "Hello, Mark." OMG, why the hell was he standing in front of her? She surveyed him from top to bottom. Damn, he looked good. She laid the sticky bun on a napkin, still trying to process the shock of seeing him. "Don't you live somewhere else, like out of state?" *Or in Siberia?*

"I moved back a month ago." He displayed that million-watt smile she'd managed not to forget and moved to a table next to her, plopping a tan leather briefcase on the top. "Would you mind watching this while I get a coffee?"

"Sure, no problem." What else could she say? "No, jerk ex-husband, you broke my heart" didn't seem appropriate for a coffee shop, even if it was true. She stuffed more of the sticky bun in her mouth. A sugar rush might give her energy or at least keep her hands busy.

She went back to her work. With her gaze glued to her laptop screen, she read a couple of paragraphs to re-orient herself with her location in the story. This scene had issues and—

"How've you been?" Mark pulled out a chair, the legs screeching on the tile floor. He settled at the table. "It's been a while since I've seen you. Ten years, maybe?"

Avery wanted to curl into a ball and roll away from him. Why-oh-why did he have to walk into her favorite Starbucks? She looked into his milk chocolate eyes and knew in the deepest, most remote corner of her heart that he still owned a piece of it, even after so many years. But he didn't know that so she squared her shoulders and reminded herself she was a successful forty-something cozy mystery writer who'd had her latest series optioned for a television show.

"I'm not sure." She struggled to keep her tone steady. "I can't remember the last time I saw you." She stuffed the last piece of the sticky bun in her mouth and washed it down with coffee. That's right. Keep yourself occupied—anything to avoid throwing her arms around him, or smothering him with smoldering kisses. Oh God, she was an idiot for even imagining that.

Mark stared at the ceiling, as though looking for answers then snapped his fingers and faced her. "It was at Memorial Park. You and your sister were running and I nearly ran you over."

"Hmm . . . I do remember that." She'd never tell him she remembered exactly how wonderful he looked with his tee shirt tied around his waist and his tanned chest glistening with just the right amount of manly perspiration. He'd gained some weight and had obviously started going to a gym. He looked just as good today, sitting calmly and drinking his coffee. At least this time he was fully clothed.

"I'd come home for my parent's wedding anniversary. I was staying at the corporate apartment downtown."

"You still work for Capital First?"

"Yep, got a promotion and transferred back here from Denver. Decided to live in Sugar Land to be close to the folks and my brothers." He bit into a muffin and chewed. "I love these things."

She remembered all too well how much he loved to eat and never seemed to gain an ounce. Most of their happiest memories had been related to food—her cooking and him eating. She ignored his comment.

"You live around here?" It would be a disaster for her emotional psyche if she continued to run into him.

"Uh-huh," he said between bites. "I bought a townhouse off Sweetwater. Easy access to the freeway to drive downtown."

"Aren't you late for work then?" She displayed her favorite Mickey Mouse watch to him. Maybe he'd hurry up and leave if she reminded him of the time. "It's past nine-thirty."

He placed his coffee cup on the table and looked at her, a smirk crossing his face. "Are you trying to get rid of me?"

Damn right. "No, of course not. Just don't want you to be late . . . for, uh, whatever."

"Not to worry." He winked at her while slugging down coffee. "I'm wasting time before heading to DPS to get my Texas driver's license."

"Right." He might have time to waste but she didn't. A manuscript deadline loomed in front of her. She shifted in the chair and tried to concentrate on her story. She re-read a few lines from yesterday's writing. Crap, this wouldn't work at all and she began pounding on the Delete key.

"Avery."

She faced him again, not bothering to hide her irritation. "What?"

"Am I keeping you from something?" He ran his fingers through his light brown hair, pushing it off his forehead. It curled around his ears, longer than she remembered.

"Yes, actually. I came here to work, and you are keeping me from doing just that." Not to mention causing her heart to gallop like a spooked mustang.

"Don't you still work at HCU?"

"I resigned a couple of years ago. I write full time now."

"You write?" He smiled slowly then leaned over to kiss her cheek, but she pulled away from him. "Congratulations. I remember how much fun you and your sister used to have thinking up imaginary characters."

She bristled at his comment. Writing for a living wasn't child's play. "It's not imaginary any longer. I earn my living from writing now."

"What do you write?"

"Google me."

"I'll do that." He tossed something on her table. "Here's my card. What's your phone number?"

She hesitated, should she? Oh, why not. She opened her laptop case and pulled out her own personal card with her phone number and address. She slid it across the table toward him.

He picked up the card and looked at it. "Last name is the same. You haven't remarried?"

She shook her head.

"Same here." Mark rose and walked to a trashcan, tossing in the remains of his breakfast. He slung the briefcase's long strap over one shoulder, and sent Avery one of his trademark grins, his lips curved in a sexy smile, his eyes shining with pleasure. He moseyed back to her table. "I'm glad I ran into you today. Since we both live in Sugar Land, there won't be any awkward moments next time it happens." He stroked a finger slowly down her cheek then drew it back. "And it will happen. See you around."

Avery watched him exit through the main door and climb into a white SUV parked right in front. Damn that man, he still had the knack for getting primo parking spots.

~~*

Mark Burke chuckled as he headed south on Highway 59 to Rosenberg and a mega center for getting a Texas driver's license. Things sure had changed since he'd moved to Denver ten years ago. But the truth was he'd jumped at the chance to move back and a promotion had sweetened the deal. Plus his many years of traveling back and forth across the country as an IT consultant were no longer required with his new position.

He'd noticed Avery the minute he'd walked into

Starbucks. It was as though a transparent laser had dinged after registering her presence. He figured he'd run into her eventually but not so soon. Hopefully not until he'd analyzed how he'd react and what he'd say. And how he'd handle how damned good she looked. God, she hadn't changed at all in the last fifteen years, maybe a little thinner and her dark hair was longer.

Those deep, ocean blue eyes still sparkled with amusement. In fact, they were what he first noticed about her the day they met at Texas A&M's freshman orientation. Many years later, and after everything that had happened, he still considered it the best day of his life. He treasured the memory of that first meeting.

They'd been standing in line for a barbeque lunch. He was behind Avery and her twin sister, Ashley, and Ashley's boyfriend, John or Joe, something. During the course of their time-killing conversation someone had mentioned Sugar Land, and they discovered they'd attended competing high schools. The group of four ended up sitting together. His relationship with Avery had started over Texas brisket and ranch beans. For him, it truly had been love at first sight.

They dated throughout college and moved in together after graduation. Mark started working at Capital First Consulting and Avery at Houston Cullen University in the development office. They were engaged a year later and married a year after that. Life was good. They worked hard and enjoyed to the max what little downtime they had together.

Their married life was damned perfect, until Avery got pregnant. She had a miscarriage at ten weeks and took it as a personal defeat that had to be overcome. Regardless of trying and talking to doctors and going through fertility treatments, Avery didn't get pregnant again.

Mark massaged his jaw with one hand. Why was he thinking about all this stuff? Their relationship ended in too much pain and the death of their marriage. The decision to divorce had been mutual. Although from his point of view, Avery had been more eager to end it than him. It hadn't been for a lack of love between them but a lack of living. After two years of trying to get pregnant, their interactions focused entirely on that one goal. Ultimately, they'd gone their separate ways.

He'd never forget the haunted look in her eyes as they performed the final separation of their belongings that last Saturday of living together.

"You can take all the VHS movies and recorder," Mark said, placing his golf trophies in a box.

Avery looked at him suspiciously. "Why? Are you going to buy one of those fancy DVD players?"

"No." Everything she'd said to Mark sounded like an accusation. He was tired of the pressure of trying to make her happy and finally admitted to himself he couldn't. "I know you like those girly romance movies and I won't watch them again."

She'd thanked him and set the recorder in the bottom of a box then started piling the tapes on top of it. "What about the kitchen stuff? You said to leave it for last." Her voice had been devoid of emotion, like a conductor announcing the next train's stop in Boringville, USA.

"Yeah, I know. You can have everything. I doubt I'll

be doing much cooking." He smiled sadly. "It'll be hard to beat your cooking. I'll make do."

She spun around like a tornado. "Are you accusing me of causing this divorce? Damn you. You're right, like always." Tears started to roll down her cheeks and he had no clue what had set her off. "I'm the one who can't get pregnant. You shouldn't have to suffer because of my failing. I—"

"Stop it. It's not anyone's fault. It just happens." He stepped toward her and she backed away from him, looking like a wounded waif from a bad B-movie. He couldn't take it any longer. The pain in her eyes would stay with him for the rest of his life. "I'll leave you alone. Let me know when you've moved out everything you want and I'll let the management office know the apartment is empty."

"Fine." She'd turned and walked to the bedroom, slamming the door behind her.

Why was he thinking about all this? His fist pounded the steering wheel. They'd been divorced fifteen years and he still thought about Avery almost daily. What the hell was wrong with him?

He sighed and switched lanes for his upcoming exit. God, why were relationships so difficult? Over the years he'd not met a woman who could stand up to Avery's memory and now that he'd seen her again, the reason why had been reinforced a thousand times over. He was still deeply and unequivocally in love with his ex-wife.

He signaled right and exited onto the feeder road. A thought came to him. Was he an idiot or a loser for still being in love with her? If he asked his oldest brother,

Ellis, he'd say "hell no, all love is glorious, go for it." Of course the next oldest, Klein, would tell him to count his cards and make the safe bet. He turned right, and soon pulled into the Department of Public Safety's parking lot, finding an open spot in front of the main door.

He sat for a moment, analyzing the situation: pro—he'd loved Avery for more than half his life and he wanted to be with her again, con—he'd have to win her over. He could do this. Meeting out of the blue at Starbucks was an omen, especially since he'd already decided to get in contact with her.

Yep, kismet sang, they were meant to be, now and forever. And he knew exactly how to inaugurate his win-back-Avery plan. The one he'd just now decided might have a snowball's chance in hell of succeeding. Not bad odds considering she hated his guts.

December 3, Wednesday

Avery hunkered down at the small oak desk in the study aka bookroom, close to the kitchen and the coffee pot. She diligently worked on increasing her word count to a level that would have the first draft of her new book finished by five p.m. on Friday. She'd let it rest over the weekend and then begin her revision process on Monday. Her copy editor expected it by the twenty-second. Her well-honed writing method gave her confidence that she'd have no problem meeting the deadline.

This was the twelfth book in this cozy mystery series and she intended to stop the series at book thirteen. She had another series slated to go live the day after Christmas with the first two books. It was another cozy mystery series centered on a family's gourmet deli store located in a fictional Texas Gulf Coast town. She loved the idea of this series being on the coast rather than in the Texas hill country.

Avery found her writing zone and typed word after word for two hours before she realized her coffee cup was empty. She rose and walked the few steps to brew another pot. As she pushed the button, the doorbell rang.

Opening the front door, she gasped. A huge vase of pink and white daises filled the space in front of her. A head poked around the flowers.

"Miss Burke?"

"Yes, that's me."

"Could you take the pad from under my arm and sign at the line with your name?"

Avery signed as requested then took possession of the vase and closed the door with her hip. This was the nicest arrangement of flowers she'd ever received. Maybe it related to her book sales. She hurried to the kitchen and set the heavy vase on the counter. Curious as to the sender, she ripped open the accompanying envelope and read the card.

What the hell?

She never should have given her card to Mark. But he'd sent her beautiful flowers and asked her to go to dinner with him that evening. Oh . . . oh, good grief.

She started pacing from the front door, down the hallway, and turning at her bed, back and forth three or four times. Walking helped her think, but this wouldn't do. She grabbed her keys, threw on a jacket, exited through the front door, and headed for the community mailbox. Of course her insides were anything but calm, jumping from one end of the teeter-totter to the other and then back again.

Her brain worked better in mobile mode so once on the sidewalk in front of her house, Avery turned the opposite direction of the mailboxes. A few extra steps couldn't hurt even after her three-mile run earlier that morning. This time she'd be thinking and not listening to her favorite playlist. *[See EC on page 271]*

She set off with her arms swinging and her mind focused on the issue at hand: should she go to dinner with her ex-husband?

First of all, why had this happened? For what reason had the cosmos concocted a plot point to bring her and Mark together? It made no sense. The Christmas decorations in her neighbor's yard caught her attention and brought a smile to her face. A huge Santa sat in the middle of colorful three-dimensional gifts. If she'd been blessed with a child, she'd decorate as well. She turned away and focused straight ahead.

She hadn't put up a single Christmas decoration since her divorce from Mark. What was the point when there were no children in the house? And that led her back to Mark since the reason for their divorce was her failure to produce a child. Produce? That sounded appalling.

It didn't matter now; the marriage was way past done. Nothing had stayed with her after fifteen long years but silence and the eventual calming of her mind.

She was long past mental screaming and crying. Time does heal after all.

She rounded the block and turned back. She had nothing to lose by going to dinner with Mark. Her long ago feelings for him, although true and eternal, would stay buried. They were the feelings of a young girl not a mature woman of forty-four. She grimaced as she reached her front walk, forgetting about checking the mailbox. She was much too old to experience love a second time. That she'd leave to the heroines and heroes in her novels.

~~*

Avery pulled into a space in the parking lot of Carrabba's, one of her favorite restaurants in Sugar Land. When she'd called Mark to accept the invitation, he'd asked her to choose the restaurant. She'd opted to drive herself as her home was currently a man-free zone and she intended to keep it that way.

She met him exiting his SUV, close to the front door of course. She shook her head.

"Something wrong?" Mark met her on the sidewalk.

She chuckled. "I see you still have your knack for parking spots."

He shrugged and sent her a grin. "Yeah, still got it."

Five minutes later, they were seated at a table against the back brick wall, a bit out of the way and conducive to conversation. She wondered what they had to talk about.

Once the menus were delivered, Mark opened the wine list. "Would you like a glass of wine?"

"Sure."

"Red or white?"

"Pinot noir."

"Good choice." Mark flagged the waiter and ordered a bottle.

Now that she was seated across from her ex-husband, Avery couldn't think of a thing to say to him. What did they have in common? Rather than talking, she studied him studying the menu. Food had always been a serious subject for him. That was one of the reasons they clicked—she loved to cook and he loved to eat.

In fact, he'd been an excellent guinea pig for her experimenting with numerous recipes. She remembered one in particular, halved boiled eggs topped with a cilantro-tomato sauce. It was awful but he managed to eat it without gagging. To this day she had no clue why she'd prepared that particular dish. It was on her top ten list of loser-do-not-make-again recipes.

"What are you smiling at?" His question jolted her from her musings.

"Nothing." She would never let him know she'd been thinking about him. That would only create a problem or unwarranted expectations. "Have you been here before?"

"A couple of times with my brothers," he replied. "What do you usually order? I recall you have favorites by restaurant."

Avery shivered, amazed that he remembered her little idiosyncrasy. This dinner, which had barely started, was getting too intimate, too familiar, and way too fast. *Too scary.*

"Nope, don't do that anymore." Of course she went

to a restaurant for a particular dish. He didn't need to know that was still true. Some things in her life hadn't changed over the years. "Do you like shrimp and garlic sauce?"

"Uh-huh," he said as he continued to look at the menu. Yep, Mark still really liked food. In a small way, that was comforting.

The waiter, a tall middle-aged man with a serious demeanor, arrived with the wine and bread. He uncorked the bottle and intended on pouring in the glass next to Mark's water glass but Mark put his palm over the top.

He nodded to Avery. "The lady selected pinot noir, she can taste it." The wine was poured as instructed.

Avery raised her eyebrows at his tone, flirty almost. She twirled the wine in the glass then brought it to her lips. She swallowed then nodded. "Very good."

The waiter allowed a small grin then filled their glasses, set the bottle in the middle of the table, and moved on.

Mark picked up his glass. "Let's have a toast. It's been so many years since we've shared a meal."

She wondered what he might be up to. But whatever, a toast was harmless enough. She collected her glass and held it in front of her chest. "It has been a long time. What's the salute?"

He pursed his lips, focusing on something just over her shoulder. After several seconds, his gaze returned to her. He raised his glass a tad higher. "Mm, let's toast to living life to the fullest and embracing new beginnings."

"Very nice." Avery tapped her glass against Mark's. That was it? Life and new beginnings? She'd expected something more eloquent. Perhaps something significant had happened during the years since their divorce and he'd toned down his tendency for making speeches or giving lectures when asked about a subject he enjoyed.

She sipped her wine, sending him covert glances in order to study him as he again reviewed the menu. His face hadn't changed, other than a few lines around his eyes and sexy creases on the sides of his mouth. The years had been good to Mark.

"Are you ready to order?" He placed the menu over his plate. She nodded and the waiter appeared within seconds.

"What would you like this evening, Madame?" He smiled at her, flashing very white teeth.

"I'll have the quattro formaggi pizza and a small Caesar salad."

"Very well. And you, sir?"

"The filet marsala, medium rare, garlic mashed potatoes, and a small house salad. Add an antipasti plate as an appetizer." Mark nodded and threw a grin at Avery.

"Excellent choices," the waiter said as he scooped up their menus.

Many times when they were first married and money was scarce, they'd go to an Italian restaurant and order the cheapest bottle of wine with an antipasti plate. With that and the bread, they'd had an inexpensive meal in a fabulous setting. *Aarrgh*. Avery clenched her fists in her lap, vowing to stop thinking about the past. Nothing could be gained by dancing down memory lane.

"You're awfully quiet," Mark commented.

"Just thinking."

"About what?"

"Nothing."

"How can you be thinking about nothing if you're thinking?" Mark looked amused at his own question. He hadn't lost his sense of humor.

"It's not anything, really." She paused for a beat. "I don't want to share my thoughts with you."

"Why not?"

"Seriously?" She put a hand over her mouth to hide a repressed smile. It wasn't exactly a strange question, for Mark. He'd always gone after whatever he wanted. But still. "My thoughts aren't any of your business."

He sipped his wine, considering her over the rim of his glass. His gaze was direct, intense, as he seemed to contemplate her statement. "I remember a time when you couldn't wait to tell me everything on your mind."

"Uh-huh." She would not be drawn into a conversation about the past. "I remember when I believed in the Easter Bunny and Santa Claus. Those days are long gone, too."

Thankfully, the waiter stopped their conversation with the appetizer. They loaded their plates and tasted the food. The softness of the accompanying silence surprised Avery. It was comfortable. She felt no need to break it. As she popped a piece of prosciutto rolled around a slice of cantaloupe in her mouth, she considered how she could use this situation with Mark in a plot for a future book. It was the reunion story without the happily-ever-after. Maybe a murder-mystery—the ex-wife is accused of murdering her ex-husband . . . he dies after falling down a very long flight of stairs or when a hot air balloon crashes in the desert.

"Tell me how you started writing full time." Mark interrupted her thoughts with a question related to them. He'd always had a knack for that, almost zeroing in on her brain activity. She'd never liked it but what difference did it make now?

"A couple years after we split, I transferred to financial aid at HCU. Over-time wasn't required as much so I had a lot of free time. I got tired of reality shows on television and eventually decided to write a short story to fill the hours after work. I wrote another and then decided to try a novel."

"Did you publish the short stories?" Mark popped a trio of Greek olives in his mouth.

"Actually I did. I sold several to a women's magazine." She considered how much she should tell him. Well, she'd been honest in interviews so she could at least tell her ex-husband what she'd said to a random reporter. "Those sales are what prompted me to write my first novel."

"And the rest is history."

"No, the rest is a ton of hard work and dedication to the craft of writing." Once the words were out of her mouth, Avery wanted to take them back, too prickly.

He topped off their wines glasses then spoke. "I'm happy for you. Your hard work and dedication have paid off."

"You Googled me."

"Yeah, apparently you're quite the success story for self-published authors." He dipped a piece of bread into the olive oil and herb mixture in a small bowl. "I'm proud of you."

The waiter arrived with their salads and Avery swallowed her response to Mark being proud of her. He had no right to be proud of her. He had no right to be anything related to her. They weren't even friends. She forked romaine lettuce in her mouth and thought about that. Why hadn't they remained friends after the divorce?

"Thanks for that." She might as well be nice to him. Avery reminded herself, she *was a nice person*, even to her ex-husband who had walked out on her. "I have a question for you: Why didn't we stay friends after our divorce?"

Mark's fork stopped halfway to his mouth. "Friends? I thought we were."

"I haven't seen or talked to you in ten years and the last time was a chance occurrence. Friends don't do that."

"I guess you're right." He put his fork on the plate and sipped his wine. "It's entirely my fault. I'm the one who moved to Denver and didn't let you know my new address or phone number."

"And why didn't you?"

He sat back in the chair and rubbed his jaw with his right hand. She'd always loved his hands. They were big and strong and had made her feel safe when one was entwined with hers. She missed holding hands with a man. Missed holding Mark's hands. Damn it. She had no business allowing her mind to ramble down this particular road.

"Well, Mark, why didn't you stay in contact with me? Living out of state is no excuse."

He opened his mouth then shut it. She'd finally managed to render him speechless.

~~*

Mark had never been happier to see a waiter arrive and serve the entrees, the perfect diversion. He couldn't lie to Avery and he didn't want to tell her the truth just yet. They needed more time to get to know each other again. He had no intention of screwing that up.

The waiter left and he dug into his filet, thankful he'd managed to avoid her question. He needed time to gain her trust and to show her how much he still cared and would continue to care about her. Project "gaining trust and showing love" would begin now.

"While I was driving over here, I had a thought," he said.

"About what?"

"I was wondering what we might have done if we hadn't gotten married so soon after we graduated college." He'd thought about this many times over the last couple of years. Figured it was a middle-aged thing.

"I'd have gone to law school." She smiled then sipped her wine.

"Really?" She'd managed to surprise him right off the bat. "I never knew that."

"I thought I'd enjoy working for a big corporation in their legal department."

"I wish you'd told me about this. We could have made law school work."

She shrugged. "Hard to know. I chalked it up to bad timing."

"And you never found the right time."

"Nope," Avery said and smiled. Her smile could light a Christmas tree. "But now, I'm happy with my work. If I couldn't find the time when I was younger, it wasn't meant to be."

"That sounds philosophical."

"One of the bonuses of getting older."

"We're not that old." He avoided thinking about his age or aging at all costs. Aging was depressing and unavoidable. Why worry about something he couldn't control?

"I turned forty-four my last birthday."

"I know." He chuckled.

"Right, I forgot our birthdays are a week apart." Avery smiled again and Mark's heart picked up a beat. Reminding her of the good things was next on the agenda.

He cut a small piece of filet then scooped a bit of potatoes on the fork with it. He reached across the table. "Here, taste my steak." Back in the day they would always share restaurant dishes—double the foodie fun Avery had said.

She accepted the bite and briefly closed her eyes. "Hmm, very good. I love garlic mashed potatoes." She placed a slice of the pizza on his plate. "Now you try my four-cheese pizza. And tell me what you didn't do because we got married after college."

He took a large bite of the pizza, chewed, and nodded. "Good, very cheesy. What I would have done is take a year off before starting work and bum around Europe."

"I had no idea."

"It was my dream year." He sighed. Damn, he hadn't thought about that particular fantasy in a long time. "But you were more important to me so I concentrated on getting a job, saving money, and proposing."

"Have you considered that you might have made the wrong decision back then?"

"Not a chance. I'll never regret marrying you."

~~*

Avery's nerves were tingling. Sitting so close to Mark during dinner had her resisting the urge to jump out of the chair and cover his face with kisses. An unexpected reaction for sure—a surprise from the past or the result of her lack of male companionship the past year or two? She'd been on a hiatus from dating and had spent all her time cranking out books for her cozy mystery series.

She'd refused a coffee or cappuccino and now walked out the front door of Carrabba's with Mark behind her. Stopping at the sidewalk near his SUV, she turned to him.

"Thank you for dinner." She extended her hand. "I enjoyed the conversation."

Mark took her hand, his thumb slowly skimming over the top. Her nerves escalated from tingling to all out body slapping.

"My pleasure." He pulled her hand gently, and she moved a step closer to him.

"Um . . . it was good seeing you again." Avery attempted to tug her hand from his, but he held it, stepped toward her. Sirens went off in her head. They were too close. She'd suffocate from the bombardment of memories. "I need to get going."

He leaned closer, his woodsy cologne surrounded her, and the subtle nuances of spice tickled her nose. His mouth brushed feather soft over her ear, his voice barely a whisper. "See me again, please." He held onto her hand. "We can do whatever you want."

Avery's mind clouded and moved in circles. Mark's touch wasn't helping to clear her head. She hadn't anticipated seeing him after this one dinner and wasn't sure whether it was a good idea. Their marriage was long over, all communications cut. But . . . he *was* a huge part of her past.

She pulled back her hand then placed both hands on his chest and pushed him back. She needed space to think. What could they do? Keep it simple. "How about dinner and a movie? My treat."

"I like that idea. Will Friday work?"

"That's fine." She backed further away from him. "I really need to go. I'll see you around six-thirty." She turned and escaped to her car.

Driving home she reflected on her decision to see Mark again. Why should she? Why did she agree to it? She knew the answer as easily as she knew her birthday. Because she was nuts and still had feelings for him no matter how hard she worked at keeping them buried. Those feelings bubbled up at the worst times.

She needed to talk with her sister and punched Ashley's name on the car's phone contact list. Her husband, Dustin, answered as Ashley had a child throwing up right then. Avery sighed; her sister always had all the fun.

December 5, Friday

Avery had worked her butt off all of Thursday and Friday morning to have the first draft of her current manuscript completed four hours ahead of her five p.m. deadline. This constituted the best part of her writing process—completing the guts of the story and then looking forward to refining and polishing during the revising phase, scheduled to commence first thing on Monday morning.

After putting the book to bed she'd taken a shower and visited the grocery store. Mark didn't know that her version of dinner and a movie was a home-cooked meal and a romantic comedy or action film. She had quite the collection of movie DVD's along with a wide-screen television.

She'd reviewed her stash of favorite main dish recipes and decided on shrimp scampi over angel hair pasta with grilled asparagus and mozzarella-parmesan bread. Due to a hankering for chocolate yesterday, she'd made her favorite chocolate mousse late last night. It would be a nice dessert after the shrimp and pasta.

With an hour to spare, Avery had everything ready in her compact kitchen to prepare a simple dinner for her ex-husband. She poured a glass of wine and walked the few steps to the fireplace. The temperature was still cold outside so a blazing fire seemed perfect to set a cozy and friendly mood for her home.

Avery's house was on the small side, square footage-wise, yet she had added her own touches to make it seem much larger. The living room furniture consisted of an Aggie-maroon leather couch and chair and turquoise tables. A bookcase of her favorite books and family photo's added a homey touch along with a twelve-inch sculpture of a mother and child she'd picked up at a garage sale.

She stepped to the fireplace, turned on the gas, and swept a long match against the dark red brick of the hearth. After poking the match into the kindling, flames built quickly along the base of the logs. She nodded in satisfaction.

Resting on her favorite chair with her feet on the ottoman and sipping a glass of pre-dinner wine, Avery finally relaxed and focused on the evening ahead. She'd purposely given little thought to Mark since arriving home Wednesday night. Her manuscript had taken precedence until the next deadline, which thankfully, had been achieved.

She had two full days of no writing. She was fortunate being a fast writer and could produce books at a steady pace. Although she wasn't even close to the same sales or award level as say, Charlaine Harris or Sue Grafton, Avery was trying like crazy to gain new readers with her books and through her marketing efforts. Promotion was the curse of every writer, whether writing mystery or romance.

Sipping her wine, she transitioned easily from writing to Mark. He'd looked really good Wednesday evening. Frankly, that was expected. But the fact that he hadn't remarried surprised the hell out of her. Why another woman hadn't reeled him in seemed weird. He was quite the catch in her opinion. But then again, she'd not allowed a man to reel her in during the past fifteen years. She rose and prodded the logs with a poker tool. Flames rose higher, cupping the sides of the logs. Good, she mentally checked "start a fire" on her to-do list.

Grabbing her wine glass, she went to her bedroom. The turtleneck sweater she wore was too hot. She stripped it off and looked at her closet for a replacement. A white long sleeved shirt would work. She buttoned it in front of the bathroom mirror, turned side to side, and unbuttoned the top button to show a little cleavage.

No. This wasn't a date.

On the other hand, she could show cleavage if she wanted to. It was a free country. She applied a little lip-gloss and went to the kitchen. She pulled a pot and a skillet out of the cabinet and placed them on the stove.

Why the heck was she doing this? Five days ago she hadn't given a thought to Mark in weeks, and now she struggled to keep him out of her head. This simply wouldn't do. They'd eat dinner. He'd leave. That would be the end of it. Her ex-husband needed to stay in her past—where he belonged.

~~*

The sky darkened with a heavy cloud cover as Mark pulled in Avery's driveway, five minutes early. He hadn't realized how close they lived to each other until he entered her address into the vehicle's navigation system. Thus, he was early for their date. He exited his vehicle and rang the doorbell.

Before he could say "Merry Christmas" three times, Avery opened the door and invited him in. He handed her a bottle of wine.

"Thanks for this," she said as she studied the label. "Chianti Classico Riserva, sounds good."

"Hope so, the guy at the liquor store said it's a popular Italian wine."

She ushered him through a wide foyer to a living-family room that opened to the kitchen. The rooms weren't overly spacious but comfortably furnished and inviting. He liked it. She turned to him. "Let me take your coat."

"Shouldn't you be putting yours on?"

"I thought I'd cook for you rather than going out."

"Oh, sounds great." He loved the idea and quickly shrugged off his coat. She draped it over the back of a chair at the oak table in the breakfast area.

"Would you like a glass of wine or a cocktail," she asked.

"Wine sounds good."

"Have a seat in the living room."

Mark settled in a corner of the sofa and looked around. He really liked the colors. Of course, Aggie-maroon would always be a favorite. He noticed a framed photo on the side table and leaned closer for a better look. My God, he remembered the day it was taken. He, Avery, Ashley, and her boyfriend had gone to Schlitterbahn Water Park in New Braunfels their senior year at A&M. They had all been laughing at the end of the day and vowed to stay friends after graduation. Right. That didn't happen, in—

"We're having shrimp so I opened chardonnay," Avery said as she handed him a glass. "It won't take long to cook." She settled in the chair adjacent to the sofa.

"Thanks. I was looking at the picture. I forgot the name of Ashley's boyfriend."

"Dustin Evans. They're married with four kids."

"Wow, four kids. That must have happened after we split. I thought they broke up after graduation." A flare of sadness rolled through Mark. What else had he missed over the years? At that moment his life seemed empty.

"They got back together after seeing each other at a Rolling Stones concert. And it wasn't long before they decided to get married. In fact, they married the day our divorce finalized."

"Ouch. That couldn't have been easy for you."

"No, it wasn't at the time." She turned toward the fireplace and sipped her wine. He wondered what she was thinking. Did she have regrets about their divorce? Her gaze slid to him and she smiled. "It was hard . . . but like anything else, you deal with it. My sister means more to me than my hurt feelings."

He was stunned by her words. "Hurt feelings? That's all the impact our divorce had on you?" Jesus, he could barely function for almost two years. How could she be so cavalier?

She looked at him like he'd grown horns. "Do you really want me to sit here and whine to you about how the divorce devastated me?" She rose and leaned over to pick up her wine glass.

His gaze zeroed in on the tantalizing display of cleavage, via her open shirt . . . nice, very nice. Avery straightened, taking the view with her.

She walked to the kitchen. "I'll start cooking."

He rose and followed her, seating himself on a high

stool at the granite countertop across from the sink. The kitchen was small but seemed organized as she moved from the gas stove to the counter by the sink. The appliances were stainless steel and the cabinets were painted an ivory color. He liked it.

Ignoring any talk about their divorce seemed like the best avenue for him. He'd treat this dinner as a real date and use the opportunity to get to know Avery. Right. He'd think of it as the next step in his win-back-Avery plan.

"Anything I can do to help?" He hoped her mood would lighten after his bonehead question.

"Nope, I've got everything under control."

If her tone was any indication, she was good and pissed at him. Definitely time to switch tactics.

"Tell me about your writing, how do you come up with the stories?"

She threw him an irritated glance before sliding a cookie sheet into the oven. "Don't ask unless you really want to know. Writers love to talk about writing."

"Of course I want to know." He'd talk about anything as long as she'd talk with him and wasn't mad.

She dumped spaghetti in a pot then poured something in a wide skillet soon followed by big shrimp. *[See EC on page 272]*

He'd always loved watching her cook. It fascinated him, seeing how comfortable she was in a kitchen. He'd been the guinea pig for many recipes she had to try. "Do you still enjoy cooking?"

"Uh-huh, always looking for that next killer recipe." After stirring the shrimp for a bit she dumped them in a bowl.

"What did you pour in the pan before the shrimp?" He watched her do it again.

She glanced at him then sipped her wine. "It's olive oil."

"Oh, should have known that. Guess I'm more of a take-out guy."

~~*

Avery topped off their wine glasses then sat across from Mark at her breakfast table. The occasion didn't quite merit the use of the dining room. Although she did love to show off the oak sideboard she'd purchased in New Orleans not long after moving in. She doubted he'd be interested in knowing how long she'd saved to buy her first house and its accessories.

"This looks fantastic," Mark said as he dug a fork into the shrimp scampi.

"It's one of my favorite recipes."

"What else do you like to do besides cooking and writing?"

"That's pretty much it. My life revolves around writing or researching for one of my stories." And how boring and sad did that sound. "I attend a writing conference about every quarter. I had to limit them as they're a time suck."

"Time suck?"

She watched him stuff shrimp and roasted asparagus into his mouth. It was nice to see a man enjoy her cooking. That simple thought made her sad. Why hadn't she cooked for the men she'd dated over the years? She knew why—it was too personal, too intimate. Yet here she was in her own home, sharing a meal she'd prepared with her ex-husband. Yep, she was certifiably nuts.

"Avery." Mark waved a hand in front of her face. "You okay?"

"Sorry, what was the question?"

"You mentioned something about a time suck."

"Oh, right. After I had some success with my books, I had a lot of speaking requests at conferences and workshops. As long as they were expenses paid, I attended." She took a bite of shrimp. "The exposure to readers and other writers was fantastic, but my writing time took a hit from all the traveling. So after three years, I decided to limit them to four per year."

"That sounds wise. What do you speak about?"

"The craft of writing, developing characters, having a career as an indie writer." She sipped her wine then pulled off a piece of bread. "I have several talks I give and I keep thinking up new ones. I've thought about doing monthly workshops but don't have enough time to do them justice."

"You sound busy."

"I've worked hard at gaining readers. Keeping them means publishing new books on a regular basis." That was enough talking about her life. She'd already shared too much. Her response to his question made it sound like she did nothing but work. Unfortunately, that was close to the truth.

"You didn't answer me before. How do you come up with ideas for your stories?" Mark was on his second helping of scampi—yes, she talked too much.

"Everywhere. You'd be surprised how much the

news can stimulate a writer's mind."

He chuckled. "That doesn't surprise me. People do some pretty crazy things."

"That they do."

"Tell me, what have you ever done that's crazy?" His eyes narrowed just enough to confirm the teasing tone in his voice.

"That's easy, cooking one of my favorite recipes for my ex-husband." The comment was out before Avery had a chance to filter her words. "Oops, sorry."

"No problem, I totally understand."

"Really? What have you done that's so crazy?"

"Asking my ex-wife out on a date." He had a "so-there" look on his face.

"This isn't a date."

"It is to me."

"It shouldn't be."

"It is.

"Is not." She suddenly realized how ridiculous their conversation sounded, and couldn't hold back a low chuckle. "We sound like twelve year-olds."

He grinned, but kept any thoughts or comments to himself.

She took her last bite and rose to clear her dishes. "Are you full? I have dessert."

"Yes, I'm full and yes, I'd love dessert but can I have a few minutes to rest?"

"Sure. You put the movie in while I clean off the table." Avery pointed to the mantel over the fireplace. "I selected a few options from my collection. You choose. The DVD player is in the bookshelf."

"I can handle that." Mark rose and carried his dishes to the sink despite Avery's protest. "I'll get out of your way and pick our movie."

"And I'll start a pot of coffee." She accidentally bumped his hip, and he placed his hands on her shoulders to steady her. She froze for a moment, licking her lips at his nearness—at the scent of his cologne as it swirled around her head. She stepped back and he dropped his arms. "Sorry. I don't usually try to knock over my guests."

"No problem." His voice sounded rough, a little edgy and hoarse. "I'll go check out your movies. Hope you've got something besides chick flicks." He went to the fireplace and picked up the stack of DVD cases on the mantle.

Avery took advantage of the separation. She released the breath she'd been holding since she'd bumped into Mark. The feel of his hands on her shoulders had elicited the strongest urge in her to wrap her arms around him and to hug him like crazy. Thankfully, common sense ruled and she'd stepped away. But the urge had definitely been there. What was wrong with her? She could not— would not—allow her feelings for Mark to bubble to the surface. That had all the makings of a full-blown disaster. She no longer lived through disasters, she wrote about them.

She started a pot of coffee then quickly rinsed the plates and silverware, stowing them in the dishwasher. Everything else she left soaking in the sink. Walking into the living room, Mark held up a DVD case.

"How about this one?"

"Mm, love Tom Cruise and Val Kilmer without their shirts. Put it in." She stoked the fire and added a log before sitting in the chair, leaving the sofa for Mark.

"I could have done that," Mark said, pointing to the fire.

"No problem, I'm quite the fire builder now." She pulled the remote for the DVD player out of a drawer of the little chest next to her chair. "Are you ready?"

"You bet. It's been years since I watched *Top Gun*."

"You picked a good one."

Forty-five minutes into the movie, Avery remembered the coffee and dessert. She hit the pause button. "Let's take a few minutes. I'll get dessert. Restroom is down the hall."

While Mark took a bathroom break, she poured coffee into tall mugs and retrieved the chocolate mousse bowls from the refrigerator. She situated everything on a wide tray along with cream, sugar, spoons, and a plate of lemon crisp cookies.

He re-entered the kitchen in time to take the tray from her hands. "I'll get that."

"Thanks. Set it on the ottoman."

Back on the sofa, he immediately reached for a dish of mousse while Avery opted for coffee.

"This is good." Mark said. "I'm happy you've continued to enjoy cooking."

His comment surprised her. "I didn't cook just because I was married to you. I started when I was a teenager."

"Sorry, what I meant is that I'm happy you didn't stop because you didn't have anyone to cook for."

"Mark, just so you know, while we were married, my world didn't revolve totally around you."

"That's not what I meant. I've always thought . . . well, the main reason we got divorced was because we started dating at eighteen. We never developed as adults outside of our connection to each another."

"Oh."

"There was never a fully developed adult me, or a fully developed adult you," he explained. "As a result, we always resisted working on the 'us' part of our marriage."

"I see."

"And not having that resulted in our lack of, um . . . our lack of properly dealing with us not getting pregnant."

"How could we have dealt with it better?" Avery didn't like the direction of this conversation.

"I've thought about this a lot, even talked to a therapist." He picked up a mug and drank. "I think we should have considered adopting."

"Adopting? I can't see you accepting a child that wasn't your own."

"That shows how much you don't know about me. Like I said before, we were too young."

She pursed her lips. "I don't think age had anything to do with it. We didn't have a strong enough marriage to deal with my issue."

"Your issue? It was *our issue*. And you not realizing that shows just how young we were."

"No. It wasn't age. We were twenty-seven. We didn't fit together in the ways that mattered."

"What the hell does that mean?" Mark appeared to be getting riled up.

"It means we were too different." How could she make him understand? "We couldn't even agree on where to buy a house. We—"

"You are so wrong. We couldn't *afford* to buy a house." His voice had risen.

"Whatever. It's silly to argue about it now. Would you like more coffee?"

"No, no more coffee. Thank you. Avery, I think we need to talk about all of this . . . talk about the real reason we got divorced."

"The *real* reason?" That was it. She wanted to dump her coffee over his head.

"Yes, since time has passed I think we can look at everything more objectively." Now he sounded like a prosecuting attorney giving his summation to the jury.

No way on earth would Avery discuss their divorce. It was fifteen years too late. "It's almost ten, and I don't think this is a good time for a discussion." She rose and walked toward the kitchen with her cup. "I've had a long day."

"Avery, stop."

She turned around. "What?"

"Don't walk away from this."

She rolled her eyes. "Mark, there's no need to rehash the past. We married. We divorced. We're over."

From the darkening of his eyes, she guessed her words didn't please him. He opened his mouth, and then shut it. After a moment he spoke. "This discussion isn't finished." He carried the tray to the kitchen. "Thanks for dinner." He gathered his coat and shrugged it on.

She clenched her jaw and walked to the front door. After reaching for the doorknob, she felt a hand on her arm.

"Avery, wait." Mark's much too large frame stood too close. His cologne once again swirled around her, creating images of them resting on a thick quilt on the floor next to the fireplace. He was taking off her sweater and—

"I want to see you again," he said, his voice low and sexy. He stepped closer to her.

Oh, dear God. She'd just described her ex-husband's voice as sexy. She was mad, out of her freaking mind mad. "I'm not sure that's a good—"

He bent forward and captured her lips, silencing her attempt to keep a distance from him. His arms circled her waist and he pulled her closer as his mouth moved to her ear. "I've missed you so much," he whispered.

Avery once again pushed at his chest and he had the good sense to draw back. "What the hell is wrong with you?" She stepped away from him and hit the wall with a soft thud.

Mark reached an arm toward her but didn't move closer. "You okay," he said, his voice low.

"I'm fine."

"Are you sure?"

"Yes." She rolled her eyes.

"I'm sorry. I got carried away." He dropped his arm away from her. "I keep doing that with you. I'll head out then." He opened the door and stepped onto the porch.

"Thanks again for dinner. I hope we can get together again."

Standing in the doorway with the porch light illuminating the small space, she considered his suggestion and didn't know how to respond, didn't know how she felt about it. "I'm . . . I'm not sure. Seeing you again has confused me. I need to think about all this, about things you said."

He smiled that sexy grin he'd used on more than one occasion when they were married to turn her concerns and doubts to mush. "Of course." He leaned forward and kissed her cheek. "I'll call you in a few days." He turned and walked to his truck, waving at her before he climbed in.

Once his vehicle hit the street, she closed the door and locked it. Damn, double damn. He'd somehow managed to turn her orderly life upside down. She was tired in both body and mind so she'd think about it tomorrow. Her brain needed time to evaluate his words, as well as his actions. Then she'd do her usual analysis of the he said-she said. Only this time the analytical acrobatics would be for real, not for fiction.

Well, she might as well have a glass of wine while she watched the rest of the movie. Tom Cruise was the perfect distraction for an unsettling evening and an unsettled mind.

December 11, Thursday

Over the last month Mark had tried several different routes for his morning run. He liked the variety of scenery to dull the humdrum of running for exercise. Sure the morning business report on the satellite radio pounding through ear buds helped keep him awake, but running was running.

He did it for exercise. He'd much rather hear the daily report munching a bagel and drinking a good cup of coffee. He exercised because it was good for his health, not because he was a saint.

He rounded a corner and a familiar figure came into view. Perfect. He wouldn't need to call Avery after all. He jogged a few yards and stopped, waited a moment for her to reach him. He knew when she recognized him by the slight raising of her right hand. Good, she wasn't in a totally lousy mood at the sight of him.

"Hey, Mark," she said as she stopped in front of him. "I figured I'd run into you one of these days."

"Yeah, how've you been?"

"Good, working on revising my latest book before it goes to my editor. Tedious work."

"Not sure I know what that means." He looked at the ground for a moment, noticing the cracks in the sidewalk and the leaves scattered across it. "I had planned on calling you this morning. Would you like to go to the Nutcracker Ballet?"

"The one at the Wortham Center in Houston?"

"Uh-huh, I have a pair of box tickets for this Saturday's afternoon performance." He wondered if it was too lame for a guy to ask a girl to the ballet. Somehow it seemed weird, but he did have the tickets, provided by his job as a Christmas employee bonus.

Something flashed in her eyes—admiration or disgust or sympathy. Damn, he couldn't read her as well as he used to. But he could tell she was conflicted about his suggestion.

"Hmm . . . well, okay, I'd like that. What time is the performance?" She jogged in pace as she talked.

"It's at two. I thought we could go to dinner after."

"Okay, sounds good."

"Great. I'll pick you up at twelve forty-five."

"Fine, see you then." She headed past him toward the corner where he'd first noticed her. He turned to watch her. She had a very nice running stride, aka a good ass that minimally bounced with every step. He enjoyed watching her run down the block in the opposite direction.

He hoped she'd eventually run toward him, full of desire and wanting.

~~*

Avery rested the back of her hand on her forehead as she walked in the door, twenty minutes after bumping into Mark on her morning run. She figured she must be sick since she agreed to see him again. Why was she putting herself through this? She didn't feel feverish, so she couldn't blame it on illness—just stupidity.

Once she showered and dressed in her favorite cable knit sweater and jeans, she poured a cup of coffee then headed to the study for another round of revising. It had been going so well she might meet her deadline a couple of days early. Her landline rang as she settled in the desk chair.

"You have time for lunch today?" Ashley wasn't one for pleasantries; she always got right to the point.

"I guess, my work is progressing faster than normal."

"Good. After we eat, I need help choosing a new cocktail dress."

"What's the occasion?"

"Dustin's Christmas office party is a week from Friday. I haven't attended in a couple of years and want to wow his co-workers."

Avery chuckled. Ashley had always been the more competitive twin. "I can't take all afternoon."

"Great. Meet me at the Black Walnut Café at eleven-thirty." Ashley also had a tendency to determine where they'd eat. Avery had long since abandoned the thought of changing her sister's selection of restaurants. No point since she always made excellent choices.

~~*

After Caesar salads with grilled chicken and glasses of iced tea, Avery and Ashley entered First Colony Mall to find the perfect cocktail dress. Avery followed her sister from store to store, looking at one dress after another but none caught the made-to-party eye of Ashley.

Avery groaned and massaged her neck. "We've been moving so fast from store to store I might have whiplash. Tell me again what you're looking for."

Ashley sifted through another offering of cocktail dresses in a rainbow of jewel colors. "I told you I'll know it when I see it."

"Then why am I here?"

"Moral support, of course." Ashley squeezed Avery's arm as she turned away from another rack, shaking her head. "This isn't the day. Maybe I need to go to the Galleria Mall in Houston. Could you—"

"No, sorry, I can't take the time to go with you. My revised manuscript is due in a week."

"All right, let's go."

They threaded their way out of the store and through the busy mall to the same door they'd entered. They exited and Avery had a thought as she wrapped a scarf around her neck.

"We didn't stop in Talbots. Let's give it a try." The store was in the newer outdoor part of the mall.

They walked in silence for a minute and entered the store. Avery immediately moved to a table of cashmere sweaters while her sister walked to the back in search of that to-die-for dress. She lightly ran her hand over a stack of black sweaters, so soft. They were vee-necked with a trim a white crystals and beads matching the sweater color along the neckline. Avery headed to the changing room with three different colors.

Shrugging off her jacket she reminded herself she didn't really need another sweater. But since she was there she might as well try one on and pulled her old sweater over her head. The black one went on first. Oh my, it fit her perfectly and the neckline was the spot-on mix of fancy and tailored. No way could she pass up this sweater. They were on sale, two for something, so two it would be, black and red.

Outside the fitting room, she found Ashley in front

of a mirror and wearing a gorgeous dress. The white sleeveless top contrasted perfectly with its narrow black skirt. Avery walked around her sister admiring the way the dress fit, making Ashley look like a model.

"Yes ma'am, this is the one. You look incredible."

"Thanks, I like it, too. Let me go change." Ashley was back in less than five minutes carrying the dress over her arm and beaming. "Thank you for suggesting we come in here. I'm taking you out for a glass of wine and pizza. All this shopping has made me hungry."

That sounded just fine to Avery since her feet hurt. It wouldn't hamper her schedule to spend a little more time with her sister. "Sounds good to me. How about Grimaldi's?"

"Absolutely." Ashley carefully handed the dress to a store clerk. "Isn't this gorgeous?"

Within fifteen minutes, they sat at Grimaldi's long oak bar studying the menu; their shopping bags deposited on a stool next to Ashley.

Ashley closed her menu. "Small pizza and wine?"

"I'll choose the wine and you select the pizza."

"Fair enough." Ashley beckoned the bartender who arrived promptly with a friendly smile. "We'd like a small thin crust pizza with Kalamata olives and pesto."

"And two glasses of Napa Vines Chardonnay," Avery added and handed over the menu.

"Excellent choices, ladies, your wine will be right out." The bartender nodded and moved to the other side of the bar.

"This was a good idea," Avery said. "We haven't been out in a long time."

"And who's busy all the time writing fabulous books?"

"And who runs a household with four active kids and a fabulous husband?"

The bartender brought their wine.

"Okay, you're right." Ashley tasted the wine and nodded her approval. "At least with Christmas coming we'll spend plenty of time relaxing."

"Relaxing? You're nuts." Avery started listing items on her fingers. "Decorating, shopping, cookie and candy making, entertaining, and cooking meals—what's relaxing about that?"

"Oh, poo, all that stuff is fun. It's a blast with the kids."

Avery turned away from the look of happiness masking her sister's face. Of course everything was more fun with kids. And without them there was no need to really get into the holiday spirit. Tears threatened and she chastised herself. After all these years she should have grown a thicker skin about being childless. She felt a hand on her knee and turned toward her twin.

"I am so very sorry . . . that was a stupid and thoughtless comment. I know the Christmas holidays are rough for you."

"You'd think after fifteen years I could be an adult about it." Avery sipped her wine for a bit of courage. She'd not told Ashley about her time with Mark and felt out of sorts for not sharing it. She was surprised her sister hadn't picked up on it.

"You are a wonderful adult and it hurts. Own your feelings as Dr. Phil or Dr. Laura or somebody says. You feel what you feel." Ashley settled back against the barstool, her eyes narrowed at her sister. "However . . . *I get the feeling* something is going on that I don't know about."

Ah, she'd picked up on it after all. "Actually there is. I ran into Mark at Starbucks last week."

"Mark? Oh, ex-husband, Mark?"

"That's the one."

"How did it go? Did you kick him in the nuts or break his arm?"

Avery shook her head, throwing back the last of her wine. "Nope, I cooked him dinner."

Ashley caught the bartender's attention. "Two more glasses of the same, please." Her focus quickly shifted. "Why am I just now hearing about this?"

"It's complicated. Talking with him has been weird, but kinda cool, too." She shrugged, scrunched her face. "He's moved back to Texas and—"

The bartender arrived with their pizza and refills. "Here you go, ladies. Let me know if you need anything else."

Ashley served them each a slice on small plates. "Has Mark moved to Sugar Land?"

"He bought a townhouse over on Sweetwater. He got a promotion and transferred back from Denver."

"How was it? I mean . . . was it strange talking to him?"

"When I saw him at Starbuck's it was so fast that I didn't really have much of a reaction, good or bad. But when he sent the flowers I—"

Ashley's arm shot out and scuffed Avery's arm.

"Shut up. He sent you flowers?"

"A vase of pink and white daisies. Anyway, we went to dinner that night and it was nice. No arguing or nasty words." Avery hadn't even admitted that to herself—seeing Mark had been pleasant. "We had a nice talk on Friday at my house. He enjoyed the shrimp scampi and chocolate mousse, but he always was crazy about my cooking."

"You *cooked* for him?"

"Uh-huh."

"So you pulled out the big guns." Ashley's eyes narrowed again. Avery could see the gears turning in her sister's mind, imagining that something was, when clearly, something wasn't.

"Do not go there. Nothing is happening between Mark and I, nor will it."

"How do you know that? He's always had a special place in your heart . . . even after the divorce." Ashley wagged a finger. "Sisters know these things."

"Yeah, and some sisters have over active imaginations. After we go to the Nutcracker Ballet on Saturday, I'm not seeing him again."

Ashley nearly choked on a piece of pizza. Once the coughing subsided, she sipped her wine and smiled. "Another date, huh?"

"No, it's not a date. He got the tickets from work and I'm going with him because I haven't been to the ballet in years."

"Right. And I'm a forty-something virgin."

December 13, Saturday

Avery worked a few hours Saturday morning to re-write a crucial scene that was giving her indigestion. This was a normal occurrence for a writer during the polishing phase of producing a reader-loving book. She checked the time on her laptop monitor, and shut down the computer. She had one hour to get ready before Mark's arrival.

After a warm shower she wrapped a terry robe around her and sifted through her closet. What to wear? It was still cold outside so a sweater would work and decided on the new black one with sparkles around the neckline. She added skinny black jeans, black ballet flats, and some dangly earrings.

After moisturizing, drying her hair, and applying make-up, she dressed. She studied her reflection in the full-length mirror, and spared a smile for herself. She looked good for a woman her age. She had maintained a slim figure and had no lines on her face. She ran her hands over the soft cashmere covering her flat belly, her slim hips, and nodded in approval. The new sweater was perfect.

The doorbell rang. She spritzed Chanel No. 5 on her wrists and headed for the front door.

"Hey." Mark's impressively handsome presence filled her doorway. "Are you ready for some ballet?"

"Absolutely. Hold on, I need to get my coat and purse." She hurried inside and slipped into her black pea coat, wrapped a white scarf around her neck, and grabbed her purse and keys off a stool.

"Okay, I'm ready." She shut the door behind her and walked with Mark to his SUV. Within minutes they were on the Southwest Freeway, headed north to Houston.

"How have you been this last week?" Mark asked.

"Good. Working, making solid progress." Avery wondered if she had anything else to talk about besides her writing. Seems like that was all she thought about—how boring. "I'm looking forward to getting a break for the holidays."

"Are you going somewhere?"

Why would he think that? She never traveled for fun these days. "No. I'll be relaxing at home and researching a hot tub."

"Thinking about having one put in?"

"Yes, I thought it would be nice after I run or need to relax." She imagined herself kicking back with a cold beverage and letting the water soothe her aches. "I figure I'll get a better deal if I have it installed off-season. It's a Christmas gift to myself."

"I like the way you think. I'm considering buying myself a road bike. I need to cut down on the running miles as my left knee is giving me problems."

"Really? Sorry to hear that." Avery was fortunate she'd not had any knee problems herself . . . but maybe it would be good to try something new. She made a mental note to check out bikes. "Do you have a doctor here? I know a great orthopedist.'

"I could use a referral. What's the name?"

"Actually, you already know him . . . it's Ashley's husband, Dustin. He's on staff at Methodist Hospital and works at their sports clinic on Highway 6."

"You're kidding me." His mouth gaped open. "That skinny guy who loved beer is a medical doctor?"

"Yep, and he's a good doc, too."

"That is awesome."

It didn't take long to exit the freeway and reach downtown Houston via Louisiana Street. They parked in the Theatre District underground garage and were soon taking the beautiful escalator up from the first level of the Wortham Center to the lobby area for the Brown Theater.

A ballet market with nutcrackers of all sizes and various dance-oriented gifts stood in the middle. A few mini-ballerinas and costumed mice we circling the area posing for pictures with excited children.

Avery watched a little girl with blonde curls and a magenta dress pose with a ballerina in front of her mother's camera. She turned away from the sight as Mark touched her arm.

"Would you like something to drink? We don't need to find our seats quite yet."

"Sure." She turned her attention to Mark. "I'll take a latte or a cappuccino if they have it."

"I'll be right back." He walked to the bar area.

She turned back to the child and the posing ballerina but they had disappeared into the crowd. Avery sighed as she thought about the fun in dressing a little girl in fancy clothes to go to the ballet. She looked around the lobby, noticing all the children. How exciting it must be for them. Something she'd never experienced with a child. She sighed again and walked toward Mark.

~~*

Mark wasn't really a fan of ballet. But the bonus of sitting through the Nutcracker so close to Avery made it worthwhile. He took full advantage of their proximity to each other and even held her hand on his knee. It surprised the hell out of him that she didn't pull it back. But now at Pappas Steakhouse, they were seated across from each other in a cozy booth, no handholding.

They'd ordered Crème Brule for dessert and were waiting for it to arrive. Avery had talked about her writing during dinner. It seemed well rehearsed, like she'd given talks about it. He wanted to get under that outer layer of public charm. But how? He knew he still wasn't her favorite person, although he intended to eventually change that.

"Come on, Avery, you've given me the public version of your accomplishments. What was it like to have such instant success?"

"If you'd been listening you'd realize it wasn't instant."

Damn, he needed to watch his words. "Sorry, bad choice of words. What I meant is how did it make you feel when you did hit the big time?"

"Well . . . I'd paid my dues by submitting to contests and agents and I paid attention to any criticism. I'd written a dozen manuscripts before I published five at one time." She lifted her coffee cup then set it on the saucer and leaned forward, her eyes sending off sparks. "Actually, when those five books took off like a rocket, I felt like I was on top of the world."

"And what did you do to celebrate?" He hoped it was something crazy, like dancing naked in the rain or going without a bra for a day.

"I did drink champagne. Ashley and Dustin bought me a bottle of Dom Perignon and we had it with chocolate and almonds."

"Almonds?"

"Yeah, I love them. Geez, you don't remember that?"

"Sorry, sure, I remember." Mark realized right then just how much he loved her. It was weird. He nearly blurted it out but that would only turn her off. He needed to be smart. He needed to convince her she needed him in her life—just as much as he needed her in his.

"No problem. Things have been great since I first published."

"Sounds like you're satisfied with the way your life has turned out."

Avery scrutinized him with narrowed eyes and smiled. "You're fishing. What do you really want to know?"

"Are you happy, Avery?" He hoped she'd talk to him rather than blow off his question. He gave her a slow smile. "I mean, are you truly happy?"

"Yes, I'm happy . . . truly happy." She tilted her head, her gaze searching his eyes. "Why are you asking?"

The waiter arrived with dessert and he avoided answering her question. He'd leave it be for now but his gut told him she needed to spill her guts about their divorce before they had any chance of creating a happily-ever-after together.

~~*

Once they'd taken a Sugar Land exit off the freeway going back home, Avery's stomach became queasy. Should she ask Mark in for a cup of coffee or a nightcap? Would he try to kiss her goodnight? Did she want to kiss him again?

Too many questions, too many unknowns, she shook her head. Life had become complicated.

"Everything okay?" Mark glanced at her briefly before patting her leg.

"Yeah, all is good."

They drove in silence until he pulled in her driveway. She gasped at the sight of water running down her front porch onto the walkway and then the driveway.

"What the hell?" Mark said, throwing his SUV into park.

Avery jumped out as the truck jerked to a stop. Mark followed her. "Where's your main water valve?"

"By the street, to the left of the driveway." Thankfully the sprinkler guy had shown her the valve last summer.

"I'll turn it off. Don't go in the house."

Mark sounded calm and in control. In contrast, her stomach had plummeted to her toes. Her hands were clammy and shaky. This had disaster written all over it. Something must have exploded or broke or . . . or, burst. Was it even safe to go in?

She waited on the porch for Mark to appear. When he did, the two of them peered through the beveled glass window of the door. Water. Everywhere. Crap.

"You've got a leak somewhere. Water heater would be my guess." Mark stepped back. "Any electrical outlets on the floor?"

"No."

"It should be okay to go inside."

Mark had correctly diagnosed the disaster as a burst water heater in the attic. The ceiling over Avery's bed had collapsed and two inches of water covered the floors of the majority of rooms in her small home. She chose not to think about the damage and the considerable amount of cleanup in her future. There'd be enough time to think about that tomorrow morning.

Mark suggested she stay with him for the night, and after a half-hearted attempt to argue, she agreed. After all, he had a guest room, unlike her sister. Avery gathered clothing and toiletries in a rolling suitcase, along with her laptop. Mark tuned off the electricity to be safe.

Less than thirty minutes later they headed to Mark's townhouse. While they drove, she called her insurance company and submitted a verbal claim. They'd call her in the morning as to the arrival of the claims representative and the cleanup company.

Mark turned off Sweetwater onto Wedgewood Way and made a sharp left to a short driveway with a metal gate. He punched a control on the visor and the gate slid open. Avery noticed a sign that read "Wedgewood Townhomes" as they drove into the small complex. Mark turned right and drove down a bit before pulling in a driveway, with the garage door opening.

"Here we are," he said as the SUV stopped in the garage. "Home sweet home. I'll get your stuff."

He jumped out before Avery had a chance to open

the door. He lifted her bags from the back and stood ready to help her out of the vehicle.

She accepted his hand and climbed down. "Thanks." She followed him through a door into the townhouse. He turned on lights as they walked down a short hallway to the kitchen. The first thing that came to her mind was "wow."

Mark set her bags in a corner. "Would you like something? You still like limoncello?"

She wasn't listening, as her focus was one hundred percent on the kitchen. OMG. It was huge and had all stainless appliances and beautiful cherry cabinets. A big island in the middle had a sink on one side and an eating bar on the other. Man, could she cook in this space. In fact, she would love—

"Avery!" Mark yelled. "Are you okay?"

She cleared her head from visions of roasts and canapés. "Sorry, I was admiring your kitchen, it's spectacular."

He shrugged. "Thanks. Would you like a limoncello? We can relax in the family room."

"Sure." She moved to the adjoining room while he opened the freezer. A light stone fireplace dominated one wall with a large flat screen television over the mantle. A U-shaped sectional couch sat in front of it with a low round dark oak coffee table in the middle. She rubbed the nubby light-sage fabric on the top of couch. It was nice. The wall to her right was wall to ceiling cabinets and bookcases—terrific storage. The wall to her left had a pair of reading chairs with a table and lamp between them and French doors. She walked to the doors and peered out the glass at the patio. She turned as Mark spoke to her.

"Here we are." He handed her a small glass with the liqueur and moved to the left side of the fireplace. "I'll start a fire." He flipped a switch on the wall and pushed a button. The fire immediately flamed.

"That was easy. You must use those ceramic logs." Avery settled on the sofa with a good view of the fire.

"They were already here. I'll eventually switch to wood." Mark joined her, with a foot or so of space between them. "It's nice to relax."

"Yeah." She leaned her head back on the sofa cushion, closed her eyes briefly. "I can't believe my water heater broke. How exactly does that happen?"

"You're asking the guy who can't change the oil in his own car. No clue. But a leak sure does make a mess. At least you weren't out of town and it's not the middle of August."

She tapped her glass to his; amazed at the simple reasons he'd shared to be thankful. "Small blessings, right?"

He chuckled. "Right, small blessings. If you don't like your floors, now will be the chance to change them."

"I hadn't thought that far, but I guess you're right. Hmm, maybe change the color, or go with hard wood." She couldn't think about new floors right then. "I don't know. I like my floors."

He leaned forward and wrapped his arms around her. "It's okay. You don't have to change anything if you don't want to. You're in charge."

The pressure of his arms enveloped her in a cocoon

of safety. She sank into the luxury and realized how fortunate it was that he'd been with her. How helpful Mark had been at her house. How very much she appreciated his concern for her and her home. She snuggled into his arms. Damn, her ex-husband had improved over the years.

December 14, Sunday

Avery parked on the left side of the driveway at Mark's townhouse as the garage door opened. She'd dealt with the insurance issues for the burst hot water heater, handed over a house key to the restoration company, and prayed the work wouldn't take more than the week they'd estimated. The timing sucked, but stuff happens. In situations like this she was a realist. Sometimes things simply happen. And then you deal.

Mark waited for her in the garage and retrieved the suitcase she pulled out of the backseat of her car, setting it by the door to the house.

"I need your help," he said with a leisurely grin.

"With what?"

"Decorating my house for Christmas."

"Oh, no," she said, raising a hand in front of him. "I am the worst decorator on the planet."

He gawked at her. "How can that be? You're a girl, it's in the DNA."

The utter disbelief on his face poked at her and she started to laugh.

"Please come with me. I need your help," he

pleaded.

Oh, why not. Just because she didn't like to decorate didn't mean she didn't know how. Her life had been turned upside down since she'd met Mark at Starbucks. Maybe it was time she nuked her personal ban on Christmas. What would it hurt to help him?

"Okay, all right. When?"

"Right now." He walked to his SUV and opened the passenger door. "Come on, let's go."

She shrugged, nodded. A few hours of spending Mark's money might be fun.

The first store they tackled was Michaels off Williams Trace Boulevard. Shortly after entering the store, Mark's eyes glazed over. Shelf after shelf of greenery, ornaments, ribbons, and Christmas themed knickknacks must have been a sensory overload for him.

Avery stopped next to a tall shelf of ornaments. "Do you have a theme or a color preference?"

He looked at the display then at her. "Huh? Um . . . Christmassy?"

She put a hand over her mouth to hide a giggle. "Okay, let's go middle of the road. What size of tree do you intend to buy?"

"I already have an eight foot mountain spruce that has those twinkly lights installed. My parents bought it for me as a housewarming gift."

"Good for you." She pointed to a shelf with angels, snowflakes, and stars. "Why don't you pick out the tree topper?"

While Mark shook boxes, Avery selected boxes of red and clear glass ornaments, white snowflakes, and thick gold hearts. She found wide green and red plaid ribbon for garland circling the tree. She threw in a bolt of red ribbon and greenery for the mantle. Candles would be nice as well and then she stopped with a new thought.

She pushed the shopping cart to him. "Have you considered outside lights?"

He frowned. "No. I guess I could put some on the bushes and around the front door. Would that work?"

She nodded. "Guess we need a door wreath." She watched him as he studied the assortment of twinkly lights. Would he select clear or colored lights? He shook each box he picked up. Why do men do that? She moved over an aisle and chose a pretty drop wreath with fake pinecones and a big red bow.

Mark joined her and tossed several boxes in the shopping cart. "I got one of those outdoor cord plug-in things with a timer. What else?"

"Candles for the mantle," Avery replied, pleased at how easy this shopping trip was progressing. Over the past fifteen years, she'd never imagined she and Mark would be able to get along so easily and do an everyday thing like shopping for Christmas decorations. Blessings, indeed.

After Michaels, they stopped at Pier 1 Imports for Christmas accessories and a couple of Santa themed dishes.

Walking out of the store, Mark grabbed Avery's hand and brought it to his mouth for a tender kiss. "Thank you for doing this. I owe you big."

"No," she said quickly. "No, you don't owe me anything. It's been fun." She was helping him decorate not because she wanted something in return, but because it was helping her. Helping her erase a decision made long ago to never celebrate Christmas at her home as long as there were no children to enjoy it. Yes, it was time to shut the door on the past and go forward. After all, she had so many wonderful parts of her life. She gazed at Mark from a new point of view. Perhaps her life had just turned a corner.

He kissed her palm again then released her hand to open the lift gate of his SUV. "Are you hungry? Let's get a couple of to-go sandwiches at Jason's Deli."

"Great idea." She jumped in the vehicle with a grin on her face, her heart feeling a little lighter.

December 20, Saturday

"I do not believe this." Avery tossed her cell phone on the counter and paced from one end of Mark's kitchen to the other then circled the middle island. "Damn it. Why in the hell does the Christmas holiday stop work on my house?" She released an exasperated breath and looked at Mark who stood near his wine refrigerator.

"It sucks for you, I know," he said, obviously trying to make the best of the situation for her benefit. "Another week isn't so bad. The day after Christmas is Friday. I bet you'll be back in your house no later than a week from this Monday."

He opened the door of the wine cooler and retrieved a bottle. "How about a glass of wine? It's after five o'clock."

"You're right. I'm acting like a baby. The restoration crew deserves a Christmas holiday just as much as I do." Mark was a wise man and kept his mouth shut. Avery appreciated that.

She pulled two wine glasses from a cabinet and placed them on the island counter. She'd been surprised at how comfortable she'd felt in Mark's house during the past week. They'd had a blast putting up the Christmas decorations and his house now sparkled with Christmas cheer.

Her completed manuscript had been turned over to her editor yesterday and she expected a draft cover by Monday. The last book in the series was already outlined so she would start writing it tomorrow if she had time. She accepted a glass from Mark, leaned against the counter, and smiled. Yep, things were good, for now.

"I'm hungry. Should we go out or order a pizza?" Mark said.

"I'd planned on cooking."

"Really?" He didn't even attempt to hide his pleasure at her announcement. "What are you making?"

"*We* are making pasta carbonara, salad, and cheese bread."

"The bread you made at your house?" *[See EC on page 273]*

"Uh-huh," she said as she opened the refrigerator. "I figure we can make dinner together."

"Just tell me what to do. I'm at your command."

Avery liked the idea of Mark being at her command, for about five seconds. "This is a team sport. I'll do the pasta and bread, and you do the salad."

"Fair enough." Mark sipped wine as he leaned against a counter. "How do I make a salad?"

She stared at him with her mouth open, and then she shut it. "Have you never eaten at home the past fifteen years?"

He rolled his eyes. "Of course I have."

"What did you eat?"

"Take out, PB&J sandwiches, and cereal."

Avery shook her head then pulled a large pot for the pasta out of a lower cabinet. How was it that a man who didn't cook had such a fabulous set of pots and pans? She asked and he said he got them for his birthday from his parents. Why not a power drill?

Two hours later their stomachs were full after the pasta dinner and apple pie for dessert. They settled on the sofa to watch a Saturday night college football game on TV. The Christmas tree glowed in a corner by the French doors and white candles burned on the mantel above the fire Mark had started earlier. His home looked festive and comfortable.

After several minutes of watching, he reached his arm around Avery, drawing her closer to him. "It's been great having you here this past week." He kissed the top of her head.

She snuggled against him, enjoying the comfort his muscular body gave her. They fit together so well. Funny how she'd become accustomed to his touch and his physical closeness these past three weeks, especially this last one at his townhouse. Definitely strange, considering their past.

"I appreciate you taking me in like a stray puppy."

He pulled back from her and cupped his hand around her chin. "You will never be a stray to me."

Before she could blink, his lips were on hers, seeking and savaging her mouth. She pressed closer to him as swirls of pleasure zipped straight to her toes. Making out with Mark had become her favorite sport when she wasn't thinking clearly.

She moaned as she felt his hand skim up her side, the thumb caressing the underside of her breast. Wait, hold on. She scooted back from Mark, her breath ragged. "What are we doing?"

He looked at her with confusion in his eyes. "I say we were enjoying each other."

Avery scrambled off the sofa and stood with her back to the fireplace. "How can you say that? *We are divorced* and shouldn't be enjoying anything about each other, especially not that."

He sat at the edge of the sofa cushion. "And why the hell not?" he asked. She glared at him with her arms folded tightly over her chest. "What I mean is that, yes, we're divorced. But there is no reason that fifteen years later we can't . . . care about each other."

"What does that mean?" Avery did not understand what was going on between them. Mark was acting like he was dating her. No way.

He threaded his fingers though his hair, frustration pinching at the corners of his mouth. "Avery, please, hear me out." He patted the cushion next to him. "Sit down so we can talk about this."

She nodded and sat at the end of the sofa, across the coffee table from him. "Okay. What is it you want to say to me?"

~~*

What *did* Mark want to say to his ex-wife? With so many years for preparation he should have had a speech memorized. Instead his thoughts were jumbled together like a plate of spaghetti. All he knew for sure was that he'd always loved her and still wanted her as his wife.

"I've always thought our divorce was a mistake."

She stared at him, disbelief shadowing her face. "What did you say?"

"We should never have gotten divorced."

She leaned toward him, fire in her eyes. "Then why the hell did you fight so hard to get it?"

"You were the one who wanted the divorce so badly. I didn't want it." That was a fact. He had tried to talk her out of splitting up, but she simply wouldn't listen. Eventually he gave in. He'd had no other alternative.

"You're insane. You filed, not me." Avery's voice increased in volume.

"Because you gave me no choice."

She rose hurriedly. "That is nonsense. I gave you plenty of opportunities to change your mind."

"How? By not talking to me and kicking me out of the apartment?"

"That's it. I'm not discussing this any further." She marched down the hallway toward the bedrooms and he heard a door slam. He remembered the last time she'd slammed a bedroom door. He'd never forced himself on a woman and he wouldn't start now. Plus, she obviously needed time to cool off.

He looked at the dancing flames of the fireplace.

Damn, what had just happened? More importantly, how did this happen? He still thought the time had finally come for them to have a real discussion about why their marriage had disintegrated into a pile of crap. He'd talk with her in the morning.

He rose and went to the kitchen. He pulled out a short glass and a bottle of scotch. He poured two fingers and went back to the fireplace, sipping as he walked. The scotch burned all the way down. So far, his plan to win back Avery hadn't worked, but he wasn't about to give up now—no way in hell.

December 23, Tuesday

Avery pushed the chair away from the hotel desk and checked her watch. It was almost four o'clock. Her mind simply couldn't concentrate on the new story even though she knew the characters so well. She'd been at the Sugar Land Marriott since Sunday morning, after departing Mark's townhouse without talking to him or leaving a note. They needed a clean break. Or so she had thought three days ago. Now she questioned whether her abrupt departure had been wise. It definitely wasn't polite or gracious.

Mark's face, when she walked out of his family room last Saturday, kept playing in her mind like a flashing neon sign—Dumb Ass, Dumb Ass, Dumb Ass. Why couldn't she have a civil conversation with him like a mature adult?

She rose and moved to the window. Sugar Land's

City Hall, with its bubbling fountain, sat in all its glory across the street from the hotel. The huge Christmas tree sat squarely in the middle of the plaza, giving the area a festive appearance—none too subtle reminder of the season. The entire Town Center development, with its eclectic array of shops and restaurants, and office space, had been a wonderful addition to the city. Avery had been thrilled when good restaurants had opened, eliminating the need to drive to Houston. Yep, she loved living in Sugar Land. It was home.

But all that was irrelevant to the issue at hand—Mark and their new "relationship."

She'd managed to put the divorce into a tight little box fifteen years ago. The box hadn't been moved, kicked, or opened in the ensuing years, until now. Until Mark had moved back to Sugar Land and concluded they should rekindle their relationship and spark their romance.

And what was wrong with that? Now, after three days of feeling lower than an armadillo on a dry west Texas road, she realized he was right. They did need to talk.

She turned away from the window and retrieved her water glass from the desk. She needed more ice. At the small bar, she took the lid off the ice bucket and heard a knock at the door.

She opened the door a smidge and her heart skipped a beat.

"Is this a bad time?"

"Yes, it is," she said, seriously debating whether to slam the door in his face. She hated surprises. But good manners won out and she opened it wider. "But whatever, come on in."

Mark walked past her and stopped in front of the television. "Okay if I sit on the loveseat?"

"Sure." The room was overly large with a king-size bed and a small seating area next to the desk and bar.

"I hope you're not mad at me for coming here."

"You talked to Ashley."

He nodded and half-smiled. "I checked your house several times before I called her. It took a good bit of convincing before she'd tell me where you'd gone."

"Why are you here?" Avery had a good idea why Mark had sought her out. He was a good man and no doubt wanted to clear things up between them. She could do that—best to get it over with and make a clean break. How many times in the last month had she said that? God, she was wishy-washy.

"We need to talk," he said with a shrug. He glanced at her laptop on the desk. "You've been writing here?

"I have to keep at it. My readers expect a new book every three months."

"Sounds like a grueling schedule."

"I guess, but I like it. Can you work in your pajamas?" Avery considered that a huge plus for working at home.

"No. I don't think I could work at home though. I like moving around, talking to different people."

"See, that's one of the reasons why we weren't meant for the long term."

"You seriously believe that crap?" Mark had the look of a man who didn't believe one word she said. "I'm an extrovert and you're an introvert and therefore we can't make it together. That's ridiculous."

"I disagree. We enjoy different things."

"Give me an example."

Avery thought for a good minute. When they'd first started dating one of the things he'd commented on was how they were "likes attracting" not opposites. History proved that wrong. "An example is that you like to deer hunt and fish, and I don't."

He rolled his eyes. "You don't like to hunt and fish because you're a girl, not because you're more of an introvert than me."

"Bad example." She thought some more. "Okay, I've got a real difference—you eat crawfish and I can't stand the idea of those little suckers."

"Uh-huh, and you like carrot cake and I don't. So what?" He leaned over and took her hand. "What keeps a man and a woman together isn't the same tastes in food or outdoor activities, it's what's in their core and their heart. You'll never be able to convince me we don't have the same heart."

She slowly pulled her hand out of his and rose, walked to the window. She noticed the Christmas tree lights had come on, so pretty. Watching the people meander around the plaza, she spoke. "We may have the same heart but it wasn't enough to keep us together. We were so young. Hell, I hardly knew myself." She turned back to him. "I don't see any reason to rehash our divorce."

"And I disagree with you."

"Why? What do you hope to accomplish?" She

leaned her butt against the desk.

"We were young and both of us shut the other out when you couldn't get pregnant again."

The way she remembered it, he wouldn't talk. "It's hard to get past something as a couple when you don't communicate."

"Exactly," he said. "Why wouldn't you talk with me? Every time I tried, you started to cry."

"And why didn't you hold me until the tears were gone?"

"Because it broke my heart." His voice was raw with emotion.

"I'm sorry for that. But do you have any idea of how . . . how worthless I felt back then?" She picked up a water bottle left on the desk and took a long swallow.

"Worthless, why?"

"See how different we are . . . you don't even know."

"Jesus, Avery, you wouldn't talk to me." His eyes flashed with anger. "How the hell would I know your feelings . . . we didn't *talk*, damn it. And I wasn't a freaking psychic. Not then, and sure as hell, not now."

"Don't you yell at me."

He jumped from the loveseat and got in her face, gripping her forearms. She dropped her gaze to the floor, unable to face him.

He shook her gently. "Avery, look at me."

She couldn't.

"Please."

Avery remembered the last time she saw Mark while they were still married. They'd been talking about splitting up the kitchen stuff and she'd had a beautiful blue serving bowl in her hands. His aunt had given them the bowl as a wedding gift. She'd told Mark he shouldn't have to suffer and stay married to her. After all it wasn't his fault she couldn't get pregnant.

She recalled the tears sliding down her face and how helpless she'd felt. How lonely she'd felt. Mark just stood there and stared at her. That had infuriated her. She dropped the bowl on the floor of tiled linoleum and ran into the bedroom, slamming the door.

She shook her head to clear the memories.

He hadn't gone after her then but here he was now. He'd come after her today. And he wanted her.

After a moment, her shoulders slumped and the anger she'd carried since the divorce evaporated. Why now? She didn't know the answer but her soul understood the time had come to face the past and Mark, as a mature adult. She raised her face, tears threatened but she managed to hold them off. "I'm looking at you," she whispered. "Maybe for the very first time."

"Aw, babe." He wrapped his arms around her and kissed the top of her head.

She snuck her arms around his waist. Simply holding each other was like drinking a frozen margarita on a Texas afternoon in late August. They stood wrapped around each other for what seemed like an hour until Avery stepped back.

"Let's talk," she said as she ran a finger down his chiseled face.

Mark sat back on the sofa and Avery returned to the desk chair.

She kept thinking about Mark's statement that she wouldn't talk to him. He had to be referring to the time after the last in vitro fertilization. She'd shut down emotionally and refused to discuss her heartbreak with anyone, including Ashley.

Her heart stopped cold for a brief moment. Clarity coursed through her. She'd never given Mark the chance to work through her fertility issue with her—together, as a couple, as a united entity and thus, possibly, avoid the divorce. A month ago this realization would have stopped her world and she would have taken on the veil of "it's all my fault." But not now. The time had come to let the demons fly from the closet.

"Mark, you've been right all along. I think we were too immature to deal with a fertility issue," Avery said. "And that lead to the divorce."

"Why couldn't we talk to each other back then?"

"I don't know. Now, it seems silly that we couldn't."

"Maybe we should just leave it," Mark said quietly. "We made mistakes but they were so long ago."

She regarded the picture on the wall behind him. It was one of those modern things with crisscrossing angles and blocks of bright colors. Could she leave the past in the past? Go forward as though it hadn't haunted her for the last fifteen years.

If it would help Mark, then yes, she could. Her gaze slid to her handsome ex-husband. How in the world could she have let him go?

"I think letting the past float into cyber-space is a fine idea." But not before she told him the truth. "But first I need to say something to you."

He nodded, his gaze riveted on her.

Avery blew out a shaky breath, wiped tears from her cheeks, and straightened her shoulders. "I want to tell you I'm sorry. Sorry for not listening to you. Sorry for ignoring your pain. And sorry for acting like a spoiled brat. We should have considered adoption."

He grinned that sexy grin. "Thank you for that. I'm sorry for being immature and unable or unwilling to try harder to keep our marriage going."

"Enough talking about the past. Let's move forward," she said, reaching out her hand. "I'll shake on that."

He took her hand and shook it. "Deal." He rose, still holding her hand and she stood as well.

"I'm really glad you came to visit," she said, lightly stroking his chest with her fingers.

"Me, too." He cupped her face with his hands. "I want you to know I never stopped loving you. Actually, it's been the one constant in my life." He planted a sweet kiss on her lips.

"Thank you for saying that. My heart has been full of love for you."

"And I'm sorry you felt worthless after all the fertility—"

She placed a finger on his lips. "That's over. Let's concentrate on now, here, today."

"I agree," he said while gently pushing her backwards until they both fell on the bed. "Let's get to know each other better." He had a wicked gleam in his eyes as he kissed her like it was the very first time. Sweet. Hot. With promises of more to come.

"I like your style," she said, her tone low and seductive.

He rolled on top of her, his forearms supporting him as his gazed at her. "You are so beautiful. I love you."

Actually, Avery wasn't surprised to hear those words as they mirrored her own feelings. "And I love you. I have since that first day we met at A&M."

"Mm, that's my girl." Mark's head lowered and the kiss wasn't gentle, it was meant to ignite. Passion flared between them as their hearts and their souls met. And when he took her a few minutes later, they flew on the wings of desire and lust. Hot and hungry. Fast and furious. The greed and the excitement mimicked first-time lovers, destined to make up for the years of separation. Avery closed her eyes and breathed in Mark's scent . . . without a doubt, this was where she belonged.

~~*

Four hours later, after a marathon session of catching up, Mark was hungry. Good lovemaking was the perfect appetite creator. He rose from the bed and looked for his jeans.

"What are you doing?" Avery whispered.

"I'm hungry. Wouldn't you like a hamburger?" he said while pulling up the zipper.

"Hmm, I like that idea. We can call room service." She sat up, retrieved her sweater from the floor and pulled it on. "Burr, it's chilly in here."

He sat next to her on the bed. "I can warm you up." He'd always had fun playing with her. She had such a quick sense of humor.

"Which you just demonstrated." She laughed and

kissed his shoulder. "Come on, order food, I'm starving, too."

He found the room service menu, made his selection, and placed his order. Avery was in the bathroom when he called so she didn't hear about the little extra surprise of champagne and chocolate he'd requested with the meal. He moved to the window and admired the Christmas tree across the street. Although substantially larger, it reminded him of the tree he and Avery had decorated in his family room. The fact that she'd helped him had given him the confidence that they'd eventually arrive exactly where they were now.

He turned from the window as she walked to him. "We should have food in thirty to forty minutes."

"Good." She sat on the corner of the bed.

"There's something I want . . . well, I have a proposal for you."

"Ooh, a proposal, la-de-dah."

"I think you should move in with me." He said what he'd been thinking for two weeks and continued before she could reply. "My townhouse is twice the size of your house, you love my kitchen, the study is yours for your writing, and we can install a hot tub in the back." He stopped to take a breath.

"Whoa, I—"

"Please don't think, just say yes." He sat next to her on the bed.

Avery twisted her hands in her lap. Not a good sign. Then he realized what he hadn't said.

"I'd like to revise my proposal." He took her hand and brought it to his lips. "Please."

"Okay, go ahead."

"I didn't say the most important part." He squeezed her hand and prayed she'd agree with him. "I suggested you move in with me because . . . I want us to live together as husband and wife." He took her other hand and held them gently in his. "Avery Burke, will you marry me?"

She blinked and a single tear ran down her cheek. "Absolutely." Her arms wrapped around him and she pressed against his shoulder. He hugged her back and her floral scent swirled around him. He'd never forget this moment.

"Aw, babe." He swallowed hard, his heart thumping like a jackhammer. "I'm so damned happy right now."

"Me, too. I love you."

December 24, Wednesday

Mark departed from the Marriott mid-morning, while Avery checked out near noon. She appreciated the time alone as she had a mission to achieve—a Christmas present for Mark and the Apple store at First Colony Mall had exactly what she had in mind. She walked out carrying a small shopping bag and sporting a huge grin. He would be amazed when he opened her gift.

On the way home, which she now considered the Wedgwood townhouse, she stopped at Panera Bread for salads and sandwiches. No cooking on Christmas Eve other than one of her favorite appetizer. They were due at Ashley's house later for dessert.

The car radio blared non-stop Christmas carols and she sang along. Laughing at her terrible singing voice, she understood the one-eighty she'd made concerning the holidays. It felt good to get in the spirit and she was truly thankful for the plot twist her life had taken the last few weeks.

Thankfully, Mark was home to let her through the gate when she arrived. After parking in the driveway, she jumped out of the car to hide the Apple shopping bag behind her computer tote. He quickly arrived on the driveway.

"Finally, you're home."

"Sorry, I wrote for a couple hours after you left then made a quick stop for dinner." She stretched the truth only a couple of inches. She pulled her suitcase from the back seat. "Can you get the bags out of the front?"

While Mark did that she hurried into the house and to the guest bedroom she'd previously used. She slid the Apple bag under the bed.

"Hey, wrong bedroom, you're with me at the end of the hall." Mark stood in the doorway grinning.

"Right, of course, show me the way."

Once Avery settled into the master bedroom as best she could, she took a shower and dressed for Christmas Eve. She slid on her new red cashmere sweater and black leggings along with her favorite red ballet flats. She studied herself in the framed mirror over the bathroom vanity. She looked happy and that was very good. Very good, indeed. She checked her watch, after four o'clock. It was time to put together the appetizer.

The kitchen and family room were empty. Mark had

to be somewhere and would probably appear once he smelled the spinach-artichoke dip baking. She'd picked up the ingredients several days ago in anticipation of this night. Of course, she hadn't known Mark would propose to her but she'd assumed they'd spend Christmas Eve together.

She searched all the cabinets and couldn't find a food processor. Well, she'd chop the artichokes and spinach the old fashioned way with a knife and a cutting board. This recipe was one of her favorite dips and she made quick work of putting it together. Mark opened the French doors as she put the baking dish in the oven.

"I was wondering where you were," she said, tickled to remember that he would soon be her husband. They *really needed* to talk about those wedding details.

"I was measuring the back for a hot tub when George, our neighbor to the right, came out and we were talking about the Texans."

"Oh, manly conversation," she teased.

"That's right, woman." He hugged her and gave her a loud smack on the lips. "What did you put in the oven?"

"Spinach and artichoke dip. I thought it would go with the salads." Avery decided now was a good time to give Mark his gift. "I'll be right back."

She retrieved the wrapped package and brought it to the kitchen. Mark sat in a stool with a wrapped gift on the counter next to him.

"Looks like you had the same idea as me," she said as she handed Mark his gift. "You open yours first. I can't wait to see your reaction."

"Okay." He shook the box near his ear and seemed satisfied with what he'd heard. He ripped the paper off in one long tear. He stared at the box then gazed at Avery. "Wow, this is incredible . . . an iPhone 6, thank you. How did you know I needed a new phone?"

"Just a guess," she said. If the ecstatic look on his face was any indication, he really was thrilled with the phone. "It's got some cool stuff on it."

"Thank you." He gingerly lifted the remaining gift from the counter and handed it to her. "This is for you."

The gift was four inches or so square. She untied the red ribbon and carefully removed the green paper. After removing the lid from a black box, she pushed aside red tissue paper. A round clear globe sat in the box. She pulled it out.

"Oh my God, this is perfect . . . it's so unusual." A miniature skating rink was inside the globe with children on the ice, a dog on the side, and Christmas trees bordering the rink. "Where did you get this? I've never seen such a fantastic ornament."

"I found it at a new gift store over on Chestnut Street. I thought it was time to start a tradition of adding a new decoration to the tree each Christmas. I hope you agree."

"Of course, it's a wonderful idea." She was stunned and delighted at his thoughtfulness.

"There's something else in the box."

She peered inside and sure enough there was a little pink bag at the bottom. She drew it out and felt something round. OMG. She looked at a beaming Mark, and handed the bag to him. He opened it and dumped the contents in his left hand.

"This isn't a Christmas present but I thought now was a good time to give it to you." He quickly slid a diamond on the ring finger of her left hand.

She threw her arms around his neck. "This is fantastic . . . thank you."

"Look at it before you get too excited." He stepped back. "You may not like it."

She rolled her eyes as she held her hand in front of her, turning it from side to side. The diamond was a square-cut solitaire, probably close to three carats on a plain platinum band. Her heart galloped around the kitchen. "Mark, oh . . . it's beautiful. I love it."

"Whew, good. I thought we could get the wedding bands for both sides and you can make them as fancy as you want."

In a bit of a daze she nodded, still looking at her engagement ring. She hadn't been dreaming yesterday at the hotel, she was marrying Mark. Which meant a wedding would be happening, and soon she hoped. "We need to discuss a wedding date."

"The sooner the better." He kissed her firmly. "How about we go to Las Vegas next week? We already had a big wedding with all our families and friends. Let's do it for us this time."

Hmm, she'd never thought about getting married in Vegas but it wasn't a bad idea. They could take a few vacation days, relax, and have fun. "I like that idea. We can do a party here in a month so no one gets mad at us or feels left out. But wait, I have two books coming out the day after Christmas. I'll need to do some online promotion."

"No problem, we'll leave on the twenty-seventh. I like the idea of a party." He took both her hands in his. "There's one more thing I need to discuss with you."

Avery's heart flopped, he sounded so serious. "Okay. What is it?"

He pursed his lips and gazed at her with something, uncertainty maybe, etched on his face. Finally, he smiled. "I'm going to be blunt . . . I'd like for us to look into adoption."

"Oh, Mark, I'm too old to be the mother of an infant."

"I wasn't thinking about a baby, an older child."

"I'd never thought of that. What age?" A slow whirl began in her stomach.

"Eight to twelve." He stroked his thumbs over the tops of her hands. "Plus, I was thinking maybe we could adopt more than one child, siblings hopefully."

The whirl picked up speed and excitement pumped through Avery. "You're serious about this. Where do we go to adopt? I've never researched this."

"I have and I think we should start with DePelchin Children's Center in Houston." *[See EC on page 274]*

"I think Ashley knows someone who adopted a little boy from them. I wonder if it's hard to qualify."

"I've checked into that a bit. Hopefully, we won't have a problem."

Two hours later, after turning off the oven then retiring to the bedroom for an official engagement celebration followed by a quick dinner, Avery and Mark prepared to leave for Ashley's house. On the way to get her coat, she walked to the Christmas tree in the corner of the family room. She'd earlier placed the new ornament prominently on a top branch. The glass reflected the twinkly lights and sparkled.

And that's exactly how she felt about herself—sparkly and new. The diamond on her finger signified her love for Mark and the hope she felt deep in her core for their future. As a mature woman with a good dose of life wisdom, she knew in her soul that their decision to re-marry was a good one.

Mark walked behind her and wrapped his arms possessively around her. "You're awfully quiet."

She rubbed his hands on her stomach. "Thinking how lucky we are that we found each other after so many years."

He kissed the top of her head then the side of her neck. "I think the fact that the neither of us re-married says something. This was meant to happen."

She turned around, placing her hands on his chest. "Oh, yeah? You seem pretty sure of yourself." He cupped her face with his hands and leisurely kissed her, his lips igniting a smoldering fire deep in her heart. This is what she'd been waiting for, after holding her breath for fifteen long and lonely years.

His lips moved to nuzzle her neck and he hugged her tightly. "What I'm most sure of is how much I love you." He pulled back from her, grinning like a fifteen-foot alligator scoping out a bass boat full of tourists. "In fact, Miss Burke, I adore you."

"That's just fine, Mr. Burke. Cause this girl is not letting you go."

"Good, we agree." He motioned for her to put on her coat. "Come on, let's go. We have people to tell we're getting married next week."

Avery stopped forward motion and turned back to him. "I just had a thought. I won't need to change my name for social security or get a new driver's license. How cool is that?"

"And why are you thinking about that?" He helped her with her coat.

"I'm a writer, I always think about the details." She slipped away from him and wagged a finger. "Be careful, Mr. Burke. I've been known to kill people in one of my books."

"Uh-huh, right. You'd be better off using me as your inspiration for a hunky-billionaire-stud-muffin."

She grabbed him and planted a hot kiss on his lips. "Now you're talking, Mr. Stud Muffin."

* * * * *

CHRISTMAS BY CANDLELIGHT

Dating? No Way

Nervous excitement bubbled in Cara Allen's chest as she shook her blond curls and took a deep breath. Her fingers clenched then opened as she muttered, "I can do this." She exited her car and nearly stumbled while stepping onto the sidewalk but managed to cross it without her usual display of slips, trips, and falls.

She secured her purse strap over her shoulder and pushed open the glass door decorated top to bottom with rainbow colored paw prints. The pungent aroma of rose potpourri floated through a door open to the interior of

Sammy's Small Dog Rescue. Barking followed the scent through the opening.

Her eyes scanned the stacked display of pet food and the bulletin board of notices as she approached the reception desk. A young woman with bright red hair and white cat-eye glasses pounded on a keyboard.

Cara waited a moment to catch the woman's attention then finally spoke. "Please . . . excuse me; I'm here to adopt a dog."

"Why didn't you say so?" The young woman stood so quickly her chair pushed backward. She stuck out her hand. "I'm Amber, part-time proprietress of this pet establishment. How may I help you?"

Cara sucked in a breath. Why the hell was she so anxious about taking home a little dog? "Like I said, I'm here to adopt a dog."

Amber pushed the glasses down her nose and narrowed her eyes. "Are you sure about that?"

"Yes, of course I'm sure. I've done my research and Sammy's seems like the perfect place to find my dog."

"Okay, great." Amber realigned her glasses. "Have you completed an application?"

"I did it online a few days ago and received an adoption confirmation."

"What's the name and address?"

Cara recited the requested information and began to tap her foot. Although her nerves were on high alert, she was eager to start her search. She'd waited too many years. Her husband had been allergic to dogs yet when he'd died three years ago from a heart attack she still couldn't bring herself to adopt. But the months had passed and she'd made a vow to add a puppy to her lonely household of one before her next birthday, the big 3-6.

Amber waved a hand. "You're right here on our listed of approved adopters. Let's find your little darling. I'll get a volunteer to help you." She spoke into a walkie-talkie.

Less than a minute later, a tall man walked through the door. Amber pointed towards Cara and the volunteer stopped in front of her. Cara twisted her hands together. She'd imagined a teenager or a little old lady helping her, not this hunk with deep blue eyes and sandy colored hair that curled over his collar.

He smiled and nodded toward the kennels. "I'm Jake Kennedy. Ready?"

Hell, yes, she was ready—ready for those biceps and that killer grin. Oops, spontaneous girl reaction.

"Nice to meet you, I'm Cara."

"Okay, let's look for your baby. I understand you want a female around a year old."

"That's right." She followed him through the door and unfortunately noticed his jeans molded to his backside. It had been a long while since she'd noticed a man's butt in a pair of jeans.

Once in the kennel, he made a quick turn to the right and stopped.

"This is the section holding the young ones. Take a quick look around and then we can discuss the individual dogs." Jake motioned for her to go down the aisle between the cages. "Take your time. I need to check on something and I'll be back in a couple of minutes."

Cara waved her hand at him. "No problem."

She preferred to look at the dogs alone. That way she wouldn't be influenced by anyone else's opinion as to the right dog. Actually she didn't need the perfect dog, just the dog that was perfect for her. The plan was to walk down the right side and then the left. She took a deep breath, slowly released it, and moved in front of the first stack of cages.

Ugh. She hated the word "cage." She'd think of them as kennels instead, or even better, a doggie hotel. Regardless, the kennels were stacked vertically in three's, with four stacks on either side of the walkway. And every kennel was full. Her hand automatically gripped her purse. How in the world would she choose the right dog?

Once she took her first step, pandemonium erupted. The dogs barked, whimpered, jumped on the door of the cage, or huddled in a corner. It was as though they had been waiting for her to declare her intent.

She took another deep breath before pushing out her hands and mimicked a quiet down motion. "Come on guys, settle down. Yes, I'm here to find a dog and I can only take one of you home. Okay? Hopefully, y'all can understand." She glanced at a few cages and noticed the dogs had moved to the center or a back corner and were either sitting quietly or lying down. Good, they did understand.

She made a quick survey, taking note of the kennels with small dogs. There were three. The first dog had a pointy muzzle she didn't like and the second one turned around with its back to her. Huh? She walked to the last kennel and viewed the dog, her name was Gracie. Cara like what she saw.

Gracie's head was cocked to the side as her dark brown eyes watched Cara. She stood and stroked her paw on the floor, and then she barked as though saying "hello." Jake arrived just as Cara debated whether to open the kennel herself.

"How's it going? Any of these fine animals strike your fancy?"

Cara turned at the sound of his voice or was it the scent of his musk aftershave? "Actually, yes, I'd like to get to know Gracie."

"Ah, good choice, she's a sweetheart." He opened the door, pulled out a hopeful-looking Gracie and plunked her in Cara's arms. "Cara, this is Miss Gracie, cutest dog on the block."

Cara nestled the half-pint dog in her arms, surprised at how light she felt and the softness of her wiry hair. *So far so good.* She re-positioned the dog to get a good look at her face. She had a shiny black nose, a square muzzle, brown hair with patches of black here and there, and those soulful brown eyes. Yes, this might be her dog.

"Do y'all have an outdoor area where Gracie and I can get to know each other?"

Jake led them down a hall to a scratched door leading to the back of the building. Cara managed to step over the doorjamb without tripping and entered the small yard. She leaned over and set Gracie on the patch of grass. "Just in case you need to pee."

Gracie licked Cara's hand then performed one of those head rolls that the cool girls do and pranced off, swinging her little stub tail.

Cara crossed her arms over her chest and watched the pup move from one section of the yard to another, sniffing bushes and flowers as she strolled. Cara` glanced at Jake standing next to her. "Tell me about Gracie."

"She was found wandering the streets, in the old section of Sugar Land, no tags and no chip. She's a well-mannered dog and seems intelligent. I think she got a rough deal from someone, some asshole. She'll make a fine addition to a new family."

Cara watched her squat to pee then continue her survey of the smells in the yard. For a small dog she had a big presence. Cara's heart fluttered, she had a good feeling about her. Gracie stopped and turned her head towards Cara. Her left ear hitched up and she barked. Cara hunched down and Gracie ran over to her, placed her front paws on Cara's knees, barked almost a whisper, and then winked at Cara.

That was the sign. Cara scooped Gracie into her arms, kissed the top of her head, and rose. "Okay. I've made my decision. Do I need to sign something?"

Thirty minutes later, at the local pet store, Cara pushed a shopping cart through the aisles with Gracie sitting in the upper basket. The goal was to get accouterments fitting a doggy princess. Cara knew without a doubt she had made the right decision in adopting Gracie. She'd talked in the car nearly non-stop, telling Gracie all about her house and her friends. Gracie had the good manners to simply nod and wag her tail.

The cart was soon full of an oval bed, a pink blanket, dog toys, snacks, and bags of food. They were almost at the checkout register when Cara remembered a leash. She fully expected to lose a pound or two walking Gracie around the neighborhood. She tossed two in the cart, one for the house and one for the car, and retraced her steps to the front of the store.

Once she'd stowed everything in the back of her car, Cara headed home. She turned to a country station on the radio. Gracie seemed to approve of the music as her head bopped up and down, almost in time to the beat of the song.

Cara grinned. Having Gracie in the house was going to be just what she needed. *[See EC on page 276]*

~~*

"Stop by for a glass of wine after work," Cara said to her best friend Susan. "I want you to meet Gracie."

"She's a dog. You don't meet dogs." Susan chuckled over the phone. "But I will accept your happy hour offer."

"Good. I'll see you around five-thirty."

Cara clicked off and reviewed her to-do list for the day. Gracie slept on the pink blanket in a corner of the sofa. Today was a test of sorts. She would leave Gracie alone in the house for the first time. She hadn't bought a crate so Gracie would have free reign of every room. Cara didn't like the idea of penning up her dog even though the experts said it was a good idea.

Gracie was different. Cara *knew* she wouldn't get into any trouble. She gathered her purse and a stack of mail, and rattled her keys to wake Gracie. "I'm going to the post office and then the grocery store. You mind your manners while I'm gone, okay?"

Gracie yawned and rolled over on the blanket, burying her head against the sofa.

"Good, she understood me," Cara said as she walked to the garage.

First stop was the post office. She had thank you cards for a few clients plus a signed contract for another. Naturally, she had to wait in a long line for certified mail, which meant she could jot down a grocery list while she inched forward.

After digging a small notebook and pen from her purse, she concentrated on what she needed to buy for happy hour, or dinner in Susan terms. It was late-October and that translated to a warm appetizer. "Hmm, which recipe?" she muttered, chewing on the end of the pen.

"Recipe? You cook?"

Cara turned at the male voice behind her. Well, of all the post offices in Texas, who would have imagined she'd run into the dog rescue volunteer, in the line from hell, at this particular one in Sugar Land.

"Jake, hi."

"I was on my way to a job and need to mail some cards." He raised a stack of envelopes in his hand.

"I didn't know you worked around here."

"Yep, both my office and my house are in Sugar Land. You, too?"

Cara nodded, "I work out of my house." She stepped forward as the line moved closer to the counter. "I'm a freelance writer."

"I guess we have something in common, I own a business, too."

"What do you do?"

"Landscaping and pools, decks, all that outdoors stuff."

"I could use you at my house. I'm not much of a gardener."

They both shuffled forward as the line shortened. Jake leaned toward her. "Anything in particular you need help with?"

"How about everything?"

"Everything? Hmm, that sounds interesting." He cocked an eyebrow as he spoke.

"I didn't mean everything, everything. I was talking about my yard."

"Oh," he said with a mischievous grin. "Do you have time for lunch? There's a sandwich shop down the block and you'd save me from getting fast food. We could talk about gardening."

Cara snuck a glance at her watch. She hated getting off schedule but she could swing a quick lunch. She calculated forty-five minutes for it and she'd still have plenty of time for the grocery store.

"I'd love to have lunch with you."

"Good. We shouldn't be here all that much longer," he said.

The line moved again and Cara stepped to the busy counter. She turned back to Jake. "I'll meet you out front."

A few minutes later they entered the sandwich shop and shortly slid into opposite sides of a shiny blue booth, each carrying a sandwich basket and a soft drink.

Cara soon wondered if Jake regretted his impromptu lunch invitation. He dove into his turkey and cheddar on whole-wheat and kept his head down or directed toward the wide store window bordering the oh-so interesting parking lot.

After another minute, she couldn't stand the silence. It reminded her of her husband and his refusal to talk before he had a cup of coffee in the morning. She said the first thing that came to mind.

"How long have you volunteered for Sammy's?"

Jake's head turned slowly toward her, his blue eyes glittering in the sun light streaming through the window. "I guess it's seven or eight years now. I started a couple of years after my divorce."

"Oh, you're divorced."

"Almost ten years now, college sweethearts who didn't marry for the right reason. What about you?"

"My husband died three years ago, heart attack." She stuffed a pickle in her mouth to refrain from revealing anything else. She didn't feel comfortable talking about Justin with another man. Three years was not enough time to heal the hole in her heart.

"I'm sorry to hear that. Were you married long?" Jake seemed genuinely interested.

"That's old news." She was not talking about her marriage. Losing a spouse who had just turned thirty-six was an absolutely horrific experience. The subject was off-limits to Jake or anyone else. "How did you decide to go into landscaping as a business?"

His face froze for a mere second then he recovered. "That's easy, my grandfather, David 'Green Thumb' Martin. He's a master gardener and loves to grow vegetables and flowers."

"Sounds like a cool guy. Does he live close by?"

"Oh yeah, he retired a couple of years ago from the Rosenberg police force. He was chief for over twenty years." He sucked on the straw of his drink. "I spent a lot of time with him growing up."

"Working in the garden?"

"Right, mowing a huge lawn and weeding a ton of flowerbeds. Gramps believes in the old adage that children are to be seen and working their ass off."

"And with all that ass working you fell in love with green things?"

He laughed, a rolling carnival erupting from his chest. "That sums it up."

"That's a wonderful story. Do you see him often?"

"Oh yeah, he's my number one consultant on large jobs."

"Very cool. My grandparents live in Florida and I see them once a year at the most."

"Bummer. He's a good guy, just too opinionated sometimes."

"I know what you mean. My Mimi loves giving me advice, usually about clothes or cooking."

"You really do like to cook?"

"It's a hobby for me and I blog about recipes I try. One of these days I'll put together a cookbook from all my blogs."

"You said you're a freelance writer. Do you ever work on advertising copy?"

She nodded. "I've had a few assignments."

"Good." Jake pushed his basket to the side and placed his elbows on the table. "You're hired. This is what I need."

Cara relaxed against the back of the booth and simply watched. As he talked, there was something about Jake that invited her scrutiny. His hands orchestrated the ebb and flow of his words while the planes of his face reflected the knowledge behind his words. It was easy to see his passion for landscaping and building backyards for families. She liked that.

They talked about flowers and patios for another two hours. Cara finally checked her watched and realized she was way behind schedule. As they exited the shop, Jake asked her to a high school football game and dinner on Friday night. She quickly said yes, concerned about not being ready for the happy hour with Susan. Once she thanked Jake for lunch and headed to the grocery store, she realized what she'd agreed to. Holy crap, she had a date.

~~*

Cara hurried to answer the door, wiping her hands on a dishtowel.

"Come on in." She held the door open for Susan. "I was just about to uncork the wine."

"Good, I'm thirsty."

"I have snacks, too."

Susan took her usual spot at the breakfast bar. "I'm glad I came for happy hour. Much appreciate the buffet."

Cara chuckled and placed two trays on the counter. She poured the wine, a delicate chardonnay. "This is from a new vineyard near College Station. I think you'll like it."

Susan sipped and smiled. "Yum, I do like it." She

turned her head from side to side, her gaze directed at the kitchen floor. "Didn't you tell me about a new roommate? Where's the puppy?"

"She's in time out."

"Time out," Susan sputtered. "A dog can't be in time out, that's for toddlers."

"Gracie acted like a toddler this afternoon and deserves her punishment."

Susan swung a foot back and forth. "Oh boy, this is gonna be good. What did poor little Gracie do that made her momma angry?"

"She chewed through the strap of my favorite designer purse. It was totally uncalled for."

"I see. You left her at home alone, right?"

"Yes."

"She had free reign of the house?"

"Yes, it was the first time I didn't keep her in the utility room."

"And you left the door to your closet open." Susan pumped her arm with an "ah-ha" movement as Cara nodded. "It's like you sent her an invitation to chomp on some tasty leather."

Cara popped a bacon wrapped shrimp in her mouth. Chewing it gave her a few seconds to think about how not to sound like a complete idiot when she explained her logic for not locking up Gracie. She knew without a doubt that whatever she said would sound lame.

"I don't agree with putting dogs in kennels, owners need to train them properly. I accidentally left the purse on my bed and—"

"Oh . . . this is so your fault. Too funny." Susan rose

from the stool, walked to the utility room door. "I think it's time I bust Gracie out of doggie-jail."

Before Cara uttered a word, the door opened and Susan stood looking at Gracie who sat just inside the doorway. Gracie's head was cocked to the side and she had a "what the hell" look on her face, er, muzzle. After a moment she nodded, stood, stepped around Susan, and walked to Cara. She sat again and extended her left paw, her sweet face looking up to her owner.

Susan grabbed her wine glass and stood behind Gracie. "This is one talented dog. Interesting, she has the same eye color as you."

Gracie barked, just one woof. Cara was a goner, all over again. She knelt in front of the pup, patted her head, and scratched a floppy ear. "Okay, you're forgiven."

Gracie rose and wiggled her back end. She barked again.

"I believe your dog understands human speak," Susan said with a sloppy smile.

"Yes, she does," Cara agreed. "But I need to be more consistent with my training. This can't happen again." She rose and shooed Gracie to the living room. "Go lay on your blanket while I talk to Susan."

Gracie woofed, turned her head to Susan, then sashayed out of the kitchen.

"Did you see that? She just winked at me," Susan said.

"Right," Cara said. "Have more wine."

Susan returned to the stool and surveyed the tray of appetizers. "She'll grow out of the chewing phase. What do you call these bread things?" She popped a snack in her mouth.

"That's crostini with dried tomatoes, basil, Greek olives, and feta cheese. I tweaked a recipe I found online. Try the spiced almonds. I may give jars of them to my clients this Christmas."

"You are so nice to the people who pay you."

"That reminds me, I have a new client and a date."

"A date? Shut the front door . . . finally." Susan playfully pounded her fist on the counter. "Tell me everything and don't leave out one detail."

Cara sipped her wine and took a deep breath, blowing it out slowly. This conversation was truly a first during the past three years. All of their talk about dating had revolved around Susan's escapades, although she had dated her current boyfriend for six months. That, too, was a first. Usually they didn't last longer than two or three months.

"Remember the man who helped me when I adopted Gracie?"

"Uh-huh, you said he was a volunteer at the shelter and on the hunky side."

"I met him today at the post office and we had lunch and then he asked me out for Friday night, a high school football game and dinner—"

"Hold on a second." Susan raised a hand. "You met this volunteer guy at the Sugar Land post office? He lives around here?"

"He owns a local landscaping business and lives over in the Commonwealth subdivision. He's divorced, no kids."

"You learned a lot at the post office," Susan teased.

"We went to lunch, nothing special, the sandwich shop down the street."

"He invited you to a high school football game? That's interesting with no kids." Susan popped a crostini in her mouth and performed a thumb's up while chewing.

"It's his sister's son who's playing. Apparently he's the star quarterback and only a junior so that's a big deal. Jake goes to all of his games, being a supportive uncle."

"He sounds like a nice guy. How long has he been divorced?"

"I think he said ten years, not sure," Cara explained with a shrug. "He mentioned they didn't get married for the right reasons in college. No clue about the divorce"

"Hmm, she probably got pregnant. Why don't people use birth control?"

Cara threw up her hands. "Who knows? College students are known for doing dumb things. I remember a time or two you used lousy judgment."

"And more times than not, you were right next to me."

"True, except for that time you decided to cook soup in the pot thing for heating scented candle pieces. You almost burned down our apartment."

"Whatever. So you're going out with Jake, the hunky dog shelter volunteer and landscape business owner. Cool. I'm happy for you." Susan topped off their wine glasses. "Notice I haven't said it's about damn time you had a date."

"I did notice that. Good restraint." Cara laughed and stuffed a couple of almonds in her mouth.

"You said client. Has he hired you?"

She nodded. "He asked me to revamp the marketing program for his business including a new logo, copy for TV and print advertising, and a couple other things. It's a great opportunity for me."

"Do you think it's a good idea dating a client?"

"I hadn't even thought about that." Cara leaned against the edge of the counter across from Susan. How could she be so stupid? Of course she couldn't date a client. "I need to call him and cancel the date. You're right, this is totally unprofessional."

Susan again raised her hand. "Hold on, I didn't say it was unprofessional. Let's think about this. If you do work for him it will be a job with a set beginning and an agreed upon end date. Right? Freelance work doesn't go on forever."

"I see what you're saying. He won't be a client for more than a couple of months at the most." Cara pressed her palm over her heart and briefly closed her eyes. Things would be okay. "If Friday night goes well then I'll plan my work for him to be completed as quickly as practical."

"There you go. Problem solved."

Gracie barked in the living room. She must have agreed with Susan. The only problem was the fact Cara hadn't touched a man in over three years and had no clue how to prepare for a date as a thirty-five year old widow.

~~*

Jake drove his sedan to Cara's rather than his truck as it was habitually dusted with soil and grass. Not good for taking a lady on a first date. He turned into her neighborhood, knowing exactly where to go. His company had several lawn maintenance clients in the area. He'd always liked the houses, mostly one story with well-tended lawns and kids' toys strewn over the front walks.

He turned in Cara's driveway and soon rang the doorbell. He tugged at the waistband of his jeans. He hoped the white shirt and cowboy boots looked okay. First dates always made him nervous.

The front door opened. Cara stood in the doorway like a yellow daisy gracing a spring garden. Uh-huh, she looked hot. Her top exposed a bit of cleavage, very nice.

"Come on in and you can see Gracie," she said.

"I'd like that."

She moved to the side and he walked past her into the foyer. It wasn't big but had a side table with a tall vase of silk flowers. He hated silk flowers. He'd bring her real flowers next time.

Cara walked beside him. "Gracie's in the living room. We just had a little talk about her being good while I'm gone. Had a problem the last time I left her alone."

Gracie was indeed in the living room, sitting like a princess on a pink blanket on the sofa. Jake bent over to rub her ears. "How ya doing, Gracie? Looks like you've settled into your new home."

She licked his hand then woofed.

"I think she remembers me." He gave her a final scratch on her tummy and turned to Cara. "Are you ready? We don't want to miss kick off."

"Let's go." She grabbed her purse and they were quickly on their way.

Within ten minutes they entered the parking lot next to Mercer Stadium. Jake hadn't said much other than comment on the weather and mention that Cara would meet his sister who always got to the games early and would be saving seats for them in a prime location.

The band played a rendition of *We Are the Champions* as they got their tickets and walked up the ramp to the stadium's seating area. The lower section was individual seats in boxes and the upper section was bleacher seating.

He led Cara to the box where the family usually sat and sure enough his sister was there, holding her cowbell, ready to cheer. They went down the steps and Jake made the introductions.

"Janet, this is my friend, Cara Allen." He watched the two women shake hands and say hello. Janet, defying her usual standoffishness, surprised him by acting pleased to meet Cara and smiling for once. For some reason, she seemed genuinely happy to meet her.

"Where's the rest of the crew?" Jake said as they took their seats. Janet's husband and their daughter were usually at the games.

"It's just me tonight. Bob had an emergency at the hospital and Julie has a slumber party that she couldn't miss. I'm glad you two are here to help me cheer on the Wildcats."

The band marched to the sidelines as the cheerleaders ran to the middle of the field. The opposing team ran out first, followed by the Wildcats. Both sides of the stadium went nuts with cheering, whistling, and the ringing of cowbells. *Gotta love Texas high school football.* Within minutes the Wildcats had won the toss and elected to receive the ball. Jake rubbed his hands together; this should be a good game.

"Here we go." He patted Cara's knee as the ball soared into the air headed toward the waiting Wildcats. The ball was caught at the fifteen-yard line and carried almost twenty yards before the player was tackled.

"That's a good start," Cara said.

"Sure is," Janet said, addressing her remark to Cara. "My son, Carter, is the quarterback, number six. He's a great player."

By the time halftime rolled around, Carter had thrown two touchdown passes to put the Wildcats ahead 17-3.

"I need to stretch my legs. You want to come with me to the concession stand?" Jake rose at Cara's nod and pulled her up by her hands, enjoying the way they fit in his. It felt right. They headed to the ramp, but it was slow going. He didn't mind a bit, since he took the opportunity to hold his hand against her back.

When they finally reached the bottom, Cara headed to the restroom and he headed to the long line at the concession stand for soft drinks. After shuffling forward for several minutes, he winced as an all-too-familiar voice called out his name. Oh crap. This was all he needed. He turned reluctantly as his ex-wife sashayed to him like she was auditioning for a job at a men's club.

"Oh, Jake, it's so good to see you." Meagan wrapped her clinging arms around his neck, and squeezed like she wanted to choke the life out of him.

He removed her arms quickly and stepped back to

put some distance between them. "I don't remember you liking football."

"Oh, silly, you have the worst memory. Of course I love football. Janet asked me to come and watch Carter." She swung her hair back and grinned liked a small child. "And as usual, I'm late." She stepped toward him again and reached out to encircle his waist. "It's *so good* to see you."

"Jake, I'm back."

He turned, noticing the puzzled look on Cara's face and separated himself from his ex-wife's death grip. It was impossible to miss the smug look on Meagan's face. Damn.

"Cara," he said and stepped close to her side. "This is my ex-wife, who came to watch the game with Janet."

"Nice to meet you." Cara politely offered her hand which Meagan had no choice but to shake.

"Right, same here." She scrutinized Cara like a python stalking a pig and smiled at Jake like sex on a stick. "Sweetie, I didn't know you'd started dating again, especially after that last disaster. Didn't you make a vow or something?"

Thankfully, the line moved forward bringing Jake to the order counter. "See ya." He turned Cara toward the counter, hoping Meagan would take the hint and go home. He spoke softly near Cara's ear. "Sorry about that. What would you like?" From his peripheral vision, he viewed Meagan stomping childishly toward the ramp.

Soft drinks in hand, they headed back to the stands. As soon as they rounded the corner of the bleachers, Jake realized that Meagan was in the box with Janet. Damn it.

Why the hell had Janet invited her?

Cara went down the steps to their seats first and noticed Meagan. "Oh, you're here."

Janet waved. "Hi, y'all, the second half is about to start. Meagan came by to watch Carter."

Something strange flashed on Cara's face before she sat next to Janet. Jake could only imagine what she might be thinking. He checked his watch. If things got too weird they could always leave early claiming a dinner reservation, that would work. The teams trotted back on the field and the crowd stood and roared.

The Wildcats kicked the ball, chased it like a battering ram, and tackled the receiver at the five-yard line. The spectators cheered like crazy as Jake gave Cara a one-armed hug. "Now that's a football team."

Cara leaned into him and wrapped an arm around his waist. "I agree. Thanks for inviting me to the game."

"My pleasure." He planted a kiss on her cheek, amazed at how good and how right it felt.

~~*

"I love this restaurant," Cara said, placing her fork across her plate. She was stuffed with excellent food. "I can't believe I've never come in here before." The décor reminded her of a bistro she'd visited in Rome many years ago. She had no idea why it stood out in her mind, other than a fantastic meal.

"I'm glad we came. David Lombardo, the owner, and I went to high school together," Jake explained. "I went to A&M and he enlisted in the army."

"Not only is he an excellent chef, but this ambiance is fabulous. I like the Coliseum theme."

"His wife Jenny is the decorator. I'd introduce you but they're not here tonight, family emergency."

"Is everything okay?" Cara hoped the emergency was a small one.

"David's mother broke her leg and had surgery this morning."

"Sounds painful."

"She's a cool lady and tough. I'm sure she's ordering the nurses around, and keeping everyone on their toes."

"Are you close to them?" She was now very curious.

"They're like family. Mrs. Lombardo was my mother's best friend. She was almost a second mother to me after my parents died in a car accident."

Cara placed her hand over his and rubbed her thumb along the side. "I'm so sorry. I know it must still hurt."

Jake nodded. "It's something that's always with me—a big hole in my gut that I've learned to live with."

"Believe me, I understand. I lost my parents almost ten years ago."

"What happened?"

"It wasn't long after my wedding. They finally took a European vacation they'd put off for years and were on a train that was bombed in Madrid. It was awful." Cara didn't talk much about that time.

"Crap. I hate that we have the loss of our parents in common."

A resigned sadness touched Cara's smile. "I know, but sometimes people can draw strength from a shared experience."

~~*

Jake rubbed a finger over his lips and smiled, thinking maybe Cara was on to something. Commonality of human emotion—an excellent reason the two of them should spend time together.

"I agree. Not everyone understands the sudden loss of parents."

The waiter returned after the last dish was cleared and they declined coffee or Italian liquor.

Cara tried, but couldn't quite manage to stifle a yawn.

"Are you ready to head out?"

At her nod, he rose and stepped back for her to exit in front of him. He did like the looks of her from the rear, especially in a tight pair of jeans.

Within a few minutes he'd pulled in her driveway. "I'll walk you to the door." He debated with himself whether or not to kiss her, which in itself was stupid and lame. Jesus, he was thirty-eight years old, not some middle school kid.

They stopped on the small porch and Cara offered her hand. "Thanks so much for the game and dinner. I had a good time."

He took her hand and brought it to his lips, kissing the top. "Me, too. Perhaps we can do this again. Do you like professional football?"

"Sure, totally rooting for the Texans."

"Good. I have tickets for the home game two weeks from Sunday. Would you like to go with me?"

He loved that her face brightened at his suggestion. She seemed to show her emotions for all the world to witness.

"I'd love to. I haven't seen them play in person."

"It's a date then." He leaned toward her planning only a quick kiss, but the spark of excitement in her eyes made him rethink his strategy. Instead, he wrapped his arms around her waist and she snuggled into his embrace. The deep, soul searing kiss he gave her, as well as her response, told him everything he needed to know. Mm, this had all the makings of something very, very good.

This Could Work

Cara closed the door behind her and floated to her kitchen. After that kiss she was suddenly wide-awake and in need of something—something to drink or something to do. Not a chance could she get to sleep. Gracie came running after her and skidded on the tile in the kitchen before plopping on her butt, her head cocked to one side as she released a single bark.

"Yes, I had a good time with Jake. The Wildcats won the game and dinner was delicious."

Gracie's head bobbed and she patted her right paw on the floor.

"I guess you're happy for me." She bent over and gave her dog a good ear scratch. "In honor of your support, I'm going to make those dog biscuits I told you about." *[See EC on page 278]*

Gracie barked, ran in a circle a couple of times and headed back to the living room.

Cara chuckled as she pulled on her apron and

grabbed the recipe off the refrigerator. Maybe she'd have a glass of wine while she baked.

A few minutes later she'd poured a glass of chardonnay and assembled all of the ingredients for the biscuits. Her plan was to take several dozen to the shelter before Christmas. It was the least she could do to thank them for arranging her adoption of Gracie. This was the test of the recipe.

As she mixed the ingredients in her favorite yellow bowl, Jake came to mind. He had such a nice smile and well, he looked great in a pair of jeans and cowboy boots. She'd always been partial to men who wore jeans and a white shirt. That image made her think of George Strait, her all-time favorite country artist. Justin had hated country music and refused to attend any of George's Houston concerts.

"I wonder if Jake likes George," she muttered as she began to spoon out pieces of dough and roll them in her hands to make small balls. She quickly had a cookie sheet full of the balls and popped it in the oven, then sipped her wine.

Then again, it wasn't important whether or not Jake enjoyed country music. It's not like she was composing a list of things they had in common. Even though she'd enjoyed their date, the Texan game would be the last one.

She wasn't ready to devote her time and energy toward dating Jake or anyone else. That kiss had proven to her that she simply wasn't ready. She'd enjoyed their interactions way too much, plus she wasn't ready to deal with the emotional toll of a relationship with Jake. Frankly, he scared the hell out of her.

Even if she did have a great time with Jake, was she ready to push Justin's memory aside? He'd been her first love and the man she'd hoped to raise children with. How could she go out with someone else when Justin still filled her heart?

She should probably back out of the Texans game date. But she'd never been to a game in person. She laughed out loud; amazed she could see the humor in her inability to make a solid decision. Well, she'd already said yes to Jake and she did have a job to do for him. *That's it.* The game wouldn't be a date but business entertainment. That happened all the time. Problem solved.

It was well after midnight before a batch of biscuits had cooled enough to try. Cara bit into one of the super hard creations, the first requirement of any decent dog biscuit. She nodded, deciding the flavor wasn't half bad. She took one to the living room for Gracie who was the official taste tester.

Cara found her in the usual spot on the sofa. The pup rubbed her eyes with her paws then rolled over.

"Hey sweetie, I have a treat for you."

Gracie accepted the small round biscuit. Her eyes focused on Cara as she chewed. Cara held her breath, waiting for a reaction.

"If you like the biscuit bark three times."

Gracie's head wobbled and she sat up. After a beat she barked, "Woof, woof, woof."

"Excellent. They've passed the taste test. Thanks, sweetie. You can go back to sleep."

Gracie lifted a paw then stretched out on her pink

blanket and closed her eyes.

Cara went back to the kitchen to take the last batch out of the oven. These dog treats would be perfect for the shelter. She stowed the cooled biscuits in a storage container to save for her sweet dog. Actually Gracie was more than a dog. She had almost human mannerisms and seemed to understand everything Cara said. That was ridiculous, of course. Dogs learned from their humans based on repetition of the same words. She had no special powers. Gracie was simply a very smart puppy.

~~*

Monday morning came much too fast and after a long dog walk, Cara had to get to work. Gracie kept guard of the street from a footstool by the front window in the dining room. All of the Halloween trick-or-treaters ringing the doorbell last night had brought out a protective streak in her.

Cara entered her office, once again amazed at how much she loved the space. Justin had helped her decorate and they had combined two opposite styles—she was country chic and he was wood and leather—into a new style they called "country meets downtown." The desk was an old door from his parents' farm they had sanded smooth and then clear varnished.

She opened the electronic calendar on her computer. She had plenty to keep her busy this week and all the very important drop-dead due dates were next week. Excellent, she could start working on Jake's project. The quicker she had the first draft for him, the quicker their "professional" meetings would be over.

She reviewed the notes she'd written at lunch. He

wanted a complete overhaul of his website, brochures, print advertising, and all the associated branding materials. The first task was to think about his brand and how it compared to his local competitors. She opened her Internet search engine and began to work.

The phone rang and Susan's office number displayed on the caller ID.

"Hope you're having a good Monday."

"So far so good," Susan said. "Sorry I didn't call you yesterday. My friend and I had our first overnight date and it lasted until after dinner yesterday."

Apparently Susan was smitten. Smitten enough to rush one of her own rules about what she would do with a man and when. Overnight dates were usually at the bottom of her list, even after six months of dating.

"You sure took your time getting to this step," Cara teased. "Hope you had a good time."

"Sure did. What about you and Jake? How did everything go?"

"It was good. He's a nice man. I met his sister and his ex-wife and—" Susan cut her off.

"You're kidding, the ex-wife already. What was she like?"

"She and his sister are still good friends." Cara thought that was strange but what did she know about ex-wives hanging onto ex-husbands. "She's pretty but seems on the high-maintenance side. Don't know if she works or re-married. Jake doesn't have a lot of patience with her."

"He probably has good reason for that. Are you seeing him again?" Susan said.

"Probably this week, I'll have a first draft of his branding and marketing material. We're going to the Texans game a week from Sunday."

"Aren't you the lucky girl? Sounds fun."

"I'm looking forward to watching a game in person but it will be the last date. I'm not ready for a relationship," Cara admitted. "I haven't put Justin's death behind me and it's not fair to Jake or anyone else."

Surprisingly, Susan agreed. "You know best."

"Wait, no argument from you? I expected some push back."

Susan laughed. "Sorry, gotta go, my other line is ringing."

Cara turned back to Jake's project and continued to research landscape companies, broadening the search from Sugar Land to the state of Texas. She jotted ideas in a spiral notebook as she clicked on links and viewed dozens of websites. She loved doing projects like this where her imagination could run the gamut. Most of her freelance work focused on producing work according to specific guidelines from her clients.

This project for Jake was feeding her creative juices.

She heard a bark followed by the click of Gracie's nails as she ran into the room and jumped on the leather loveseat. Cara had laid down an old throw to keep her from scratching the leather. So far she'd been a good dog.

Cara laughed as the pup wiggled her butt to get settled just right. "I guess you chased away all the bad guys on the street."

Gracie nodded and barked, then dramatically flopped

on her side and closed her eyes.

"Being a watchdog is tough work," Cara commented before turning her attention back to her computer.

By Thursday afternoon, she had a good draft of new branding along with print and media suggestions for Jake. The document was ready for primetime. Should she call him or email him? After thirty minutes of debate and drinking a homemade cappuccino, she made her decision and sent him an email, suggesting he drop by her house for dinner on Saturday evening. After all, she owed him a meal after he'd bought her lunch and then dinner. Fair was fair, right?

~~*

Over the years, Cara had prepared countless homemade dinners. Her only rule was to fit the menu to the occasion and to the guests. This dinner involved one guest to discuss a business assignment. She concluded that meant easy and no fuss—beef stroganoff over noodles, a green salad, and buttermilk biscuits. And she'd throw in her Love Drop cookies and coffee as a bonus.

Even though it was a business dinner, Cara added a nice cabernet sauvignon to the menu along with her favorite recipe for cheese sticks. Something to munch on kept her guests busy and calm. Plus everyone liked finger food.

She surveyed the kitchen, everything was ready. She'd prepare the stroganoff once Jake arrived. After dinner they'd go over his changes to the documents and set a date for the final submission. A car door slammed outside. Gracie ran into the kitchen and barked. Jake had arrived.

He walked in the door wearing a large smile and carrying a vase of yellow daisies, which hit Cara's top-ten list of sweet things a man could do. He said hello to Gracie who barked in response then sped off back to the living room. Cara had tuned the television to Animal Planet and the pup seemed to enjoy the channel.

"I hope you like flowers," Jake said as he handed her the vase in the kitchen. "Daisies suit you."

"Why do you say that?" She settled the vase on the end of the island counter.

"I often assign plants and flowers to people I meet, guess it's a hazard of being a landscape artist. You strike me as a happy person and a daisy is one of the happiest flowers in the garden."

"I see," she said, not seeing at all. She hadn't truly been happy since Justin died. She must be good at hiding her feelings. "Have a seat and I'll pour a glass of wine."

"Thanks, I've been going non-stop since seven this morning. Spending down-time with you will be a pleasure."

His last remark surprised and pleased her at the same time. She placed a glass in front of him. "This is a cabernet."

He raised the glass to his lips and smiled, then tasted the wine. "Yes, ma'am, I like your taste in reds."

She set a basket of the cheese sticks on the counter. "Nibble on these while I get things started." She set the burner under a pot of water to boil the noodles then retrieved the beef from the refrigerator.

"Do you mind me asking what you're making?"

"It's beef stroganoff." She turned to him, praying he

didn't have a problem with it. "I hope you like it."

"I love it. My mom used to make it on Saturday evenings. She'd use hamburger when times were tough and then sirloin when things were better."

"That's so odd. My mother did the same thing. I'm using her recipe." Cara wondered how many other things they had in common.

Jake snacked on a cheese stick. "Anything I can do to help?"

"No, you sit back and relax. This won't take but a few minutes."

They chitchatted while Cara prepared the stroganoff. She'd cooked the dish so many times that she was on autopilot. While the sauce thickened, she grabbed the salad and checked the biscuits in the oven.

"Would you like to eat here in the kitchen?" she asked.

"Sure," he said. "No need to go to any trouble."

Ten minutes later they had their plates full and sat beside each other at the breakfast bar.

Cara realized too late that sitting at the island put her in close proximity to Jake. There wasn't a table between them. She could smell the musk of his aftershave, one of her favorite scents. Damn, she should have set the dining room table.

She picked at her food while Jake cleaned his plate.

"Would you like more?" His enthusiasm hadn't helped matters. It thrilled her that he liked her cooking.

He nodded with a sheepish grin on his face. "This reminds me of my mother's stroganoff."

"I'm sure it was a popular recipe back in the day."

She refilled his plate at the stove. "I bet it was in one of the women's magazines."

"Along with articles on how to keep your man and maintain big hair all at the same time."

"I bet articles on men and colored polyester pants on the golf course were equally popular."

He raised his wine glass in salute. "I do believe you're correct about that."

"Thank God we're past big hair and green polyester."

"Think so? Let me tell you a story about one of my clients." Jake had an amused expression on his face as he began to relay the tale.

Cara studied his hands as he talked. In high school she'd taken several art classes and had concentrated on human hands for all of her projects. Jake had nicely shaped hands, broad palms, long and thick fingers. His palms were callused yet his nails were clean and manicured. A man who worked with dirt and yard tools had such beautiful strong hands—what a contradiction.

". . . and then she shut the door and drove off."

He finished his saga and she hadn't heard a single word he said. "That's quite a story," she said, hopefully covering her rudeness. "Would you like coffee while we discuss your project?"

"Sure." He rose and grabbed his plate and hers. "Let me help with the dishes while you make it."

"You don't need to do that."

"I've been trained well by my sister." He turned on the faucet and opened the dishwasher door.

"Okay." A man who volunteered to do the dishes

and volunteered at an animal shelter surely had to be one-of-a-kind. And that was why she needed to stay clear of him. He was too damned attractive.

They met back at the island counter after Cara retrieved her folder of printed material for Jake's project. She placed it on the counter then added two red mugs of coffee and a plate of cookies.

Jake placed his hands around the mug. "Hmm, that feels good. Seems like it's getting cold early this year."

"I was telling Gracie the same thing yesterday. I hope we don't have a harsh winter."

"You talk to your dog about the weather?"

"I talk to Gracie about everything. She's a very good listener."

He raised an eyebrow then nodded and munched on a cookie. "These are really good. What are they called?"

"I call them Love Drops." *[See EC on page 279]*

He studied the cookie in his hand. "Love Drops?"

"I thought it was catchy." She opened the folder and fanned several papers on the counter in front of him. "Let's talk about the new brand for your business."

An hour later, the coffee pot was empty along with the plate of cookies. Cara and Jake thoroughly discussed every aspect of her proposal. She jotted notes from Jake's suggestions and marked the items he approved of "as is." It was a good meeting.

"We've covered the entire project," Cara said, thrilled that he liked her proposal. "Another cup of coffee?"

"No, thanks, I'll be up all night as it is." He rose and placed his hands on the top of the stool's back. "I very much appreciate all the work you've done for my company. You really have a gift with this stuff."

"Thank you, it was fun and I enjoyed it."

"I better get going," Jake said and he walked out of the kitchen.

She followed him to the front door. He turned to her. "Thanks for dinner, and the conversation." He smiled and stroked his hand along her upper arm.

"It's nice to cook for someone other than myself."

"Perhaps we can do it again, my treat though." He leaned toward her, his head lowering slowly.

She was certain he would kiss her, like he did before. This man knew how to kiss a woman. She closed her eyes, waiting for the touch of his lips on hers.

She waited. No touch. She opened her eyes as he kissed her cheek. What the hell?

"Thanks again." He opened the door and stepped to the porch. "I'll call you." He walked to the driveway. "Don't forget about the Texan's game next Sunday." He saluted and climbed in his truck.

Cara closed the door and leaned against it pondering the non-kiss. What had changed from the football game to tonight?

~~*

Jake's project wrapped up at the end of the next week, three days before the Texans game. Cara sent the final email to Jake and leaned back in her desk chair. No matter how confused she was over Jake, she couldn't deny her pride in this assignment. She'd done a great job in an area where she'd completed only a couple of prior jobs. Of course, she'd never tell Jake that. A girl had to have a few secrets.

Her shoulders slumped. If truth were told, she had too many secrets. Like her wishy-washy attitude about dating. Jake had no idea she felt so conflicted—her loyalty to Justin versus her belief that she needed to go forward with her life. Why couldn't she let Justin go? Why did everything have to be so damn complicated?

It was at times like this, the crossroads in her life, that she especially missed her mother. Talking about a problem had been so easy with mom. They had shared so much, almost like sisters. While growing up in Sugar Land, Cara had never made the mistake of assuming that her mother was a friend rather than a parent—a parent who believed in tough love, boundaries, and discipline.

She had loved her mother unconditionally, her father as well. They weren't perfect, but had worked hard at being good parents. The gift of hindsight and adulthood allowed Cara to understand them now. She avoided almost everything on March 11 each year, the date of their deaths. Perhaps, someday, she would be able to find peace. That day had yet to arrive.

The house phone rang and Cara let it go to voice mail. She didn't feel like talking to anyone until she made a final decision about the Texans game. She was at odds with herself about which way to go—dating a client was a no-no versus she'd never been to a Texans game. In the end, she didn't have to decide.

On Saturday afternoon, she went to bed with a stomach virus after hours of horrendously painful cramping. She called Jake and he understood completely. To make up for her missing the game, he invited her to

Thanksgiving dinner at his sister's house. She agreed, simply to lay her head on the pillow. She later learned from a voice mail that Susan planned to go with her boyfriend to his parents' house for the holiday. Yep, everyone had holiday plans.

~~*

The sky was overcast, not a snow sky, but steel colored and flat. The forecast predicted rain in the late afternoon, but that didn't hamper the outdoor frying of a turkey. Cara had not yet experienced this particular Thanksgiving tradition, now demonstrated at the home of Jake's sister and her husband.

They had arrived two hours ago; an early start on the holiday was another tradition. Jake explained there was much to do for their dinner so they always began their preparations promptly after breakfast. Cara figured the real deal was to get the heavy lifting done before the football games started.

After watching the turkey slide into the bucket of oil, she waved to the group of males standing around the pot and went back to the kitchen. She'd volunteered for vegetables peeling duty. Janet greeted her and pointed to the sink.

"You can peel there. There's plastic on the bottom of one sink. I don't use the garbage disposal for the peelings."

"Okay," Cara eyed the mountain of potatoes and carrots on the counter and totally understood. "I'll get started."

"There's an apron on the stool by the desk," Janet said, a tight smile slicing her face. "Don't want you to get that pretty sweater dirty. I expect you don't spend much time in a kitchen."

Although Cara didn't understand her comment at all, she ignored it. "Not to worry. I enjoy cooking." She wrapped the apron strings around her waist and returned to the sink.

Janet stirred something on the stove. "Really? Like Chinese take-out and pizza?"

What the hell should she say? She didn't want to antagonize Jake's sister but she didn't appreciate the snippy attitude. What a change from the football game. She peeled a potato, watching the brown peel drop to the bottom of the sink. She'd take the high road.

"You're right, I do love Chinese food and pizza." Cara patted herself on the back for her diplomacy. But she was a girl after all and added. "I have a fantastic recipe for Szechuan Beef. Maybe I'll make it for Jake one of these days."

The pot lid slammed behind her and heels clicked on the slate floor. She turned around and Janet had disappeared. Damn. Not good. But why had Janet been so catty? Perhaps she was being a protective sister and looking out for her brother. Cara shrugged and continued to peel; she'd play it by ear.

A few minutes later, Jake and the other men came in through the back door. They talked and laughed over each other, something about a bet on a college game. Jake moseyed over to Cara while the rest headed toward the huge television set in the family room.

"Why are you in here by yourself?" he asked, before sneaking a quick kiss to her neck.

"I'm on veggie duty," Cara said lightly. "Your sister left a minute ago. I'm sure she has a dozen details to look after."

Feminine laughter floated into the kitchen from the front of the house.

"Oh, crap," Jake said, his jaw flexing.

"What's wrong?"

He briefly put his head on her shoulder then straightened up. "Just wait."

The laughter became louder and Janet and Meagan strolled into the kitchen, arm-in-arm, and grinning like squirrels with a winter's supply of nuts in their back pockets.

They stopped next to the long island counter, two southern belles who appeared to be two peas in a very comfortable pod. Meagan stepped forward.

"Jake, darling, I didn't realize you'd be here today." She wiggled over to him and kissed his cheek, wrapping her hands around his bulging bicep. She gazed at Cara. "Oh, and you're here, too. I forgot, what was your name again?"

Jake pulled away from her clinging hands. "Meagan, aren't you missing a party or a happy hour somewhere?"

She flicked her hand in front of her ample chest. "You are such a comedian. Why don't you run along to the family room so we girls can do the cookin'."

Jake stepped in front of Cara, his back to Meagan, and threw her a pleading "help me escape" look.

"Go ahead, sweet pea," Cara said before grinding her lips on Jake's, enjoying the confused surprise in his eyes as she pulled back. Touchdown.

~~*

Nearly five hours later, the Thanksgiving dinner had been consumed along with Cara's apple pie. Dishes were stacked on the kitchen counters as everyone transitioned to the family room to watch the kickoff of the Texans game. Jake helped Bob, Janet's husband, make Irish coffee at the bar tucked into a corner of the room. Megan volunteered to serve the drinks while Cara relaxed on a loveseat not too far from the bar.

The room was large and comfortably furnished with a variety of sofas and chairs in either tan leather or a golden herringbone fabric. Sturdy oak tables were scattered about to hold drinks and decorative accessories and family photos in thick frames. One long wall of floor-to-ceiling windows looked out to the patio and a swimming pool. Cara liked the space as it had a homey and family feel.

"Here darlin', I have a coffee for you." Megan handed Cara a glass coffee mug. "I told Jake to go easy on the whiskey as I figure you're a light weight."

"Thanks, Meagan," Cara said. "Compared to you, I probably am a light weight."

Meagan screwed her mouth into a witch's scowl and stomped off. *Good riddance.*

Someone turned up the volume of the television as the Texans lined up for the kickoff, drowning out any conversation. Jake joined Cara on the loveseat and patted her knee.

"Here we go. Finally we get to watch a Texans game together."

"You're right," Cara said, squeezing her hand on his

leg. "Thanks for inviting me. It's been a great holiday."

"I'm glad you came," he said, planting a quick kiss on her temple.

The room erupted in clapping and yelling as the Texans kick returner ran the ball to their forty-seven yard line.

Janet hurried over to them and whispered in Jake's ear. Cara couldn't hear a word she said.

He rose and touched her shoulder. "I'll be right back." He followed his sister out of the family room.

She turned her attention back to the game. The Texans had scored a touchdown in the few moments she'd been distracted. She tuned out the cheers and focused her thoughts on Jake instead. Her feelings about dating him ricocheted from still-loyal-to-Justin to let's-go-for-it. She had to make a decision and did.

The time had arrived to throw off her wishy-washy cloak and go forward with life, at warp speed. After all, she wasn't getting any younger. She'd date Jake with gusto.

Coming to a resolution about this made her feel better. In fact, the idea of seriously dating Jake or another man was exciting. What was that saying about the rest of your life starting with one step?

She realized she'd just taken that one step, all by herself, and it felt good.

She needed to use the restroom and looked around for Jake. She didn't see him and headed for the hallway next to the kitchen.

A few steps out of the family room she heard Jake's voice. It came from the study she'd toured earlier that day. She walked to the half-open door, intending to say hello, but stopped at the tone of Jake's voice. Janet spoke after him.

"I'm asking you one more time. Why in the hell are you seeing that woman? She's a loser."

Cara hadn't realized Janet disliked her so much. Sure, she got the sister-is-friends-with-the ex-wife thing, but this sounded personal.

"I told you before; it's none of your damned business who I date."

"Right. And this one will be just like the last one, and the one before that. It'll end in a huge disaster and I'll have to soothe your damaged ego. When are you going to do the right thing?"

"You are going too far, Janet." Jake's voice had lowered and he enunciated his words.

"No. You need to face reality and admit you should have never divorced Meagan. You two are meant for—"

Cara eased back from the door and hurried to the bathroom, tears in her eyes. She looked in the mirror and splashed cold water on her face. Well, so much for her first attempt at dating. It wasn't in the cards for her, at least not with Jake.

She refused to let this happen to her again. Justin had walked away from his family to be with her. She'd ended up with terrible guilt over the years he'd missed with them. She had no desire to put herself, Jake, or anyone else through something like that again. She dried her face with a hand towel. She knew what she had to do.

Jake drove Cara home during half time. She declared a major headache and Jake being a gentleman, catered to her claim. She kissed his cheek quickly in the car so he wouldn't walk her to the door.

Tears sliced down her cheeks as she watched him back out of the driveway and race down the street. Well, that was that. She turned away from the dining room window and noticed Gracie sitting in the wide doorway with her head cocked to one side. She had a "what's wrong" look in her eyes.

Cara scooped the pup into her arms and buried her face in Gracie's soft fur. She loved her dog. "It's just you and me from now on."

Dogs Rule

The calendar on the refrigerator didn't lie. It was less than two weeks until Christmas Eve and Cara had fallen into an alien vortex. She hadn't purchased a single gift, which was so unlike her normal holiday preparation. Not being in the mood for the upcoming holiday didn't even cover the true essence of her situation.

Jake had called several times and she'd let it go to voice mail each time. She hadn't returned a call or responded to one of his emails. Not answering his calls was childish but she didn't know what to say.

She couldn't see herself embroiled in a family feud between him and his sister. That was entirely too much drama and unfair to Jake.

She did manage to make a triple batch of dog biscuits and take them to the shelter. Naturally, she'd almost run into Jake in a hallway but turned a corner before he saw her.

Typically during this time of the year, her business slowed down and she had extra time on her hands. This year she planned to use the time wisely—to outline the cookbook she'd been mulling over for months. She planned to publish it herself. Everyone was self-publishing these days. Why not her?

The first thing to do was to research the alternatives available. That activity would keep her occupied for a while and keep her mind off of Jake. Not being in contact with him was for the best.

A fresh pot of coffee finished brewing and Cara added nonfat half and half to her cup. The doorbell rang. She had few visitors so this was unusual. At the front door she peeked out the side window. Her breath caught in her throat. Jake stood on her porch.

Locusts swarmed through her, leaving her incapable of moving. What should she do? He didn't know she was at home so she could do nothing and he'd go away. The doorbell rang again. Gracie came running and skidded to the door.

Oh, what the hell, she opened the door.

"Jake, this is a surprise."

"Do you have a minute?" His face looked pinched. "Hi, Gracie."

She barked once and took off running for the living room. Her favorite Animal Planet show was on.

"Come on in, I just made a pot of coffee." He followed her to the kitchen, his boots slapping on the floor.

Cara grabbed a mug and poured Jake's coffee. "Here

you go," she said, sliding the cup across the island counter to where he stood next to a stool.

"Thanks." He lifted the mug to his lips while his gaze never left her face.

Cara wanted to get this over with, and quickly. Jake's closeness sent goose bumps along her arms and caused her to exhale a shaky breath.

"What do you want to talk about?" she said, getting the ball rolling.

He set the mug down and placed both hands flat on the counter, leaning slightly forward. "What happened between us? You haven't answered my calls or replied to my emails.

"I've been busy."

"Really? If I'm not mistaken, you told me on Thanksgiving that December was your slow time."

She did tell him that. Damn. Cara sipped her coffee, stalling for time. "Okay . . . I'm not ready to date yet. I realized I haven't gotten over Justin's death. I need more time."

Jake stepped back from the counter, rubbed a hand over the manly stubble on his face. "I can accept that. But it sure as hell contradicts that mind-blowing kiss you gave me in Janet's kitchen."

Damn, again. They were going in circles and she'd soon spill her guts if she didn't get him to leave. She braced herself.

"Not really. I was just showing off in front of your ex-wife. It was a girl thing, had nothing to do with you."

His eyes briefly rounded then he smiled, real slow. "If that's the case, I'm sorry I bothered you today. It won't happen again." He turned and headed to the front door.

Why had she said such a nasty thing? She hurried after him, mentally wringing her hands. Could she be any more of an idiot in dealing with men? Perhaps she should tell him the truth about Justin being estranged from his family because of her.

Jake had his hand on the doorknob and turned back to her, his face grim.

"I'm real sorry about everything, Cara. You're a nice lady. Take care of yourself." He opened the door and strode to his truck, his boots silent on the concrete. He jumped in and within seconds, shot down the street.

Cara stared at the empty driveway, tears welling in her eyes. Why had she driven him away? Because she didn't have the guts to open up to another man and tell him the truth. She'd given her heart to Justin and he'd died so young. It was better to end things with Jake before she opened herself up to the possibility of being hurt again.

She shut the door and rubbed her eyes while walking a couple of steps, intending to go back to the kitchen. Unfortunately, her left foot caught on the fringe edge of the rug in the foyer. She slid forward and fell on her right side with the outside of her right foot and her head hitting the hard floor with a loud whack and a thump.

~~*

Gracie raced into the foyer. She circled Cara, sniffing her still body and nudging her hands with her little black nose. She licked Cara's face but nothing happened.

Gracie ran through her doggie door to the backyard,

around the corner of the house and toward the front fence. Running straight to the loose slat in the fence, she nudged it aside with her nose and belly crawled through the opening. She raced down the street, hoping to find the one person she instinctively knew could help her mistress.

~~*

Jake couldn't believe Cara had acted like that. What the hell was wrong with that woman? He turned the corner and swung into a drive-in. He needed to think and a cheeseburger and fries would help the process move along. He parked in a slot and shouted his request via the order station out the window.

Slumping against the seat and the door, he noticed through the windshield a park across the street. It had a variety of outdoor equipment built for kids, mostly empty this time of day. Wouldn't it be fun to take a child of his to a park like that?

As he waited for his lunch, he purposely didn't think about Cara. He needed time to get past this lost opportunity. He knew in his heart they had a chance for a good relationship.

Barking, very loud barking interrupted his thoughts.

He straightened up and glanced out the driver side window. What the hell?

Gracie stood next to his truck, bouncing on the pavement and barking like crazy.

He opened the door and patted his leg. "Come on girl, jump up." Without missing a beat, Gracie jumped onto his lap. Jake wrapped his arms round her and rubbed her back. "What are you doing here? Did you get out by accident?"

Gracie licked his face, her rear end moving from side to side.

"Okay, I get it. You're a runaway and I need to take you home." Jake cancelled his order then backed out and retraced his route to Cara's house.

He scratched Gracie's ears as he drove. "Your mom won't be happy you snuck out. But she'll be very glad you're home safe and sound."

Gracie barked and snuggled against Jake.

He pulled in the driveway then carried Gracie to the front door. He rang the doorbell once, then twice. Gracie began to bark. She wriggled until he lowered her to the ground. Her barking grew more excited as she jumped repeatedly against the door.

Jake stared at the dog, his chest tightening with a bad feeling of foreboding. This was not usual Gracie behavior. He tried the doorknob. When it turned, he pushed the door open and stepped into the foyer, calling Cara's name.

He paused only for an instant before rushing forward to kneel beside Cara. Gracie remained at his side, silent as a stone. He touched Cara's shoulder and said her name. She didn't stir.

"Gracie, I need to take Cara to the hospital. You stay here and guard the house, okay." The dog seemed to nod in agreement as he patted her head. "Promise me you won't leave the house."

She danced on her hind legs.

Jake bent over and scooped Cara up in his arms. He looked down at Gracie. "I'll be back as soon as I can."

He closed the front door of the house with a bump of his hip and quickly settled Cara in the passenger seat of his truck. He noticed her right foot was swollen over her shoe. That wasn't good. The nearest hospital was ten minutes away and he lost no time in getting there. He parked in the emergency room parking lot and lifted Cara back into his arms. He rushed through the doors to the reception desk.

"Please help. She's unconscious and she hurt her foot."

A nurse came around the desk and motioned for him to follow her. She waved a plastic card over a black thing on the wall and a wide metal door opened. They hurried through it to a treatment room and Jake carefully laid Cara on the bed. She moaned as he released her.

"Do you know what happened to her?" The nurse said while wrapping a blood pressure cuff around her forearm.

"I think she must have fallen, maybe tripped on a rug." He remembered the crumpled rug under her.

"Are you her husband?"

"No, a friend."

"Do you know if she's allergic to anything?"

"No."

A woman in a white coat walked in the room and bent over Cara with a stethoscope.

"Sir, why don't you go to the waiting room and we'll call you once we know what's going on." The nurse gave him the evil eye. "The doctor will do what's best for your friend."

He provided his name, Cara's name and left the

room, eyes scanning for the exit to the waiting room. He found the right door and staked out a spot on a row of uncomfortable chairs near the television.

Someone changed the channel on the television, knocking Jake out of the zone he'd been in for over an hour. His mind had circled the facts several times, hopping from the image of Cara lying on the floor, to thoughts of how Gracie must have known that something was wrong. The dog was clever as hell, that's for sure. How had she known to go searching for him, and how did she know his truck? He shook his head. Some dogs have almost human-like instincts and Gracie seemed to be one of those dogs. He checked his watch; two hours had passed since he'd entered the ER. He ran his hand over his hair. What was taking so damned long?

Half an hour later, a young woman in navy blue scrubs approached him. "Are you Jake?"

He nodded and she continued. "Mrs. Allen is asking for you. Please come with me."

His heart nearly leapt out of his chest. Cara asking for him had to be good. He jumped from the chair and followed the nurse back to the original treatment room.

Cara's eyes were closed when he entered the small space. He prayed she was okay, resting comfortably, and not in a coma. She seemed so thin under the blanket. He'd never thought of her as petite but now the term fit her perfectly. He stepped closer and took her hand. Her blue eyes opened immediately.

"Jake, you're here," she whispered. "Thank you."

"How are you doing?" He brushed hair off her forehead.

"Okay, I guess." She licked her lips. "I hit my head and broke my ankle. They put a splint on it, the ankle, I mean."

"I'm not surprised. It looked swollen. Does your head hurt?"

"Not really. How did you find me? I don't remember."

Jake told her the story and she thinned her lips, slowly shaking her head.

"What are you thinking?" he said.

"That I have an amazing dog. But how did she get out of the yard?"

"I'll check the fence for you."

"You don't have to do that. I'll get my yard guy to look at it."

"I am a yard guy." He patted his chest. "It's not a problem."

"Okay. But still, how amazing that Gracie found you."

"She's a smart dog," Jake stated.

"She's more than smart. I think she's . . . um, gifted in a people-type way."

He narrowed his eyes; it *was strange* how Gracie found his truck. "I'm beginning to think you're right."

A nurse intruded with a stack of papers in her hand. "Mrs. Allen, I have your release orders. Since you refused to stay the night for observation, we won't send you home unless someone stays with you tonight."

"Well, I—"

Jake interrupted Cara. "I'll make sure she's not alone."

"You don't need to do that," Cara countered.

He squeezed her hand. "Shh, listen to the rest of your orders."

The nurse gave her two prescriptions for pain and inflammation, and the name of an orthopedist who would cast the ankle once the swelling went down. An aid came in with a pair of crutches and leaned them against the end of the bed.

"Have you used these before?" the nurse said, pointing to the pair.

Cara shook her head and grimaced. "I'm notoriously klutzy. This will not be fun."

~~*

Actually, Cara hadn't worried about not having fun the last three days. Jake played the role of male nurse to a Hollywood, Oscar-level degree. Hiring him on a regular basis had crossed her mind, but that was probably the pain meds talking. Regardless, he'd been a blessing.

Today she'd finally get her walking cast. It would be the last day he'd have to help her and occupy her guest room. She figured she'd be able to move on her own and get back to normal. Thank heavens she hadn't required surgery.

Right then he was at the grocery store, stocking her pantry so she'd be set for at least a week. He'd easily accepted her list and hadn't squawked at its length. The man walked on water, which made her life so much harder because she knew they could never have any sort of a relationship in the future.

She would not be the cause of a family fight between Jake and his sister. Been there done that, period. But she would enjoy the time she had with him even though her heart would break when she had to say good-bye.

She leaned her head against the back of the chair for a moment and closed her eyes. Her foot rested on a matching ottoman. She intended to refresh the ice bag in a minute.

She woke from her nap to find Jake bending over her foot. "How long have you been back?"

"Long enough to stow the groceries. How's the pain? I'll get more ice."

"The drugs are good."

He chuckled as he scooped cubes into the ice pack that normally rested on top of her ankle. "Would you like a sandwich for lunch? We should leave for the doctor's office in an hour."

Yep, the man was a saint.

Nearly four hours later, she had a yellow walking cast with a black clunky shoe and a special plastic bag that slipped over the cast so she could take a shower. Walking was more painful than she'd expected. Thus, Jake had convinced her he would stay one more night and then leave her on her own the next day.

She again rested in the chair with her leg on the ottoman. Gracie sat next to her, keeping her company. Jake had been in the kitchen ever since they'd returned, working on dinner. He said he'd prepare his specialty. A man who had a special dish that didn't involve barbequing on an outdoor grill? Wow.

He came into the living room carrying a wine glass and wearing a dishtowel over his shoulder. "Everything okay out here?"

"Enjoying my yellow leg. How's it going in the kitchen?"

"Under control." Jake grinned, and sipped his wine.

"I haven't had a pain pill in hours. May I have a glass of wine?"

"Under the circumstances, that's a fine idea. I'll be right back."

He quickly returned with a glass.

"Thanks. Sit with me," Cara said. "This is our last night together."

The hard planes of his face softened. "I'll be checking up on you every other day."

"That's sweet but not necessary. I'll do okay." She caught a whiff of an aroma from the kitchen. "Mm, something smells good."

"It'll be worth the wait." He planted himself on the sofa and Gracie joined him, stretching out against his thigh.

"I hope you'll give me your recipe."

"Maybe . . . probably."

"That's a definite yes."

"I'm curious," he said. "Did you learn to cook with your mother?"

"Uh-huh, the first thing I made by myself was apple crisp. I remember my hands shaking slicing the apples with my mom's favorite utility knife. I managed to keep all my fingers."

"I bet you were a cute little girl."

"Nothing special." She shook her head yet a tingle of pleasure canoed across her stomach. "How about you? What were you like as a kid?"

"Just like you, nothing special."

She laughed. "Guess we both turned out pretty good considering with started out so non-special."

~~*

Jake had fun serving Cara dinner at her dining room table. He'd gone all out with flowers and candles along with his specialty, chicken spaghetti with a green salad and whole-wheat rolls. Her eyes glowed when she hobbled into the room.

"Look at this beautiful table. You have out done yourself."

He knew he blushed at the comment. Meagan had never appreciated his efforts when it came to meals. "Thanks, sit down and I'll make you a plate."

Their conversation ping-ponged from favorite authors to favorite basketball teams to the best vacation to take. He liked that they both favored mystery novels and preferred the beach to the mountains. They had so many things in common. Why couldn't she understand they could have a future together? Or, at least admit it was worth a try to find out.

What the hell—he wanted to know the truth.

"Cara, you said you don't feel comfortable dating because of your husband."

"Yes, that's right."

"Are you sure it's not something else?"

She set her goblet on the table in a rush and water dotted the tablecloth. "How can you even ask me that?"

He was going all the way. "What you said about the kiss, that it didn't have anything to do with me. That's the kind of silly logic my sister would use when we were kids . . . to deflect the real issue."

"Silly?"

"It doesn't make sense so I know there's another reason. Did I offend you?"

"No, of course not."

"Then what is it?"

She turned her head away from him. After a long moment she turned back with her eyes looking glassy. "I didn't want to tell you."

He parked his hand over hers on the table, and hoped his silly grin would encourage her. "Tell me anyway."

"Okay," she said, brushing both eyes with her fingers. "Remember at Thanksgiving when you left the game to talk with your sister?"

"I remember. I missed a Texans touchdown."

"I heard you arguing with Janet, about me." She played with the stem of her wine glass. "I don't want to be the cause of a family feud. That happened with Justin's parents and I'm not going through it again."

"What happened with Justin?" His gut told him if she got this out, he would have a fighting chance. His bluntness was worth the chance of pissing her off.

She looked at him, her eyes round and the color of a Texas bluebell in the spring. "Okay. I'll give you the short version."

"Go ahead."

"Justin and I met in college. We were crazy about each other, the perfect match . . . except for one thing." She sipped her wine and took a long breath. "I wasn't a debutante."

"A what?"

"Justin's parents are old Houston with money going back a hundred years. All of the women were debutantes with many invited to this big International Ball in New York City. Me, I'm middle class and could care less about that kind of thing."

"His parents didn't approve of you and that created a major family issue."

"Bingo. We ended up eloping to avoid the eventual family confrontation. After three or four years Justin and his parents resolved their differences. We'd actually attended a couple of Christmas dinners before he died. His folks were very supportive during the funeral."

"Sounds like the original problem was resolved."

"But look at all the years that were wasted," she cried. "I'm not going through that again."

"You don't have to. I guess you didn't hear me telling Janet that I'll pick my own girlfriend and to give up her notion that Megan and I will get back together. We should never have gotten married."

"You said that before. Why did you get married?"

"Junior year at A&M, first time we had sex, she gets pregnant. We tell our parents and boom, the nearest justice of the peace marries us and away we go. Months later she had a third trimester miscarriage." He rubbed his hand on his chin. "I miss not having that child."

"I'm sorry," Cara said. "Yet you stayed married."

"Dumb, I know. I didn't want to admit to myself I'd been a fool."

"Yeah, I get that."

"Glad you understand." He stroked a finger along her arm. "Will you reconsider going out with me?"

"No."

~~*

Cara loved to bake. Today she was making a batch of her Love Drops cookies for Susan to take to her boyfriend's brother's house on Christmas day. She sat on the stool most of the time, giving her ankle a time out. She'd had the cast for nearly a week and had managed to stay upright without tripping over herself.

Christmas Eve would arrive in two days and she had yet to make the final decision for her holiday menu. Although she and Gracie would be alone, she still enjoyed making a big deal out of the food. Why not? Being alone on a holiday wasn't a crime.

The doorbell rang and Gracie started barking. Cara shuffled to the front door with the dog ahead of her and peeked out the side window—hmm, a delivery person.

She opened the door and greeted a cute teenage boy.

"Cara Allen?"

She nodded and he shoved a clipboard in her hands. "Sign on the last line."

She signed and he placed a vase of yellow tulips in her hands. "Merry Christmas."

Cara was perplexed. Who in the world would send her tulips, gorgeous yellow tulips? She sat the vase on the kitchen counter and retrieved the card. They were probably from Susan to say thank you for making the cookies.

She tore open the envelope and read the message on the card: "Please reconsider dating—I'd be honored if you'd spend Christmas Eve with me, I'll cook. Bring Gracie with you. –Jake."

She slipped onto a stool and hugged the card to her chest, breathing slowly in and out. Oh my . . . Jake had touched her heart with the tulips and his request. Her heart ached to open to him and what he represented. But could they actually work as a couple?

She knew exactly what to do, that is, once Susan's cookies were cooled and boxed.

Two hours later, Cara drove into Forest Lawn Cemetery in Houston. Yes, she was driving with her left foot on the accelerator, and she was careful. It took several minutes to park and walk to the large Allen section of memorials. Justin's was on the right side, below his grandmother.

Although it was December, the day was clear with temperatures in the low seventies, perfect Texas Gulf Coast weather. She stepped to her husband's grave.

Usually Cara sat on the grass but this time she stood, not sure she'd be able to get up with the cast on her foot. She placed her hand on the top of the charcoal granite headstone, feeling its warmth on her palm. It gave her comfort. Justin had a way of doing that for her without even trying.

"Hey, sweetie, I need your help with something." She rubbed her fingers along the smooth top of the marker. "I've been thinking about starting to date . . . get on with my life. What do you think about that?"

She closed her eyes and listened to the sounds of the cemetery. She heard the crunch of car tires on the gravel road, a distant cry of grief, and the mottled voice of someone long since departed. Rubbing her arms against a sudden chill, she opened her eyes and noticed a hot air balloon rise above the trees.

Stepping away from Justin's grave, she watched the balloon float slowly in the western sky. It had the University of Texas longhorn emblem on the side facing her with cream and orange vertical stripes. How strange. Justin had graduated from UT and he'd been a dedicated football fan. She turned in a full circle, wondering if something else would appear. Nothing out of the ordinary caught her eye. She turned back to Justin's gravestone. It was glowing silver in the late afternoon light.

Cara wasn't a fool and she totally understood Justin's sense of humor. She had her answer.

~~*

Sure she had a broken ankle encircled by a yellow cast, but that didn't make Cara helpless. Yesterday, she'd phoned Jake and accepted his invitation for Christmas Eve. And she offered to bring the dessert, the least she could do considering he was cooking dinner. She'd gone through dozens of her recipes, searching for that one dessert that would wow Jake.

Finally she found the perfect dish, tiramisu, and thankfully she had all the ingredients at home—no trip to the grocery store on Christmas Eve—that was a blessing. She'd put the dessert together, rest her ankle, and get her beauty rest all at the same time.

On her way to Jake's house, Cara gave Gracie a mini-lecture on how to behave in someone else's home. The talk included the major good-dog points—don't pee inside the house, no chewing on anything that's not identifiable dog food, and don't jump on furniture without permission. Yeah, the usual stuff for a guest dog with manners.

Jake's huge house graced the end of a street with a circular driveway, wide lawns, and spectacular holiday lighting. She drove slowly along the drive, enjoying the beauty of a yard maintained by a professional.

She heard barking as soon as she pushed the button for the doorbell. Jake answered the door with an adorable white dog by his side.

"Merry Christmas," he said and leaned over to kiss her cheek. "Come in and we'll get this party started."

"Merry Christmas to you." She watched the little dog and Gracie sniff each other. "You never told me you had a dog."

"I adopted him a month ago. You inspired me. Dex, say hello to Cara and Gracie." *[See EC on page 280]*

Dex bounced on his hind paws and barked twice. Then he and Gracie touched noses, ran across the foyer, and scooted into another room.

"They made friends fast," Cara said. "Is his name really Dex?"

"Dexter. They were bunkmates for a while at the shelter. Let's go to the kitchen."

She walked behind him and once again ogled his butt encased in faded jeans. This time her heart felt no guilt while she enjoyed the view.

One step into the kitchen and she stopped, her mouth surely mopping the travertine floor. "Holy moly, I could sleep in here, it's fabulous." Between the stainless steel, the concrete counter tops, and the rich oak cabinets, her dream gourmet kitchen had materialized.

"I'm glad you like it. I plan on begging for cooking lessons down the road."

"No problem as long as the lessons are here."

He laughed and took the tote bag she'd been holding. "Have a seat at the counter and we can start with a snack and a glass of wine. Once your foot is rested, we can tour the house."

"Sounds like a plan to me." She sat in a wide leather chair and watched Jake fuss with the trifle dish she'd brought. "That goes in the refrigerator and the plastic bag is doggie treats. I thought I might need them to coerce Gracie into good behavior."

"So far so good, I haven't heard any crashes."

"The night is young," she said with a silent prayer that Gracie wouldn't create a problem.

"Have faith, they're good dogs." He busied himself for a minute before pouring a glass of wine. "Try this. I hope you like it."

She did as instructed and wanted to smack her lips. "Love it."

"This is my own recipe." He held a stoneware dish holding black and green olives, feta cheese, and grated carrots. He handed her a small fork.

She scooped a bite and tasted his appetizer. "Mm, nice, is balsamic vinegar in the dressing?"

"Yes, ma'am, it's my secret weapon."

Barking and the clicking of doggy nails on the floor caused Cara to turn in the stool. Gracie and Dex ran into the room and around the corner of the cabinet to Jake.

"They must want something," she said.

"It's called dog biscuits." He winked and tossed two

treats in the air.

The dogs ran out of the kitchen, biscuits in their mouths.

"Those two are like kids," she said, shaking her head. "Sure makes it easier they get along."

"I agree." Jake leaned across the counter and kissed Cara, sending soothing warmth straight through her. She returned his kiss as his hand stroked her arm. Then he pulled back.

"Better not get too distracted so early in the evening," he said. "Your red sweater looks nice on you."

"Thanks." She decided she liked hearing a man give her a compliment. It had been too long.

"Are you up to a house tour?"

"Absolutely, as long as it's not a foot race."

~~*

Cara didn't know, but she was the first woman Jake had invited into his home, ever. His sister or grandmother didn't count. Yes sir, it was a special occasion for him. He had high hopes this was the beginning of many visits to come and eventually, something more. He was a patient man and willing to start at the beginning to woo the woman with whom he hoped to build a strong friendship and then, well, make it permanent.

She seemed to like his house—complimented him on the décor and the size of the rooms and the backyard deck and pool. He'd almost suggested they get in the Jacuzzi later but didn't. The spa shower in the master bath was a big hit, along with the potting sink and storage cabinets in the utility room. Women, he'd never truly understood what floated their boat. Storage cabinets were cool?

The tour ended in the dining room. He liked the room but didn't use it enough. Guess he should do more entertaining.

Cara pointed to the crystal chandelier over the long table. "That's beautiful. Look how the prisms sparkle on the ceiling and walls. Where'd you find it?"

"At a store on Royal Street in New Orleans," he said, pleased she approved of his selection. "I was there for a flower and shrub conference and walked into this hole-in-the wall store one day at lunch. And there it was, smiling down at me in a corner. I had it shipped home and loaded every crystal myself."

"I love it."

"Thank you for approving of my taste in chandeliers." He bowed to her. "You look like you're ready to fall over. Let's go back to the kitchen and you can put your foot on a stool while I get dinner together."

He turned two stools facing each other so her right foot rested easily. "Do you mind if we eat in here? That way you can keep your foot elevated."

"I like that idea. What can I do to help?"

"Nothing, just relax. Tell me what you do for fun."

Cara talked about her love for travelling and a trip to Rome when she got out of college. Jake prepared their dinner while he listened. He soon set a long casserole dish on the counter, along with bowls of charro beans, and tortilla chips and queso.

"My mother made this for Christmas Eve when we were kids. I've made it every year I've been in this house." He set out placemats, plates, and silverware.

"I love Mexican food. The enchiladas smell delicious," she said and moved bowls of beans close to their plates. "You cooked your own beans, didn't you? I'd love the recipe."

"No problem." He set a covered dish on the counter and settled on the stool next to her. "That's my grandmother's rice recipe."

She smiled and touched his arm. "This is my kind of holiday food."

"Hope you don't mind, I always say a quick blessing." He placed his hand over hers. "Dear Lord, we have gathered together to share good times, good conversation, good friends, and good food. Cara and I thank you for all. Amen." He squeezed her hand then stood. "I forgot the wine. I always drink chardonnay with enchiladas and queso."

~~*

Cara needed to stretch her leg after their dinner and volunteered to load the dishwasher. Jake reluctantly agreed and said he'd take the dogs out to the backyard for a pee break. They'd been well-mannered dogs during dinner. He must have been a psychic in a former life as he was spot on concerning them—no chewed shoes, no exploding sofa cushions, and no sneaking food off of a plate.

Every minute of dinner had been enjoyable. They'd shared cooking stories, primarily the disasters, and she marveled at the ease of their conversation. Surely that had to be beginners luck.

In quick order, she had the leftovers in the refrigerator, a pot of coffee dripping, and the concrete counter cleaned by the time Jake walked back in the kitchen.

"Dogs are ready to take a nap," he said, ruffling her curly hair. He stroked his hand over her back. "How about you, ready to relax on a comfy couch?"

"I like that idea."

"Let's go to the TV room. The dogs are hunkered down already."

She didn't remember a TV room on the tour. He led her down a short hallway to a wide archway. She stopped and her hand automatically fanned over her chest.

"Oh. My. God. This is . . . it's fantastic."

She stepped into the room, taking in the flickering white candles covering almost every surface. Their glow added exactly the right touch, framed against the Christmas tree in the corner and a fresh evergreen garland with red bows draping the wide mantel. A low fire burned beneath it, filling the room with a woodsy, winter scent.

"Jake," she said, wrapping her arms tight around his waist. "This is wonderful. It's Christmas by candlelight."

He kissed her cheek. "I'm glad you like it. I thought we might watch a movie." He led her to a dark green sofa with a Christmas throw across the back.

"This is perfect," she said. She placed her right foot on the matching ottoman and he laid the throw across her lap.

"Let me get the coffee and I'll be right back."

She noticed the two dogs sleeping side-by-side in a wide chair near the window. How did that work out so well? It seemed almost too good to be true. Would she soon snap out of a dream with this perfect man as the hero?

Jake returned carrying a small tray with coffee mugs. He placed it on a side table by the sofa then sat on the edge of the sofa next to her.

"Before I start the movie, there's something I've wanted to do all day."

Cara had no clue what he meant. "Okay, go for it."

He took her hand, kissed it, and leaned toward her.

Her heart thumped as he moved closer, and closer. She could see gold specks in his blue eyes. She swallowed as his mouth moved just above hers, and he stopped.

He wouldn't do this to her again, would he? She wanted his kiss. "What's wrong?"

He gave her an irresistible look that said "come and get it, if you dare," before his mouth twisted in a sexy-as-hell grin. "I'm enjoying the view."

She wrapped her hand around his neck and played with the hair curling over his collar.

His mouth conquered hers. Lust. Longing. Crashing need. His hands ran up her sides, brushing against her breasts. She pressed against his chest, sinking into the luxury of the moment.

Jake finally broke the kiss and spoke in a voice raspy with desire. "Holy . . ."

She rested her forehead against his. "Oh God, I know, right?" she gasped, her breathing every bit as heavy as his—their hearts pounded their mutual need in perfect synchronization. *Now that's what you call romance by candlelight.*

She pulled back from him, giving herself a minute to catch her breath. "You know I'm a mess when it comes to this dating stuff. Totally out of practice."

"I can handle it." His finger nudged a strand of hair behind her ear. "It'll be an adventure."

"Mm, I like adventures." She reached up to brush his hair back from his forehead, unable to fight the urge to touch him. "Are you really as patient as you seem?"

He caught her fingers in his hand and brushed a kiss lightly on her knuckles. "Most of the time, it's my tried and true, no stress method for dealing with problems.

"I see—patience equals no stress."

"Uh-huh. And in case you're wondering, this thing we have going here, it's gonna be good. But if you're not ready to jump in yet, I'm willing to wait."

He slipped his hand to the back of her head and pulled her close for another kiss before wrapping her in his arms for a long hug.

Cara closed her eyes and breathed in his masculine scent. Could any man be this perfect, or was this a classic case of too good to be true? She glanced at the chair with the two dogs and saw Gracie watching her. After a moment, the pup nodded, tucked her head against Dexter.

The corners of Cara's mouth lifted in a slow smile. The only assurance she needed was the steady beat of Jake's heart and his willingness to take it slow. Of course, she had a hunch she'd be itching to speed things up in no time at all.

* * * *

ROCKIN' JINGLE BELLS

The Meeting

By the time the Christmas season was over, Sara McClain would be deaf and brain dead. She was certain of it. The holiday business at The Coffee Café had been fantastic thus far and that made Sara and her mother quite happy. She'd helped her mother, Joan Adams, open the café in 2008 right across the street from the Town Center Marriott Hotel and they hadn't looked back since. But . . . the holidays this year were exceptionally annoying and driving her crazy. Why? She had no clue.

The noise and the hyper-activity of the season had her wanting to pull her hair out or strip naked and run through the fountain in front of the Sugar Land City Hall. Of course neither act would help with anything, since getting naked in a public place was illegal in Texas, and losing hair wasn't a good strategy for anything. She sighed and carried empty trays from the front display case to the back of the café.

Her mother had left for the day so she worked in the kitchen by herself, washing the trays and setting up for the next day. The radio hummed to a soft-rock radio station so she swayed and wiggled a bit as she worked.

"Hey, Sara, someone out here is asking for you." Cathy, a middle-aged grandma who baked like an angel and was one of their best employees, leaned around the corner of the short hall that opened to the back.

"Oh, yeah, who?"

"Don't know his name . . . but, oh my." She flicked her hand back and forth as she chuckled.

Now Sara was curious. She knew of no man, other than Cathy's husband, who could evoke that reaction. She wiped her hands with a towel before walking to the front. As always, when she rounded that corner, she hesitated a moment to take in the beauty of the "old-fashioned" coffee shop and mini-café.

They'd used a decorating theme mimicking the soda fountain of the fifties but updated with twenty-first century technology, along with dark oak walls and furniture, and accessories in rich colors of maroon, gold, and hunter green. They were open from seven a.m. to three p.m. and were thinking about getting a liquor license for wine and beer to stay open for happy hour. Alcohol had a very nice mark-up. Sara sighed, another decision to analyze and then make. *[See EC on page 283]*

She rounded the corner and stopped. OMG. Her blood rushed to the floor and she stood motionless for several moments. Finally, she shook her head to fight off the shock. What the hell?

Kyle Scott stood by the cash register in all his rock star glory. How could Cathy not recognize him? Sara pushed hair behind her ears and wished she had a mirror. No time now, he turned around and saw her. A smile spread across his face and set his blue eyes to twinkling. Apparently, he still had the power.

She stepped around the counter and stuck out her hand. "Kyle, it's good to see you after so many years."

He accepted her hand and drew her gently toward him. She skipped a couple steps along the tile floor and confronted his chest as his arms enveloped her. Her face mashed against his shoulder and his woodsy scent reminded her of high school.

His head dipped and he whispered above her ear. "Good to see you, Sara. How ya been?" Then he had the nerve to kiss her neck before straightening to his six-foot height and grin. His brunette hair curled below the collar of a red wool shirt that he stylishly wore over a white tee shirt.

She stepped back and pointed to his hair. "What happened to your crown of glory?"

"I grew up." His smile returned as he watched her closely, his eyes slightly narrowed. "Chopped it off for a donation a few years back." He leaned against a display case, typically at ease wherever he planted himself, and crossed his arms over what looked like a solid chest. "So, how ya been? Kinda surprised you're still in Sugar Land, figured you'd be in the big city."

"You know how it goes. Things happen, plans change." She'd never spoken truer words. Eight years ago she'd been planning to move with her husband to Boston. That dream had ended in an instant.

"Isn't that the truth?"

"What are you doing back in Sugar Land?" She knew his mother had moved to Brenham after his father died and his older sister, Kate, lived in Houston.

"The band is playing a gig in front of city hall on the twenty-third."

"I heard there was a big name band playing for the festival but didn't realize it was you." Out of the corner of her eye, Sara noticed Cathy hovering behind the counter.

"Yeah, we're technically off for a couple of months but this is a no brainer for me. Kate is about to give birth to twins so I was gonna be around anyway."

"Twins, huh? I haven't seen her in a long time." Kate was a couple years older than Kyle and had been very popular in high school. Sara and Kyle had been the music nerds, Kate the head cheerleader.

Sara decided it was time to put Cathy out of her misery. She motioned to Kyle to follow her around the end of the long counter to the work area.

"Cathy, I have someone I want you to meet. This is Kyle Scott. We were friends in high school."

Kyle shook Cathy's hand. "Nice to meet you Cathy. You work for a great lady."

Cathy grinned. "Nice to meet you." She pointed a finger at him and then at Sara. "You two knew each other in high school?"

"Sure did," he drawled. "We dated for three years then she kicked me to the curb."

"What?" Sara screeched. "I did no such thing. You left me to do your band thing."

"And why didn't you go with me?"

"I am not some rock band groupie . . . then or now."

"Rock band? You're in a rock band?" Cathy had that "I've missed the party" look.

Sara patted her arm. "Don't worry that you don't know. It's not an inspirational group. He's the lead singer for Topped Off."

"Topped Off? Ooh, I know that band, Chad, he's my oldest son, loves them." She stepped back and gave Kyle a good once over. "You're the lead singer? I thought it was a young group." Sara watched Cathy's face go blank once she noticed Kyle's eyes grow round. "I'm sorry, that was thoughtless of me. What I meant—"

Kyle reached for Cathy's hand, brought it to his lips, and kissed the back before releasing it. "I know what you meant, so no worries. I'm feeling kinda old for a rock singer myself."

"Thanks, I'll go handle the customer over there." Cathy hurried to talk to Mrs. Jenkins who came in regularly before closing time for a dozen banana buns.

Sara searched his face for what had prompted his "old rock singer" comment. Nothing. Just like always, he hid his emotions too well. She needed to get back to work and finish tomorrow's set up.

"It's been great seeing you, Kyle. Good luck with the concert, I'm sure I'll be there." She almost stuck her hand out again but refrained, instead she smiled.

"Have dinner with me tonight," he said in a rush. "It would give us a chance to catch up."

Oh no, she couldn't do that. She didn't have dinner with any man. No time, no interest, no heartbreak. But she was curious about what he'd been doing the last sixteen years.

"Hmm, I can't do dinner but I could provide coffee and chocolate cake. Is nine too late?"

He laughed. "Darlin' that's my waking up time for concerts."

"Right, you're more of a night owl."

"Comes with the job. Believe me I'd rather keep regular hours." He pulled out his wallet and retrieved a couple of business cards. "Here's my phone number. Write your address and number on the card." She did and handed it back to him. "Excellent, I'll see you at nine." He leaned forward and kissed her temple. She watched his attractive jeans-clad-butt walk to the door. My goodness, Kyle's ass had certainly changed since high school.

~~*

Kyle walked out of The Coffee Café feeling like he was back in high school. No, that wasn't a hundred percent true, maybe only fifty percent true. After all he did have the girl for their last three years. Sara had hardly changed. She still wore her dark hair short, her eyes were pools of chocolate, and she was still thin but now with a bit of a curve to her hips. She looked really good.

Sixteen years ago Sara wouldn't go on the road with him to the dives and clubs where the band had honed its skills in front of a live, well mostly live, audience. After a couple of years they'd lucked out being at the right club when a record producer from Los Angeles happened to hear their set. They'd quickly secured a recording contract and, as they say, the rest was history.

He pulled out his cell phone as he walked into the lobby of the Marriott Hotel and straight to the bar. He needed to think. He touched a name on the screen and sat at the long bar, listening to the phone ring. Finally, she picked up.

"Yo, Kyle, how's it going in the country?" His assistant aka manager Melody was a smart ass but an excellent take-charge-of-everything lady. She made his life immeasurably easier in Los Angeles and wherever the band played.

"The country is fine. I need you to do a couple of things for me before you leave in the morning." She was flying in the day before the concert with the rest of the band and a small crew and would keep everything and everyone on track. There was a dinner the band was supposed to attend tomorrow night and she'd know the details.

"Sure, babe, whatcha need?"

"I need you to find a realtor and put the Bel Air house on the market and arrange for everything to get packed and moved to Sugar Land."

The bartender arrived and he ordered a scotch. He didn't normally drink during the day but seeing Sara had gotten him unsettled and needing to think.

"What the hell! Have you been drinking, man?" He could picture her lounging by the pool thinking her world was turning upside down. She was right.

"Please, just do it. Isn't there a realtor or two that all the stars use?"

"Yeah babe, I'm sure there is. I'll get right on it. I'll see you around noon tomorrow and we can have a nice long talk."

He clicked off and tasted the scotch. Not bad for the country.

He didn't worry about people recognizing him around here, which suited him just fine. He was tired of all the attention, the travel, and the hectic schedule. Fortunately he wasn't a dumb rocker, he'd made his plans. He'd given himself fifteen years once they had their first recording contract. He wanted to make a bunch of money so he'd be set for life and then teach music. That had always been his goal. He was almost there. The rest of the band would keep going without him or take a pause, up to them. They all knew his plans and were making plans of their own, which he fully supported. Maybe they'd go on a mini-tour during the summer.

He sipped the scotch and looked around the space. A big-haired blonde sat at the end of the bar. She raised her chin at him with a wide smile and he shook his head. He had no need for entanglements in his life. Those days had been over five years ago when he'd extracted himself from an eight-year relationship that wasn't going anywhere but to the dump.

Now Sara, she was the kind of woman a man would want to come home to. Even though he hadn't seen her since the year after high school graduation, he could tell she hadn't changed. She was still the sweet and smart girl he'd loved. Loved, huh? Hmm, had he carried a torch for her all these years? Is that why he could never find the right woman? God knows he had plenty of opportunities.

He drained the scotch, signed the bill and stood. He might as well work out at the hotel gym before getting dinner from room service. That should keep him busy until he drove to Sara's house for dessert.

~~*

"Mom, do I have to go to bed? We're on school vacation." Seven year-old Travis McClain performed a routine every evening trying to convince his mother he should stay up later.

"After Christmas I'll give you more play time," Sara assured him. "You know you're a bear the next day if you don't get enough sleep."

"I know," he said as he climbed into his bed. He raised his hands, spread his fingers, and growled. "I'm a big ole grizzly bear."

She pulled the covers over his little chest and tucked his favorite dinosaur next to him. "That's right but you'll always be my sweet bear. Now get to sleep. Tomorrow is the day before Christmas Eve. I think grandma has something planned and you have a play date with Jimmy."

"Yay. Good night, Mom."

She leaned over him and kissed his forehead. "Sleep tight. I love you."

"Love you more," he said as he turned on his side.

She gave him one last pat then rose and turned off the light on the dresser. She always left the light in his closet on so he wouldn't be in total darkness. She shut the door and padded to the living room. What could she accomplish before Kyle arrived?

First she loaded the coffee pot and set out mugs and plates for the cake. She'd brought home half of a red velvet chocolate cake from the café so there would be plenty, just in case Kyle still had a sweet tooth. Once that was set, she went to her laptop at the kitchen table and began to look for "happy hour" appetizer recipes. If they did add a happy hour at the cafe, they'd need light food to go along with the drinks. Food was their hook to sell beverages. *[See EC on page 284]*

Sara jotted a list of possible recipes as she reviewed her favorite cooking site. She'd have no problem selecting the right appetizers for the café. Serving alcohol was a huge change to her mother's original concept for selling great coffee and breakfast buns. Of course, adding a light lunch and gourmet-iced tea was a change as well. Staying open through happy hour would set the hours as seven to seven. That would require another employee or two and—

The doorbell rang. Kyle had arrived.

He'd changed his clothes. That was the first thing Sara noticed when she opened the door. He wore a cream-colored pullover sweater and brown slacks, not jeans. He looked more like an insurance salesman than a famous rock star.

"Come on in." She stepped back from the doorway and he walked past her into the living room. She looked at her home from his eyes—small, old fashioned, cluttered, and decorated for Christmas.

He looked around casually then nodded. "I like your

house. This is a real home, not some manifestation of one built by an interior designer."

"Thanks." He'd surprised her. He liked her 1920s house nestled in the old section of Sugar Land. How about that? "I guess your house is a lot bigger."

"Yeah, but I'm selling it. Too damned big and in the wrong state." He walked to the mantle over the tiny fireplace and looked at the pictures, then the three Santa stockings. His forehead wrinkled as he turned back to her. "You're a mother?"

"Yes, I have a son." She walked to the kitchen and poured coffee. Did it matter if she told him about Travis? No, Kyle was an old friend she hadn't seen in years, it was natural that he would be curious about her life, as she was curious about his.

"I can see you as a mother," he said, taking the mug she offered.

"Really? I never thought about having children before I met Joe." She moved to the living room and sat in a club chair next to the fireplace. This was her reading chair. He followed her and settled on the matching sofa, close to her chair.

"Is Joe your son's father?"

"Yes." And a wonderful father he would have been.

"Are you guys divorced?"

She sighed, she might as well tell him. "I'm a widow. My husband died eight years ago."

"I'm sorry to hear that. I'd heard you married but not about this."

"Guess you didn't keep up with the local gossip."

He shook his head. "Tell me about Joe. How did you

meet?"

"We met on spring break, my sophomore year of college. A group of us had gone to Destin, Florida for a few days. One night we went to a club and I met him there. He was in town on business and we hit it off."

"He was older than you?"

"Fifteen years. Anyway, we dated for almost a year. He lived in Dallas. We got married and I moved there, and became a housewife, which I loved. Took all sorts of cooking classes. I finally got pregnant; we were over the moon with joy. I—"

"How did he die?" Kyle's bluntness hadn't changed. He'd always been the kid in high school who wasn't afraid to ask the hard question.

"A hiking accident. He slipped and fell, died instantly." That was as much detail as she would tell anyone. She took a deep breath. "I was pregnant when he died. It was Joe's last big climb before he became a father. I have a seven year-old son named Travis."

"I'm really sorry, Sara. I've never been married and can't imagine how horrible it must have been." He leaned forward and touched her knee, gripping and shaking it gently. "Are you okay?"

"Of course, it was a long time ago and I have Travis. He's a great kid." He had no need to hear about the soul-sucking loneliness or the hole in her heart that had yet to be filled. "How about you? What's it like to be a world famous rock star?"

"Actually, that's about to end."

"What? I'm confused."

"I'm retiring as the lead singer of Topped Off,

exchanging being on stage for being in a classroom." He smiled like he had a deep secret behind those thick-lashed eyes of his.

She rose. "I'll get our cake while you explain why you're retiring. Seems crazy to me."

"That's a good assessment on the surface. But actually, it's part of my plan."

"Your plan?" Sara cut a large and a small piece of cake. She handed the large piece to Kyle and returned to the chair. "Tell me about this plan, sounds intriguing."

"When the band first made it big, I knew I didn't want to do this for the rest of my life. Can't see myself as a Mick Jagger still rocking away at seventy." He shoveled a large bite of cake in his mouth and nodded. "I thought about it a lot and figured out what I really want to do is teach music. Cake is good by the way."

"That doesn't surprise me. In high school, you were always the band guy who helped the kids who couldn't read music."

He chuckled. "Yeah, that was me, Mr. Helps A-lot. I enrolled in an online bachelor's-master's combo degree then a Ph.D. program at UCLA. I'll get my doctorate this coming summer, that is, if all goes according to plan. And then you can call me Dr. Scott."

Sara was momentarily at a loss for words. Wow—a famous rock start transitioning into college professor. Girls would stand in line to take his classes. "That's quite a right turn in career path. Won't you miss all the attention?"

"For the first week." He set the plate on a side table and crossed one leg over the other. "I'm not the typical rocker I guess since I don't crave the attention. I wanted to be in a band because of the music, not because of the adulation. Now the money that comes with it—that I want. But the music has always been number one for me."

"Ah, you're an honest man." The more he talked, the more the adult Kyle sounded like the dreamer teenaged Kyle. Music, any genre of music, had been the harp that plucked his soul. Apparently that hadn't changed over the years and it pleased her.

"Actually, getting financially secure is what's kept me going. At heart, I'm not a rock star kind of guy."

She laughed at that. "Seriously, you're sounding a bit pompous. I think you've proven yourself to be a suitable rock star over the years. I've seen y'all on TV more than once."

He uncrossed his legs at that. "Glad to hear you've seen me perform. You know, I wrote a song about you."

Her eyes widened. "You are kidding me."

"Nah, I never kid about my songs. The band won a Grammy for it."

"You won a Grammy?"

"Yeah, we've won a few but that one is special . . . song of the year. Guess you're my good luck charm."

Sara rose, gathered the empty plates. She was no one's good luck charm; Joe's death had proven that. Once in the kitchen she turned back to the living room. "Would you like more coffee?"

"I'm good," he said and brought her his empty mug. "I should go. I'm sure you have to get up early."

"That's one of the givens of managing a coffee shop,

early hours."

"You seem happy though." He leaned against the short counter by the sink, filling the small space with his masculine style.

Yes, she had to admit it, Kyle was no longer the high school music nerd but a sexy man who knew what he wanted. A girl had to respect that.

"I am happy. I love my son and the store. I get along great with mom. Life is good."

"Is your life today what you expected when we graduated high school?" Damn, he asked tough questions.

She moved back to the living room and straightened an ornament on the Christmas tree. She didn't want to answer his question. "The answer to that question will take much too long. Another time?" She smiled and walked to the front door.

"Sure. Thanks for the dessert," he said as followed her to the door. "You have a nice house. I hope I get to meet your son one day."

"Who knows? Depends on how long you're in town." Sara sensed that Kyle was accustomed to getting his way. Well, she was in control of him seeing Travis.

"Right." His eyes narrowed for a beat then he leaned forward and kissed her cheek. He opened the door and stepped to the wrap around porch. "Thanks again. I'll see you around."

"Yeah, see you later." She watched him walk to a black SUV before closing her front door, shaking her head.

That was the end of that. Kyle seemed like he hadn't

lost the nice guy part of him but his life was a million miles from hers. Thank heavens she knew herself and was satisfied with her life. Otherwise she'd be lusting after a high school beau turned famous rocker.

A Night Out

Sara eased a foot out of her loafer, bent over, and rubbed her foot. She'd been on her feet for six hours straight. Why she didn't put on better shoes that morning was plain stupid. Her only defense was that at 5:45 a.m. she'd been thinking about Kyle and all he'd said yesterday. And now her feet hurt. She put her shoe back on, washed her hands, and served the next order of soup and a half-sandwich. She worked alongside Joan for another hour during the lunch rush and took a quick break to get a drink of water and use the restroom.

"Mom, I'm going to the check the front."

"Go ahead. Cathy is probably ready for a change."

The rush was still on when Sara walked to the front. Must be everyone finishing their Christmas shopping. She checked her watch, only an hour-and-a-half to closing time. How would this work staying open until seven? Shaking her head she decided she'd worry about that once they were able to get a liquor license.

"Cathy, let's switch places. You deserve a break." Sara and Cathy both knew that working the front counter was a lot more nerve-wracking than plating or bagging orders. Dealing with the public had a built-in stress component. It's just the way it was. Cathy hurried to the back and Sara took over the register.

She smiled at the next customer. "Welcome to The Coffee Café, how may I help you?"

An hour later, the rush was over. A few customers remained while the crew began their closedown procedures. Sara began to remove empty trays from the display case when Kyle walked through the door and gave her a small wave.

"You have a minute?" he said. He wasn't smiling and looked on the serious side. Uh-oh, she hoped nothing was wrong.

"Sure, what's up? Everything okay?"

"You have a good day? Are you tired?" Why would he ask that?

"We've been busy which is always good."

"I have a question, or more like a proposal for you."

Now she *was curious* but couldn't imagine what he might be talking about. After last night, she doubted she'd see him again other than the concert. "I'm all ears."

"I'd like you to join me for dinner tonight. It's a group of people."

"Anyone I know?" Why did she say that? She had no business going anywhere with Kyle.

"It'll be my assistant, Melody, and George, the band's drummer. You don't know him. John and Jim are spending time with their families. You remember them, right?"

"Haven't seen them in years, but yes, I do remember those two. Anyone else?" Sara was surprised at her nosiness.

"I think the mayor and someone from Town Center

who set up our gig. Melody takes care of the details. It's at Perry's so it's really close."

Hmm, the mayor, this might be a good opportunity to mention the café's application for the liquor license and gage his support. She'd met him once when he came into check out the café. She assumed he got his morning coffee from his office or another coffee store. Maybe this could be an opportunity to change that.

"Sounds good, I love Perry's. But first I need to verify my mom can watch Travis. She's in the back. Hold on." She poured a cup of coffee, handed it to him, and went to the back. Joan was washing a plastic tub that had contained the chicken salad for their daily special.

"Mom, Kyle's out front and asked me to dinner tonight. Could you watch Travis?"

Joan's face scrunched and she opened her mouth then shut it. "I forgot to tell you something."

"About what?"

"Before Travis and I left for the Children's Museum this morning, Jimmy's mother called and asked if Travis could stay all night after their play date. I said yes and packed his little suitcase."

"Mom! We've gone over this before, you need to check with me first." Sara realized how much Joan loved her grandson and the large role she played in his life. But still, Sara was his mother.

"I know, I'm sorry. I figured it would help him pass the time until Christmas."

"You're right about that." She had a free evening after all. Interesting timing. "All right but ask next time. You need to come say hello to Kyle."

Joan smiled and dried her hands. "I'd like that."

They walked to the front. Joan went around the end of the display cases directly to Kyle. She wrapped her arms around him in a solid hug and stepped back.

"Kyle Scott, it's so good to see you. Why in the world have you been a stranger since high school?" She beamed as she spoke. Kyle had always been one of Joan's favorites among Sara's high school friends.

"Hey, Mrs. Adams, good to see you too." He rubbed the stubble on his jaw, looking like the rock star he was. "I don't get back to Sugar Land much since my dad died. Mom moved to Brenham and Kate lives in Houston."

"How is your mother?" Joan said. Sara remembered they had spearheaded a giant bake sale in high school to raise funds for the band to go to the Rose Parade in Los Angeles.

"She's doing great. Coming down tomorrow for the concert, plus Kate's about to pop with twins. She's looking forward to being a grandmother."

"You don't have children?" Joan asked innocently.

"No, ma'am. Not married either. Although I hope to change that." Kyle smiled at Sara as he spoke, which didn't seem to be lost on Joan.

"I hope you do." She quickly hugged him a second time. "I'll go finish in the back. Hope to see you again, Kyle."

"Yes, ma'am. I'm moving back to Sugar Land, so I expect you will."

"Good for you." Joan hurried to the kitchen, rubbing Sara's back as she walked past her.

"She'll watch Travis?" he said.

"He's staying all night with his friend. I'm a free woman tonight." Sara didn't know why she said that. It made her sound like something she wasn't. A mother was a mother 24/7.

"Great. I'll pick you up at seven-thirty."

"I can meet you there."

"No way. I always pick up my dates." He grinned and saluted with two fingers. "See you later, Mrs. McClain."

~~*

Sara loved to take baths but rarely had time for one. With Travis at Jimmy's, she gave herself thirty minutes to relax in a bubble bath with a glass of white wine—the ultimate luxury for a busy single mom. Once she was out and ready to get dressed, she opened her closet door. Always the issue was the outfit to wear when going out with a man, although this wasn't a real date so she had no concern about impressing Kyle. Of course that didn't mean she should look like a tomboy.

After a few minutes of threading through her clothes she went with her standby winter outfit—black slacks, a cream turtleneck sweater, a short red jacket with black ribbon and beads along the collar and down the front. She realized it didn't look very youthful but she was thirty-four with a child and much responsibility.

Kyle arrived right on time and they were soon walking into Perry's, his hand on her back. They were the last to appear. Kyle made quick work of introducing her to Melody and George. Melody then introduced Kyle to the mayor and his wife and the Town Center manager who had booked Topped Off for the Christmas concert.

His wife smiled sweetly when Kyle shook her hand, must be a fan. Melody made sure that Sara set next to her and Kyle next to the mayor.

Sara's feminine intuition was on full alert responding to Melody's probing questions.

"I hear you and Kyle were friends in high school, you know, good friends." Melody drank from a wine glass. Sara needed a glass herself to get through this dinner and the questions.

The waiter appeared and poured a glass of chardonnay from a bottle iced in a bucket behind her. That interruption gave her a moment to think of a proper answer to Melody's question.

"So . . . you guys were friends, huh?" Melody prodded again.

"We were friends in the band for three years. Had lots of fun together." Hopefully that would satisfy her curiosity.

"Hmm," Melody tilted her head to one side and considered Sara. "I'll lay money on a poker table that the two of you were more than simple friends. I bet you dated, a lot. I'm right, huh?"

Oh crap. She was good. How could she know they'd dated for three years? Kyle must have said something to her. Or, maybe she was fishing. But what difference did it make? The rest of the band, meaning John and Jim, knew they'd dated.

"We did date."

"I'm not trying to be nosy," Melody said with a sly grin. "Why didn't you go with Kyle and the others when they left here to get famous?"

Sara smiled as warmly as she could. "I'm not groupie material."

Thankfully they were interrupted and the conversation ended. Sara had a hunch Melody would try again. Why was she so interested in their history? Then the light snapped on—Melody had the hots for Kyle and was checking out any local competition. Which of course Sara was not, but Melody didn't know that. Sara would be honest if she asked questions again. That's the right thing to do because Kyle would remain in her past and not tread into her future.

The food was excellent as usual at Perry's and the conversation flowed easily. Sara did have a quick minute to mention to the mayor about the café's application for a liquor license and he agreed her plan for a happy hour made sense for the pre-dinner crowd. Kyle sat across from her and seemed to stay in tune with the various conversations she had. He smiled at her and tried to engage her in conversation but was continually interrupted. Sara merely chuckled at that, everyone loved a rock star.

Kyle suggested Crème Brule for dessert and everyone applauded his good taste. Sara observed him as he conversed effortlessly with everyone around him. His confidence and self-assuredness had grown since high school. He'd called himself a band nerd back then but he was a nice guy who didn't want to separate himself and his talent from everyone else in the school band. Yep, he'd waited until after high school to do that.

Actually she was proud of Kyle. She hoped she'd have an opportunity to tell him that.

~~*

Kyle and Sara were the last ones from the dinner group to have their car returned by the valet. Kyle hadn't had enough time alone with Sara so he had a plan as he drove away from Perry's.

"Do you need to get right home?" he asked.

"No, not really since Travis is staying over at Jimmy's house." Just what he wanted to hear.

"Okay, let's have a nightcap." He drove around the block and slid into the valet lane in front of the Marriott.

"Geez, we could have walked," Sara commented.

"I know," he said as he opened his door. "Don't want to forget where I park my vehicle. It's a rental."

They walked into the hotel and Kyle pointed to the cocktail lounge on their right.

"What's your pleasure, Madame, the bar or a table?"

She pointed to the bar. "Oh, let's go crazy and sit at the bar." Then she leaned against him. "Unless you're worried about being recognized."

"Very funny. This trip has been a breeze. No paparazzi like LA." He guided her to two stools at one end and helped her get settled.

"That must be hard, dealing with the press," Sara said.

He plopped on the stool next to her, tried to get the bartender's attention. "It's a pain in the ass. They're relentless. I know they're trying to make a living but—"

Finally the bartender appeared. "What can I get you folks?" She then did a double take. "My God, you look just like Kyle Scott, the lead singer for Topped Off."

Kyle shrugged. "I know. I get that all the time."

Over the years, he'd found that if he didn't try to hide and acted nonchalant, he could get away with being a look-alike. Plus his trademark rocker persona included a cowboy hat and dark glasses and fans hardly recognized him without them. He glanced at Sara. "What would you like?"

"Mm . . . coffee with Bailey's."

Kyle held up two fingers. "Make that two." He turned on his stool so that his knees were facing Sara. Finally he was alone with her. He'd been looking forward to it all day. "What time did you start work this morning?"

"Six a.m.—it's early but things have to get started for our opening at seven."

He blew out a breath. "That is early. I'll have to get used to it myself."

She leaned forward with her head close to his. "Once you're no longer the fancy rock singer, right?" She winked.

He raised a hand. "I know, there'll be lots of changes. Like no more chauffeured rides. Damn, I'll have to drive myself."

"Poor baby."

"It'll be easier than you think. The last five years I've kept a low profile when I'm not on stage. Thanks to the Internet I've kept up with my studies wherever we played." The coffee arrived and he took a sip. "In fact I'm kinda boring these days."

"In comparison to what?" She had the cutest look of disbelief on her face.

"Okay, I get it. You don't believe me. I can show

you the draft of my dissertation if that will help."

"No need for that. But I have a question. Why don't you have a bodyguard with you?"

"It's my disguise. If I had one, it would draw attention and I wouldn't be able to get away with denying being me." He'd lowered his voice and leaned close to Sara's ear so no one would hear. Her scent was wonderful, something floral. He couldn't help himself and brushed his lips against her neck. She stiffened immediately and he drew back casually. He ignored the kiss and her reaction. "Perfectly logical, don't you think?"

Her eyes narrowed briefly then she spoke. "Your disguise does seem to be working. Tell me about your college program. How does it work using the Internet?"

"Why are you asking?"

"I've been thinking about completing my business degree and doing it online might be the answer to my time issues."

"Good idea. It's sure as hell worked for me. I've logged in all over the world. Just need a decent Internet connection."

"I'm jealous of all your traveling. What's the favorite place you've visited?"

"Oh man, that's hard." He sipped his coffee as his attention moved over Sara's shoulder at a group of men crowded around a low table near a flat screen TV. They seemed excited about something. He concentrated on her question. "I'm thinking."

"Surely, it can't be that hard. What's your favorite city?"

"That's what makes it so hard. I have several favorites . . . Rome, Dublin, Paris, Rio, and Hong Kong. Each for a different reason."

"Wow, just wow. Now I'm really jealous."

"Where in the world would you like to go? I'll take you. We'll have a blast." The second the words were out of his mouth, Kyle knew he'd said the wrong thing. He could see Sara retreat from him.

"Kyle, I don't think so. I'm accustomed to planning my own vacations."

"I didn't mean I'd plan your vacation." God, how could he get out of this screw-up?

"Whatever. Why do you like Rome?"

At least she'd thrown him a bone. "Good question. I guess because of the history, there are ruins everywhere. But it's really something else. It's like there's something in the air . . . something that pulls you in and you feel so damned good about your life."

Sara blinked. "Very perceptive. Did you go to the Vatican?"

"We went to St. Peter's Basilica which was awesome and freaking huge. I never did see the Pope. Honestly, the history was overwhelming. I wish I'd gone to college as a history major. I also liked the Trevi Fountain and the Spanish Steps. That is until we were recognized and fans nearly caused a riot."

"I guess that happens a lot, other than in Sugar Land."

For some odd reason, Kyle found that funny and laughed out loud. "You are so right. I told you no bodyguards is the key."

"Your secret is safe with me." She turned her head at a burst of loud laughter from the group of men a few feet away. "They're having a good time."

"Uh-oh, nimrod over there saw you turn around and is coming over."

Kyle watched the man walk toward them, his gait not quite a straight line. He stopped between their stools.

"Sorry to interrupt. But we," the man pointed a finger back at the table. "We have a bet . . . you're a rock guy who sings for some lame band, Top something. Tell me you are and I win fifty bucks."

"Sorry, I'm a teacher, not a rock guy." Kyle had no intention of revealing his identity.

"Yeah, that's what they said you'd say. Going incognito." The man swayed a bit and shoved a piece of paper in front of Kyle. "Autograph this. Lucy over there thinks you're sexy."

Jesus, how many times had Kyle been faced with a drunk asshole like this guy. "Sorry, bloke. No autographs when I'm with my lady."

"Why not?" The man pushed a palm against Kyle's shoulder as he spoke again. "Come on, man, don't be an ass."

"You're the one acting like an ass, man. Shove off." Kyle glanced at Sara who looked like she was about to say something. He caught her gaze and shook his head.

"Hell no, it's a free country." The man's voice had risen. "You shove off. In fact, why don't you go to hell, too?"

That was enough. Kyle rose quickly and the man took a couple of steps backward. "Hey pal, I think you need to go back to your friends." Kyle stepped close to the man and their faces were inches apart. "Do you need an escort back to the table?"

Another man from the table hurried over. "Sorry, Bob's had too much to drink." He smiled weakly then grabbed Bob's arm and led him back to their group.

Kyle rubbed Sara's arm as be returned to the stool. "Sorry about that, happens every once in a while."

"But the bodyguards usually take care of it, right?"

"Yeah, they do." He knew this little event had been a negative experience for Sara—another reason why she wouldn't give him a chance. Well, he was determined to change that. "Would you like another coffee?"

"No, I better get home."

"Okay, let me get the check and we can go." Kyle was determined to show Sara that their lives could mesh together. He had total faith in himself that he'd find a way.

~~*

It didn't take long before they were driving to Sara's house. She was curious about something.

"Don't bands usually have a couple of buses for equipment when you're performing?"

"Good question. We have tons of equipment when we do tours. But for this gig we're renting local equipment but bringing our own guitars. It's not worth the hassle of getting stuff here since it's all stored in LA."

"How long will the show last?" Sara hoped she wouldn't be up all night keeping The Coffee Café open for the concertgoers.

"I bet it'll be close to two hours. We usually go over a bit." He glanced at her. "Why are you asking?"

"We decided to open during the show since we're right across from the plaza. Figured it might get us some new customers since we'll have hot drinks and it'll be cold outside."

"Good idea. I like the way you think."

Her heart jumped though a hoop. Kyle's complement pleased Sara. It's not that her mother never said anything positive but it was nice when someone objective approved of her ideas. She frowned—hopefully that didn't mean she had approval issues.

They road in silence until Kyle's SUV pulled in her driveway. He switched off the ignition and Sara placed her hand on the door handle.

"Thanks for inviting me to your dinner," she said, pushing on the door.

"Hold on." He jumped out, jogged around the vehicle to her side, and helped her exit.

"Thank you." Sara had hoped to get out by herself and avoid the good-night-at-the-door routine. She was now trapped. He followed her to the porch and she dug into her purse for her keys. After finding them she slid the house key into the dead bolt lock. She sighed and turned around to face Kyle.

He grinned at her and she could fully understand why fans all over the word screamed his name. The man was downright gorgeous.

"Thanks again for dinner and the coffee." She touched his forearm then drew back her hand. "I appreciate you thinking of me."

His face clouded for a moment. "Thinking of you? Sara, I want to spend all the time I can with you."

"What in the world for?" That didn't come out like she'd intended and surprise crossed Kyle's face. "What I mean is . . . we're both awfully busy and don't have much extra time."

"Isn't that life?" He stepped closer to her and took her hands in his. "Surely you know I've never forgotten about you. When I heard you got married, I got drunk and smashed a guitar."

"That doesn't sound like you." She couldn't imagine him getting so drunk he'd destroy a musical instrument.

"One and only time it's happened. Anyway, since I'm moving back to Sugar Land, I figure we can get to know each other again."

She pulled her hands from his. How could he think their lives had anything in common? "Kyle, it's truly been great seeing you after all these years. But our lives are so different now. Plus we've both changed since high school. Why waste our time?"

"How can you say that?" His brows furrowed together then he wrapped his arms around her and planted his mouth on hers. Sara was so surprised she didn't react, as she should have. Instead she sank into the kiss with rockets going off in her stomach. It had been a very long time since her last kiss from a man and in no way did it measure up to this one. Not by a long shot. He pressed closer and the kiss deepened.

She moaned in pure pleasure then realized she had her tongue in his mouth. Horrified at letting her guard down, she placed her hands on his chest and pushed.

"Kyle, we shouldn't be doing this."

His gaze slid from her mouth to her eyes while his sexy grin slowly appeared. "Believe me, that was not a waste of time." He squeezed her arms then backed away. "I better get going, busy day tomorrow. Good night, Sara." He turned and walked to the SUV. Within seconds, all she could see of it were the twin taillights disappearing down the street.

Once inside her house and after donning her pajamas, Sara couldn't settle down. She brewed a cup of chamomile tea and sat on the sofa near the Christmas tree. The house seemed empty without Travis. Lord, what will she do when he leaves home for good? Then she'll really be alone—that made her think of Kyle.

She had no doubt he was interested in rekindling their high school romance. Actually, it was flattering to her, but why? His interest made no sense to her. He'd been all over the world, always catered to like the rock star king he was, and had the pick of any woman he wanted. Why would he want to quit the band, move to Sugar Land, and hook up with her?

He must be going through some sort of personal crisis, although . . . he seemed stable. No, he probably wanted a change in scenery, a change of pace, or a change in his girlfriend. Once the newness wears off, he'll go right back to his rock star lifestyle.

Exactly, that's why she shouldn't get involved with him. He'd leave her eventually, just like Joe did. The manner of leaving didn't matter; it was the fact of leaving that counted.

She finished her tea and set the cup in the sink. After

one last look at the Christmas tree, she turned off the lights. If only she could turn off the feelings for Kyle that were starting to percolate in her heart.

The Concert

Five a.m. came early the next morning yet Sara made it to the café on time. The day before Christmas Eve was certain to be busy with shoppers and the evening with concertgoers seeking a warm beverage. Sara would work until the concert ended and then be off for two days—a luxury for a coffee shop manager.

Mid-morning they had a break in customers and Sara made herself and the crew iced coffees. Sipping her coffee, she leaned against the back counter by the register and watched the traffic on the street for a minute then turned to her left toward the plaza. The stage for the concert sat in front of the city hall steps and was filled with people and equipment. Shoppers mingled in front of it, no doubt hoping to catch a glimpse of Topped Off doing their sound check.

Sara wondered if Kyle was on the stage. It was too far for her to identify anyone's face. She noticed Melody make her way from the plaza and cross the street to the café. She entered and waved.

"Good morning, Sara," Melody said. "Nice to see you again."

"You, too. Can I get you something?" She wondered if Melody would start firing questions again.

"Sure can, I have a list." She handed Sara a piece of

paper with coffee drinks and names listed and a hundred dollar bill. "I've loads to do this morning. Could you bring the drinks over to the stage?" She turned and slipped out the door before Sara could even utter "thanks."

Well, at least she came to The Coffee Café for the order. Sara poked her head in the back. "Cathy, I need your help."

Cathy and Sara had the order done in twelve minutes and set in two cardboard trays each holding six cups. "Come on, Cathy, put on your jacket, you can help me add delivery service to our menu."

"You know, that's not a bad idea for Town Center office buildings," Cathy said.

"Hmm, I will think about that." They put on their coats and headed across the plaza carrying the coffees. Sara threaded through shoppers and workers looking for a familiar face. Finally, she saw George, the band's drummer."

"Hey, George," she yelled. He hurried over to her and Cathy. "Hi, good morning, I have coffee for y'all."

"Hey, Sara. Thanks for the coffee. Kyle bragged about how good yours is."

She handed him the cup with his name. "I hope you like it."

He turned to the stage and yelled, "Kyle, Sara's here."

Within a heartbeat, Kyle's head appeared from a crowd on the stage. He waved and hurried across it to the side closest to them. A few moments later he appeared next to Cathy and Sara as George walked away.

"Hey, good morning." He kissed Cathy on the cheek then Sara. Cathy blushed and Sara wondered what the hell he was up to.

"Good morning," she said in her most business-like voice. "We have your coffee order."

"And we're eternally grateful for that." He removed the tray from Cathy's hands and set it on the stage and did the same with Sara's. Melody appeared and began to hand out the cups to people on the stage.

"Okay, then," Sara said. "We need to get back to the café."

Kyle wrapped a hand around her arm. "Could you wait a minute? I need to talk to you."

"I'll cover for you," Cathy said with a sly smile and a wink at Kyle. She did a one-eighty turn and headed back to the café.

Sara rolled her eyes, had a bit of a peeve going on. Could Kyle charm everyone in his path?

"Sara, I do need to talk with you." Kyle now looked solemn.

"Guess that depends on the subject."

"Fair enough." He grabbed her hand and pulled her around to the side of the stage where they were secluded from the people on the plaza.

"All right, you have my attention," she said.

"I need a favor."

"What kind of favor?" She had no clue what he might want from her.

"It's about my mom." He rubbed his jaw. "She's coming for the concert and normally Kate would be with her but she's in the hospital. I was wondering if your mother would go to dinner with my mom."

"Sure, she'll enjoy that. But what's the big deal?"

"I just need mom occupied while I get ready for the show. You know how moms are and she'll want to hover and I need my space." He now ran his fingers through his hair. "To be honest, I have this ritual that—"

Sara raised a traffic-cop hand. "Enough. You don't need to go into detail." She wanted to giggle at his possible "ritual" but maintained her composure for Kyle's benefit. "Why don't they eat at the Marriott for convenience? Tell your mom to be at the Burning Pear at five-thirty. I'll make a reservation."

He leaned over and kissed her cheek. "You are an angel. Will I see you after the show? Maybe we could grab a late dinner."

"Hmm, I . . . I'm not sure that's a good idea."

"Why not?"

She didn't want to remind him before his show that any illusions he had of them ever being together were false. Doing so seemed awfully rude. "Let's play it by ear and see how it goes."

He narrowed his eyes and studied her. "Okay, I'll see you later. Thanks for helping with my mom." He stroked a finger down her cheek before bolting up the steps to the stage.

Damn. Why was Kyle Scott so infuriating? The high school boyfriend had grown into a sexy man who always said the right thing. She sighed and headed back to the café. Maybe she should give him a chance. His kissing sure had improved.

~~*

Kyle and the band waited inside the main doors of Sugar Land's City Hall with a couple of handlers. As he jumped up and down to release nervous energy, he watched the mayor talking to the crowd. Jumping was the last step in his pre-show ritual that he completed before going on stage. This gig was different from the usual tour gigs, as they weren't going on stage in the dark, hard to do on an outdoor city plaza surrounded by streetlights.

Kyle could see that the lights in The Coffee Café were on so that meant Sara was close by. He hoped she'd take a few minutes to watch the show. Knowing she was so close nearly had him doing a handstand. However, he'd be a fool not to realize she was acting standoffish towards him. She had her life organized around her son and her work and apparently didn't want to upset that balance.

No problem. Kyle's lips curved. He knew he had to take it slow with her and that was okay. He had tons of patience. He was not a man to give up—easily or in any other manner—when the end result encompassed the rest of his life and Sara. He'd play it slow and easy. After all, getting what he wanted was his special talent.

One of the handlers opened the doors and yelled, "Show time." The clock above the doors pointed to seven o'clock on the dot.

Kyle and the Topped Off band members fist-bumped each other and ran through the doors, down the steps, and up the metal steps to the stage. Kyle, Jim, and John quickly slung on their guitars and plugged them in while George sat behind the drums. Wearing his signature black cowboy hat and dark glasses, Kyle yelled, "One-two-three." Portable lights around the stage came on at the first strumming of a guitar chord. Sugar Land's Christmas concert had begun.

~~*

Close to nine o'clock, Sara and Cathy turned down the lights in the café and stepped outside to hear the end of the Topped Off show. They'd had a steady stream of customers for almost three hours but now it had slowed and they were closing for the night. Travis had actually helped cleaning tables in the café before declaring he was pooped. Joan had taken him home an hour ago after her dinner with Kyle's mother.

Sara gave Cathy a one-arm hug as they leaned against the building. "Thanks for helping me tonight. We couldn't have stayed open without you."

"My pleasure," Cathy said. "I think it's the first time we've opened at night in the five years I've worked for you."

"It's the only time." Sara laughed.

"Seems like Kyle being around has had an impact on you." Cathy looked straight ahead as she spoke but Sara knew she was curious as hell.

"Nah, it's the holidays." Sara wondered if Kyle could have an influence on her. The crowd screamed his name as he ended a song with a flourish on his guitar. Yeah, he could influence her to stay away from rock stars. She had no desire to deal with his adoring fans or his lifestyle of always being aware of who was around him and the dreaded paparazzi. No, thank you. Mom to Travis and manager of The Coffee Café had her life full and just about perfect, regardless of any feelings for Kyle that might be brewing.

That being settled in her mind, she relaxed and listened.

"Thank you, Sugar Land, home of my heart." Kyle sounded revved up, excited, he'd taken off his sunglasses. "This last song got us a very special Grammy. Hope you like it."

The band launched into *Sara's Song* and it had a new meaning for Sara. She sighed, he'd written the song for her. That was cool even though she hadn't known all these years.

"We were so very young, I left town in one direction, you left in the other . . ." Kyle sang with his eyes closed.

Sara's attention transferred from the band to the audience. People were clapping with their hands over their heads. Several couples were dancing in the street. She sighed again and enjoyed, it really was a nice song.

"Thank you, Sugar Land. Y'all sing with us." The band slid into *Jingle Bells* to close out the show. The thunderous sound of the crowd singing along was inspiring. Sugar Land loved Christmas.

~~*

Kyle and the rest of the band ran off the stage and back into city hall. They intended to stay there for a few minutes while the crowd thinned. Then they'd make their way back to the Marriott for a nightcap and something to eat at the bar. Melody had gone ahead with Kyle's mother to get her back to her room before the crowd dispersed.

Finally, the plaza was clear enough for their safety and they walked to the Marriott without being stopped by fans. The group went directly to the bar for drinks and food—on tour the concert promoter supplied this. But this was a special gig without the usual accouterments, which was just fine with Kyle. All he needed was a beer and a decent hamburger, both on his own dime.

He slowed as he entered the lounge. Melody sat at the long bar with Sara and her employee, um, Cathy. Melody noticed them and waved everyone over.

She rose, hugged each of the band members, and stood with them around her. "Excellent, my friends. You guys are the best. You've earned a long holiday."

Kyle rolled his eyes and stepped to the bar and the waiting bartender. "How about a round of Shiner Bock for my friends and baskets of chips and queso?"

The bartender nodded. "Yes sir, coming right up."

Kyle moved around George and Jim to the end stool next to Sara. "Okay if I join you?" He placed his cowboy hat on the counter.

"Of course," Sara said with a shy smile. "Great show, by the way. I've never seen the plaza so packed."

"It was fun, a good crowd." The bartender served the beers and Kyle took a long pull. "Love Texas beer."

"When will you be going back home, to LA, I mean," Sara asked.

"LA isn't home anymore. I'm selling my house. Didn't I tell you I'm buying a house in Sweetwater?" He glanced at Melody then back at Sara. "In fact, I'm gonna learn how to play golf. I hear it's relaxing if you don't get too serious."

"No, you did not tell me you were buying a house here." Sara said, surprise painting her face. "Why?"

"Huh? Why are you asking? I told you I'm retiring from touring and plan on teaching music."

"Do you have a job already?" Damn, why was she grilling him?

Kyle slugged down the rest of his beer and wiggled the bottle at the bartender. "No, I don't have a job yet. But I don't think that will be an issue for me. I have a good resume." He ignored the rest of the band talking with Cathy and Melody and a couple of fans to concentrate on Sara.

"You sound so conceited." She turned away from him toward Cathy and sipped wine.

"What the hell does that mean?" He was not accustomed to anyone calling him conceited. He was . . . well, he was confident of his chances at landing a teaching job. He had the perfect background—Ph.D. candidate and former rock star—that should appeal to any university in Houston with a decent music program. Of course, in the back of his mind he worried that his rock star background would mean nothing to a music program that leaned toward classical training.

Sara turned back to him. "Some of us have to do things the hard way—some of us don't get special treatment."

"Special treatment?" he said, peeved as well. "I'm not—"

She raised a hand. "Kyle, I'm tired and that translates to irritable. I don't want to say something I'll regret later." She jumped off the stool and picked up her purse, touching her friend's shoulder. "Cathy, I'm heading home, are you staying or leaving?"

Cathy agreed to leave as well and like a true gentleman, George offered to walk them to their cars. Kyle watched the trio walk across the street. For George it was actually an excuse for a smoke but Kyle would never tell.

He grabbed the menu off the bar. Might was well order that hamburger.

Once the order was placed, he grabbed his beer and twirled on his stool so he had a view of the band and Melody. They were in a spirited discussion with some other folks, which suited him just fine. He didn't feel all that social right then. Sara's comment had put him in a funk. Jesus, was he conceited? The thought of that gave him the willies.

She didn't say things lightly so he planned to give her words some thought. Tomorrow he'd take his mom to breakfast then to the hospital to see Kate, go shopping, and finally go to Sara's house for a surprise visit. Hopefully, she'd be all rested and wouldn't throw him out.

Until then he had some serious thinking to do. He signaled for the bartender to make his burger a to-go order. Hanging out in a hotel bar wasn't conducive to what he needed to do.

Christmas Eve

Travis was beyond excited. They'd just finished his

favorite dinner of spaghetti and meatballs and he'd rushed to the tree to select the present he wanted to open. It was a family tradition that he could open one gift on Christmas Eve and Sara had given him a choice of three to select from.

"Mom, *this is hard*. I don't know which one to choose." He bounced on the chair next to the tree, surveying each of the gifts like a puppy sniffing a new squeaky toy.

"Take your time." Sara ruffled his hair and turned on a speaker hooked up to a MP3 player in the corner for some holiday music.

"What do you think, Nana?" He looked at Joan who was spending the night with them, another tradition.

She shrugged her shoulders. "Your decision, big guy. Maybe you should close your eyes and pick one."

"Sounds like a good idea," Sara said.

"Okay." He got down on the floor in front of the gifts and studied each one without touching it. He nodded and closed his eyes tightly. His hand reached out slowly and he waved it from right to left and back over the gifts a few times.

"Are you ready," Sara said, smiling at her mother.

"I'm ready." Travis lowered his hand to the gift on the left and quickly opened his eyes. "I chose a good one."

"You sure did, now open it." Joan leaned forward to get a good view.

Travis tore off the red ribbon and the wrapping paper to find what looked like a shirt box. "I wonder what this is? I bet it's a set of Legos."

"Hard to tell from the box." Sara commented, still grinning.

He removed the box lid and pushed aside red tissue paper. Travis's face sunk as he saw Spiderman pajamas. "I always pick the box with the pj's."

"Why don't you put them on before we have dessert?" Sara put a hand over her mouth to hide a giggle.

"Okay," he said as he pulled them from the box. Underneath rested a book and his face lit up. "Mom, you got me the Spiderman book I wanted, cool." He pulled it from the box and gathered it in his arms with his new pajamas. He went to Sara and hugged her. "Thanks, I'll be right back." The doorbell rang as he scurried to his room.

"Who could that be?" She went to the front door and opened it without checking the porch from the side window. And there stood Kyle carrying shopping bags.

Her hand went to her chest. "Kyle, this is a surprise."

"Merry Christmas, may I come in?"

What could she say? "Of course, come in, Merry Christmas. We were about to have dessert." Damn, she shouldn't have said that. But what difference did it make? Geez, she was arguing with herself. He followed her to the living room. "Mom, Kyle came for a visit."

Joan rose and opened her arms. "Merry Christmas, Kyle . . . the more the merrier. Would you like a glass of wine? I was just about to open a bottle." She made a face at Sara as she moved to the kitchen.

"Sure, only one, I may have to go back to the hospital." He looked at Sara and grinned that sexy grin.

"I brought something for Travis. I hope that's okay. I was practicing for my soon-to-be-born nephews."

"It's fine. We were about to have dessert. Do you like chocolate pie?" *[See EC on page 285]*

He deposited his bags by the Christmas tree. "I love chocolate pie. Don't you remember that time you made it for my birthday?"

"Vaguely." Sara remembered everything about that day but she wouldn't admit it to Kyle. She decided she did need a glass of wine after all. "What did you open, Mom?"

They ended up in the kitchen as Joan poured three glasses. "It's a pinot noir. Red wine always goes with chocolate."

"Sure." Sara rolled her eyes. "I'll cut the pie." While Kyle tasted the wine with her mother in the living room, she pulled out plates and a knife. Once the pie was served, she poured a glass of milk for Travis. In fact, *where was* Travis?

She found him on top of his bed, reading the Spiderman book with his new pj's on the floor.

"Travis McClain, what are you doing?"

He looked at her, his face blank. "Huh?"

"Pajamas, please." She pointed to the floor. "You have two minutes to get those on and come to the living room. We have a guest."

"Really?" He closed the book and Sara left his room confident he'd be running out soon.

She found Kyle and her mother sitting on the sofa and having a grand ole time.

"Guess what?" Joan said, her eyes bright with

humor. "Kyle came bearing gifts for all of us."

"What?" Sara stopped in front of them. "No gifts."

Joan waved her hand. "Stop being a fuddy-duddy. This is Christmas."

Kyle rose and took Sara's hand. "Please don't be mad. I was shopping for my family and added to the list. It was fun."

Sara was in a no-win situation and making a scene in her own home on Christmas Eve was just silly. "All right. Thank you for thinking of us."

"Mooooom, I'm ready for dessert." Travis came running into the living room and skidded to a stop when he saw Kyle. "Who are you?"

Sara patted his head. "This is a friend from a long time ago, when I was in high school. Travis, meet Kyle Scott."

Travis stuck out his hand, which pleased Sara immensely. Kyle shook it. "Nice to meet you, Travis."

"Same here, Mr. Scott. If you guys are friends, how come I never saw you before?"

"Uh, well . . ." Kyle's gaze slid to Sara with a "help me" look.

"He moved away after we graduated and now he's moved back to Sugar Land." She moved to the kitchen. "Let's eat our pie then Travis can open the gift Kyle brought."

Travis swiveled toward Kyle. "You brought me a present? Cool." He followed his mom and sat at the breakfast table where Sara had placed his milk and pie.

Within ten minutes they were all back in the living room as Travis was eager to open a second gift.

Kyle played Santa Claus and handed a gift to each of them. "Ladies first, Travis, your mom and grandmother open before you."

Sitting on the floor next to the Christmas tree, Travis nodded and hugged the gift on his lap.

"Mom, you go first," Sara said.

"Okay, I will," Joan said as she slipped the ribbon off a rectangular box. She tore the tape at each end of the wrapping paper and the back, and then removed the paper. She looked at Kyle. "Oh, my." The box had a well-known designer name across the top.

"Take the top off, Nana," Travis added.

Joan did and found a clutch wallet in the box. She examined it and smiled at Kyle. "Thank you so much. How did you know I need a new wallet?"

"Mom said you mentioned it at dinner," Kyle replied.

"That I did. Sara, now it's your turn." Joan pointed to the gift in Sara's hands.

"Okay." She still wasn't totally happy with Kyle bringing them all presents. It seemed too intimate, too familiar, too something. She opened a small red bag and pulled out a box. Uh-oh, this looked like jewelry. She had no choice but to open the box. Inside was a silver necklace with a small heart shaped pendant. The top edge of the pendant was covered with tiny diamonds. Her hand went to her throat. She had always wanted such a necklace. How thoughtful of Kyle.

Her gaze slid from the heart to Kyle. "This is beautiful. Thank you."

"I remember you always wanted one in high school.

I couldn't afford diamonds back then."

"Is it my turn yet?" Travis whined.

Sara giggled, glad for the interruption. "Yes it is. You may open your gift now."

"Finally." Travis tore off the Christmas paper and with round eyes stared at the box that had been revealed. "Look at this! Mom, Nana, look." He held the box for them to see.

"Wow, Ninja Legos. That's very nice. Travis, say thank you to Mr. Scott." Sara wondered how Kyle knew that Legos were a favorite toy for a seven year-old boy.

Travis jumped from the floor, went to Kyle, and hugged his legs. "Thanks, Mr. Scott. I love Legos."

Kyle ruffled his hair. "You are very welcome, Travis."

~~*

Sipping his glass of wine, Kyle sat by the Christmas tree as he observed the ritual of Joan reading *The Night Before Christmas* to Travis followed by the setting out of cookies and milk for Santa Claus. He watched Travis place the plate just so on the fireplace hearth and then run back to the kitchen for a Rudolph napkin. It was so damned cute.

Once everything was set for Santa, Sara declared it bedtime. Kyle knew he should leave but it was relaxing and, well, peaceful. He'd never been through the cookies-for-Santa routine himself, as an adult that is. One more thing he'd missed with his lifestyle and one more reason why it was time for a change.

Travis hugged his grandma then stopped by Kyle. "Mr. Scott, it's been nice to meet you." He stuck out his little hand and Kyle shook it.

"It's been my pleasure, Travis. Merry Christmas." Kyle wanted to wrap his arms around the little boy but held off.

"Maybe you can come eat with us tomorrow," Travis said as he turned to Sara. "My Mom is a good cook."

"Thanks, sweetie, but you're still going to bed." She put her arm over his shoulder and guided him down the hall while Travis waved an arm over his head.

"What a cute kid," Kyle commented. So sad that Travis didn't have a father. Hopefully he could change that.

"He's a good kid, too," Joan said. "Your mom told me that you're moving back to Sugar Land from Los Angeles."

"Yes, ma'am, that's the plan. The band is taking a break for a while and I hope to get a teaching job in Houston." Fingers crossed he'd be able to land a position. He'd do his best and wasn't above throwing around a little charm.

"Goodness, that's quite a change from traveling around the world."

"Can't travel forever, in fact—" Kyle's phone buzzed and he pulled it from the pocket of his flannel shirt. "Sorry, need to get this." The name of his brother-in-law, Bill, flashed on the phone's screen. Kyle rose and walked into the kitchen.

"Hey, Bill, what's up?"

"We're going into delivery. Get your ass down here!"

"What? Delivery?" The phone was dead. Bill had

clicked off.

Sara came back and must have heard him. "Did you just say delivery? Has Kate gone to the delivery room?"

"Is that where you go?" Kyle threaded his fingers through his hair. "I need to go. I gotta get to the hospital." He rubbed his all of a sudden sweaty hands on his jeans. His big sister was having a baby—scratch that, two babies.

"What hospital is she at?" Joan asked.

"Uh . . . hmm, the one in the Houston Medical Center." His mind had gone blank.

Joan caught Sara's attention. "Sara, drive with him, please. He'll probably end up in Dallas without some help."

"I think that's a good idea," Sara said. "I'll get my jacket."

"Thanks, I'll warm up the car. Merry Christmas, Mrs. Adams." He waved at Joan as he let himself out the front door.

Thirty minutes later they crossed a bridge over Fannin Street from the parking garage to Methodist Hospital. Thankfully, once he'd gotten off the freeway he knew where he was going even though he couldn't remember the name of Kate's hospital. Sara was a trooper, too. Didn't call him a dumb ass once.

The lobby was quiet, not many visitors on this night. They walked side by side to the main elevators and were soon exiting onto the maternity floor.

After letting the volunteer at the reception desk know they were there, he sat next to Sara on a standard issue sofa; his heart pounding like it was his first show at

Madison Square Garden. Jesus, why was he so uptight? Bill was the father, not him. But Kate was his big sister and he'd missed so much the last few years with all the touring.

"That's almost over," he muttered.

"What did you say?" Sara said.

"Nothing." He settled back and stretched out, crossing his legs at the ankle. "I was just thinking about how much I've missed with my family the last few years. Once Dad died, I hardly ever visited."

"I guess you were busy."

"Yeah, but that's not an excuse." He thought about all the time he'd spent at the house in LA, both working and goofing off. Both could have been accomplished in Sugar Land. "Damn, I'm really slow. I should have moved back here years ago."

She patted his leg and shot him a lopsided grin. "Why, when you were so eager to leave?"

Leave it to Sara to point out the obvious. He sat straighter and moved around on the sofa so he was facing her. "Let me explain something to you." His voice was low. "In high school, you were the leader and I was the follower." She opened her mouth and he shook his head. "Hear me out."

She nodded. "Sorry."

"I didn't do much but go to school, play my music, and date you. When you really look at it, it was a narrow world." Kyle looked at the blue patterned carpet for several moments then continued. "In the middle of our senior year, I had an epiphany. I figured if the band could just get out of Sugar Land, we'd have a chance to get noticed, maybe even get a record deal. It was a pipe dream at the time. I had huge arguments with my folks about not going to college."

"You never told me that."

"And let you know my plans? Never." He figured he might as well tell her everything. "I knew you were set on going to Texas A&M and I didn't want to do anything to change your mind. I decided to piss you off."

"Piss me off? What the hell does that mean?"

"I figured I could irritate you enough that you wouldn't think about leaving with me after graduation." Kyle nearly laughed. How ridiculous was the logic of an eighteen year-old male?

"That's right. I said I wasn't cut out to be a rock band groupie." Sara's eyes were clouded. "You played me."

He nodded. "Uh-huh. I did what I thought was best for you. I missed you like crazy after we left."

~~*

Sara clenched her jaw at Kyle's revelation. She'd had no idea. Taking a deep calming breath, she exhaled slowly. The man was a piece of work.

"What the hell is wrong with you?" she asked.

"Huh? What do you mean?" Kyle seemed surprised at her question.

"What I mean is you had no business deciding what was right for me back then. You weren't any more mature than me." She rubbed both sides of her head with her hands. "God, I can't believe you did that."

He obviously hadn't expected her response. "I really am sorry. I thought I was doing the right thing, for both of us."

"Well, you were wrong."

"I understand that now." Kyle said, a familiar eager look flashed in his eyes. "I want to make up for everything. I want to start over."

Sara didn't know what to say. She needed a moment. She rose quickly. "I'll be right back."

"Okay, I'll be here," he said, lazily waving a hand.

She figured the restroom, a few stops away, would give her privacy. Once inside, she leaned her butt against the counter and chewed on her thumbnail. Was she ready to move past her love for Joe and open herself to the possibly of loving another man?

In her heart she knew Joe would be telling her to get on with her life—to go forth and kick some butt in the romance department. He'd lived his life full speed ahead. Maybe it was time for her do the same.

She'd wish for him to love again if the situation were reversed. She stood and turned around, looked at herself in the mirror. Yes, full speed ahead.

She was young, she was strong, and she vowed she wouldn't back away from a relationship with the right man. She washed and dried her hands and walked out.

She settled back on the couch, close to Kyle. "What did you say just before I left?"

He cocked his head. "I said I want us to start over."

Sara pointed a finger at his chest and then her own. "You mean, you and me starting again?"

"That's what I'm talking about. We're both single adults living in Sugar Land who have been known to have a certain attraction for each other. Why not fan that flame?" He laughed, must have been that awful cliché.

"You are so lame," she said. Was she willing to trust him and believe that he wouldn't leave at the first hint of a rock tour in the works? Was she truly willing to risk her heart one more time? Was she a fool? Nope. But it *was smart* to take it slow and discover if the adult Kyle personified the right man for her. "Okay. But I need to think about dating you first. Agreed?"

A man with his dark hair standing on end and wearing blue scrubs came running into the waiting room.

"Kyle, good you're here. You're an uncle. Where's your Mom?"

Kyle jumped from the sofa and shook the man's hand. "Congratulations. How's Kate?"

"Kate's fine, a little tired. Hang out for a bit and you can see my boys." He turned and ran down the hall.

"That was Bill, Kate's husband." He grinned that sexy grin. "I'm an uncle. Wow. I better find Mom." He pulled out his cell phone and moved to the window.

Sara watched Kyle as he talked. He had grown into a good-looking man who had his heart in the right place. She realized that now. It didn't matter what either of them had done or said in high school. What mattered was who they were today and would be tomorrow.

Kyle finished the call and retuned to the couch. "Mom's on her way up. She met someone in the cafeteria and was having a gab-fest, her words, not mine." He laughed and wrapped his arms around Sara. "You know, I'm glad you came with me."

"Me, too."

He kissed her the side of her head and pulled back,

meeting her gaze. "You know, I've never stopped loving you."

"You'll make me cry." His words touched her heart and spoke of a lost love probably on its path to being rekindled.

They sat silently on the sofa, side by side, Kyle's arm around Sara's shoulder. The bridge they had crossed wasn't lost on Sara. But the time wasn't right to ponder their future. The birth of twin boys on Christmas Eve spoke every word that needed to be said.

Within a couple of minutes, Kyle's mother rushed out of the elevator.

"Has Bill been back again?" she asked. "Hi Sara, thanks for coming with Kyle."

"Not yet," Kyle said.

"No problem," Sara said as she imagined how excited Mrs. Scott must be. It had to be awesome becoming a grandparent on Christmas Eve.

Sara watched Mrs. Scott walk to the reception desk and pace in front of it, the click of her heels measuring her steps. They passed the time in silence waiting for the new father to appear.

Finally, Bill strolled back to the waiting room and went directly to Mrs. Scott and hugged her.

"You're a grandma!"

She immediately had tears in her eyes.

"Can we see Kate now?" Kyle asked.

"Absolutely, we're ready." Bill said.

"I'll stay here," Sara said. "I think it should be family."

Kyle's eyebrows shot up in surprise then he nodded.

"Are you sure?"

"Yes, but I do have a question. What names did you give the twins?"

Bill beamed like a puppy eyeing his favorite dog treat. "What else?—Christopher and Nicolas."

She Said Yes

Sara was out of her element while Kyle was in his. This was her first visit to Las Vegas and she'd been twirling from one thing to another since they'd arrived two days ago at Caesar's Place Hotel and Casino. Topped Off would begin its last show, at least for the foreseeable future, in about five minutes and on New Year's Eve.

She had a special seat on the floor of The Coliseum venue inside Caesar's to the left side of the stage. Melody would join her once the concert started. The area was roped off with a nice table and a couple of comfortable chairs. It had an excellent view of the stage and was close to steps leading to it. A waiter had just poured her a glass of chardonnay and delivered an assortment of appetizers.

Sara imagined that the people around her wondered why she had such special treatment. Well, she wondered that too, and then she chuckled at herself. Being a good friend of the band's lead singer did have its advantages.

Five days ago she wouldn't have been so quick to laugh. But it had been a very good five days with Kyle. They enjoyed Christmas dinner together and took dessert to Bill and Kate in the hospital, toured Kyle's new mini-mansion on the Sweetwater Golf Course, and talked a lot about their lives during the last sixteen years.

Sara had just about decided she'd date him when he invited her to Las Vegas for Topped Off's end-of-the-year show. She figured that would seal the dating deal.

The house lights blinked and then darkened. She sipped the wine and popped a grilled shrimp in her mouth. This was exciting. She'd never had such a good seat for a rock concert.

The lights returned as the first guitar chord was played and a stick hit a drum skin. Melody slipped into the chair next to Sara and poured a glass of wine. She tapped it to Sara's glass and smiled.

Two hours later the wine was gone, the appetizers eaten, and Sara and Melody had bonded over their appreciation for the music of Topped Off. The lights dimmed again and a spotlight centered on Kyle.

"Hey, y'all, thanks again for coming out tonight. I have something to tell you. Y'all will be the first to know." The audience responded with a loud murmur followed by applause.

Sara leaned around in her chair, curious as to crowd's reaction.

George performed a drum roll and Kyle once again spoke. "This is the deal, the band is taking a break—" Loud boo's drowned out his next words.

Kyle waited for the noise to die down. "Hear me out. The band is taking a break from touring, at least for a year. That's it . . . okay?" The crowd roared, the true meaning of his words obviously not sinking in.

The warning for the fans didn't surprise Sara.

They'd discussed the break from touring more than once. The announcement over, the band began to play the melody for *Sara's Song*. *[See EC on page 287]*

"This song was written for my high school girlfriend. I've asked her out recently and I'm still waiting for an answer. Maybe you can convince her to go on a date with me." Kyle's words caught her off guard. "Sara, would you please join me on stage."

Her eyes swiveled to Melody who shrugged then rose. "Come on, I'll escort you to the stage. That's the least I can do for Kyle."

Sara allowed Melody to pull her to the steps and guide her as they marched to the stage. Melody then halted and motioned for Sara to walk alone to the middle and Kyle. She swallowed hard, the stage seemed huge and the lights were crazy. She hesitated.

"Come on, Sara, get over here," Kyle said. "Scratch that, I'll bring you myself." He started to walk toward her, guitar slung across his back. The audience clapped, no doubt enjoying this personal moment on public display.

That was all she needed to begin walking. She was not a woman who needed to be rescued on a concert stage in Las Vegas. She met him halfway and threw her arms around his waist. The crowd once again roared. They walked to center stage and a stagehand set a tall stool by the microphone stand.

Holding her hand, Kyle helped Sara sit on the stool. She had no idea what he might be up to but that was secondary to her nerves. She'd never been on such a large stage with thousands of screaming fans. Her concern right then was to stay on the stool.

Kyle took his usual position at the microphone.

"All right, all right. This is Sara." He leaned over and kissed the top of her head. "We were quite the thing back in high school in Sugar Land, Texas. And now, I've asked her out but she hasn't answered." He pointed to the audience. "What should she say?"

The crowd roared and Sara was pretty sure the fans were shouting "yes." Actually, it was exciting. She had a brief glimpse of the power of being on stage and controlling a mass of screaming followers.

"Is 'yes' your answer, Sara?" His gaze held her eyes for a moment then he grinned that sexy grin.

She nodded and the audience began to clap.

Kyle leaned over and whispered, "I love you" in her ear.

"Let's have that date after this show," Sara said, her voice low and sultry. She figured they might as well get going since they'd already spent sixteen years apart. Plus, Las Vegas was a playground for all sorts of things. Hmm . . .

* * * * *

Thank You!

Thank you for reading **Christmas in Sugar Land**. I sincerely hope you enjoyed the characters and their lives in my first collection of Christmas themed romance stories. My goal is to publish a new collection each year featuring new fictional residents of Sugar Land. If you know someone who you think would be an inspiration for a great character or who has a romantic story of their own, please contact me via my website at www.karensueburns.com. Like any writer, I'm always looking for and thinking about story and character ideas.

Also, if you enjoyed **Christmas in Sugar Land**, please take the time to leave a review of this collection via the vendor where the book was purchased. Reader reviews are one of the best ways for writers to gain new readers and gain feedback about their work. Thank you if you do post a review. Also be sure to let me know via my website or on Facebook. I'd love to hear from you!

In addition to contemporary romance, I write mystery/suspense:

2012 – **In Hot Pursuit** – When $25 million is stolen from her employer, a relationship-phobic accountant hunts for the thief alongside a handsome bachelor who donated the money. As they rush from Houston to Las Vegas, to Rome, they close in on the thief and stumble across an unexpected attraction to each other.

2013 – *The Liberation of Mr. Delaney* (Texas Ghost Stories, Book 1) – When a heartbroken bookstore manager meets a charming ghost, sparks fly and the elimination of a decades old curse becomes crucial to their futures. Along the way a murder is solved, a family is reborn, and love once again proves its far-reaching power.

2014 – *Crazy for Home* (Texas Ghost Stories, Book 2) – After leaving a promising career in Los Angeles, a thirty-something woman returns to Brenham, Texas to manage her family's B&B with the help of her younger sister. A resident ghost and a hunky boarder teach her the true meaning of home and family and love.

Planned for 2015 – *The Dancing Maiden* (Texas Ghost Stories, Book 3) and *Death by Merlot* (Coyote Cove Series, Book 1)

Note: All of my heroines love to cook as I do. Please visit my website for some of our favorite recipes – www.karensueburns.com

Enriched Content

All of the Enriched Content is arranged by story and in order within the story in which it occurs. Below are the Enriched Content titles by story:

The Christmas Star

The Story of Highlands Elementary
Homemade Christmas Tree Decorations
Christmas Eve Cheese-Potato Soup
The Night Before Christmas

A Holiday Surprise

Jogging in Sugar Land
Scrumptious Shrimp Scampi
Avery's Famous Cheese Bread
DePelchin Children's Center

Christmas by Candlelight

Why Gracie Was Special
Jingle Paws
Love Drops
Houston Humane Society

Rockin' Jingle Bells

Sugar Land's Special Coffee
Inspiration for The Coffee Cafe
Sara's Double Chocolate Pie
Sara's Song

The Christmas Star

The Story of Highlands Elementary

I chose Highlands Elementary as the grade school for Emma and Kasey to attend as it has a special place in my heart. Both my daughter and my oldest grandson attended the school. I still remember the parent-teacher conferences and attending school events. The first graders were so cute lining up in the hall on their way to the cafeteria. The school now has a fantastic outdoor play area for its students.

~Back to story, page 11~

Homemade Christmas Tree Decorations

Meg and Emma loved making homemade ornaments for their Christmas tree. These are some of their suggestions for you.

Cookie Cutters

Using inexpensive plastic or metal cookie cutters purchased from your favorite discount store, cut out the shape of the cutter on scrapbooking paper. Hot glue the paper to one side. Once cooled, poke a hole in the paper near the desired edge and run a length of coordinating ribbon or yarn through it to hang the ornament on the tree.

Unused Household Items

Look around your house for small items that match your tree's theme. For instance, a toy themed tree might involve small cars, colored blocks, or small superhero figurines. Gather your related items and spread them out on a table to arrange in the perfect order. You can hang them individually or as garland using jute twine. Use your imagination for themes.

Love To Travel

Gather together Styrofoam balls, small pins, hot glue gun, travel maps and/or pictures of favorite places, ribbon, small beads, and other ornamental items. Cut the map or photo into the same sized leaf shapes. Starting at the bottom of the ball, pin or glue leaf pieces to the ball one round at a time. Be sure to offset the rounds of leaves. At the top, pin or glue a piece of ribbon for a tree hanger. Attach beads or other decorative items to cover the top of the ball using pins or glue.

Painted Dough

Mix together 1 cup all-purpose flour, I/2 cup salt, and add 1/2 cup water. Knead the dough until it's smooth, add more flour if it's not stiff. Roll out the dough on a flat surface to desired thickness. Cut out ornaments using cookie cutters or by hand. Place on a cookie sheet layered in parchment paper. Push a straw or toothpick through the top of each ornament to make a hole for hanging. Bake at 225 degrees for one hour.

Allow the ornaments to cool completely. Decorate with acrylic paint and when dry, coat with a clear protective coating. Add a hanger, ribbon, or yarn through the hole and hang. Glitter or food coloring may be added to the dough before cutting. Note that the dough is toxic and should not be eaten.

The Old Standby

Back in the day, the go-to tree decoration was garland made from 1) strips of construction paper glued at the ends to form a chain, and 2) popcorn threaded together with a needle and a long thread. Today, the homemade garland is still easy using 1) scrapbooking paper with a hot glue gun, and 2) dried fruit such as oranges, apples, lemons and fishing wire. The materials have changed a bit but the end result is much the same and kid-friendly.

~Back to story, page 41~

Christmas Eve Cheese-Potato Soup

Serves: 6

Ingredients

1 & 1/2 sticks butter
3/4 cup flour
6 cups milk
2 cups sharp cheddar cheese, grated
3/4 to 1 pound Velveeta cheese, cubed
1 teaspoon each - garlic salt, celery salt, onion salt - or, to taste
Dash of white pepper
1 large carrot grated
2 pounds white potatoes, diced, cooked until soft

Cooking Instructions

In a large pot, melt the butter then add the flour, mix until smooth. Slowly add the milk over medium heat, stirring constantly. Once the soup is starting to thicken, add all of the cheese and stir until well blended. Add all of the seasonings and stir thoroughly. Add the potatoes and the carrot and mix until heated. If desired, you can top each serving with sliced green onions, crumbled bacon, chopped tomatoes and/or a dollop of sour cream.

Serve with a lettuce salad and garlic bread. (Just like Meg!)

~Back to story, page 45~

The Night Before Christmas
By Clement Clarke or Henry Livingston

'Twas the night before Christmas, when all through the house
Not a creature was stirring, not even a mouse;
The stockings were hung by the chimney with care,
In hopes that St. Nicholas soon would be there;
The children were nestled all snug in their beds,
While visions of sugar-plums danced in their heads;
And mamma in her 'kerchief, and I in my cap,
Had just settled down for a long winter's nap,
When out on the lawn there arose such a clatter,
I sprang from the bed to see what was the matter.

Away to the window I flew like a flash,
Tore open the shutters and threw up the sash.
The moon on the breast of the new-fallen snow
Gave the lustre of mid-day to objects below,
When, what to my wondering eyes should appear,
But a miniature sleigh, and eight tiny reindeer,
With a little old driver, so lively and quick,
I knew in a moment it must be St. Nick.

More rapid than eagles his coursers they came,
And he whistled, and shouted, and called them by name;

"Now, Dasher! now, Dancer! now, Prancer and Vixen!
On, Comet! on Cupid! on, Donder and Blitzen!
To the top of the porch! to the top of the wall!
Now dash away! dash away! dash away all!"
As dry leaves that before the wild hurricane fly,
When they meet with an obstacle, mount to the sky,
So up to the house-top the coursers they flew,
With the sleigh full of toys, and St. Nicholas too.
And then, in a twinkling, I heard on the roof
The prancing and pawing of each little hoof.

As I drew in my head, and was turning around,
Down the chimney St. Nicholas came with a bound.
He was dressed all in fur, from his head to his foot,
And his clothes were all tarnished with ashes and soot;
A bundle of toys he had flung on his back,
And he looked like a peddler just opening his pack.
His eyes -- how they twinkled! his dimples how merry!
His cheeks were like roses, his nose like a cherry!
His droll little mouth was drawn up like a bow,
And the beard of his chin was as white as the snow;
The stump of a pipe he held tight in his teeth,
And the smoke it encircled his head like a wreath;
He had a broad face and a little round belly,
That shook, when he laughed like a bowlful of jelly.

He was chubby and plump, a right jolly old elf,
And I laughed when I saw him, in spite of myself;
A wink of his eye and a twist of his head,
Soon gave me to know I had nothing to dread;
He spoke not a word, but went straight to his work,

And filled all the stockings; then turned with a jerk,
And laying his finger aside of his nose,
And giving a nod, up the chimney he rose;
He sprang to his sleigh, to his team gave a whistle,
And away they all flew like the down of a thistle

But I heard him exclaim, ere he drove out of sight,
"Happy Christmas to all, and to all a good-night."

~Back to story, page 47~

A Holiday Surprise

Jogging in Sugar Land

Naturally Sugar Land has a slew of designed jogging trails. However, both Avery and Mark were more comfortable running in their neighborhoods. Why you ask? My guess is that they enjoyed walking out their front doors to run. Driving to find a trail simply wouldn't do. When it comes to exercise, they lean toward keeping it simple. Although, Mark does enjoy lifting weights at the local fitness center. And he's looking forward to trying out a bicycle since his knee if giving him problems.

Sugar Land has many beautiful streets that are conducive to running. Of course for the long distance runner, the trails are probably the best option. Avery would definitely enjoy running along the street pictured below. And she reminds you to be safe while you run.

~Back to story, page 63~

Scrumptious Shrimp Scampi

Serves: 4

<u>Ingredients</u>

8 ounces linguine or angel hair pasta
1 pound large (16-20 count) shrimp, shelled and de-veined
2 tablespoons olive oil
2-3 tablespoons salted butter
4 cloves garlic, chopped
1 good pinch red pepper flakes (optional)
1/4 cup white wine
1/4 cup lemon juice, about one medium lemon
Salt and fresh pepper to taste
1 teaspoon lemon zest
2 tablespoons parsley, chopped

<u>Directions</u>

Start cooking the pasta according to the package directions. Heat a sauté pan on high heat then reduce to medium high heat. Swirl the butter and olive oil into the pan. Once the butter foams, stir in the garlic, and red pepper flakes. Sauté the garlic quickly, less than a minute, then add the shrimp. Add the wine and stir to coat the shrimp with the sauce of butter, oil, and wine.

Arrange the shrimp so they are in an even layer in the pan. Increase the heat to high and cook the sauce for no more than two to three minutes. Quickly turn the shrimp over to the other side, cook for no more than another minute. Remove the pan from the heat. Sprinkle the shrimp with parsley, lemon zest, lemon juice, salt and black pepper, and toss to combine.

Pour the sauce and shrimp over the drained pasta and add your favorite parmesan cheese.

~Back to story, page 80~

Avery's Famous Cheese Bread

<u>Ingredients</u>

1 head garlic, excess skins removed
Olive oil
Salt
1 loaf French, Italian, or Sourdough bread, halved lengthwise
1 stick unsalted butter, softened
1 package Ranch Dressing mix
1 cup shredded mozzarella cheese, or more if you love cheese
1/2 cup grated parmesan cheese

<u>Directions</u>

Preheat oven to 400°F.

Cut the top off the garlic head to reveal cloves. Place cut bulb in the center of a piece of aluminum foil and drizzle with olive oil and salt. Bring edges of foil together to encapsulate the garlic. Place in the oven and cook for 30 minutes or until garlic cloves are very soft. Allow garlic to cool before squeezing out the roasted cloves into a bowl.

Add to the bowl the softened butter and half of the Ranch Dressing mix and thoroughly mix together. Spread the butter mixture onto the halves of bread then sprinkle evenly with the parmesan and mozzarella cheeses.

Place the two halves on a baking sheet. Bake at 375 degrees for 15-20 minutes or until golden and crispy. Remove from oven and slice into 2 inch thick pieces.

~Back to story, page 111~

DePelchin Children's Center

Mark Burke did his research for adoption agencies in the Houston-metro area. He concluded DePelchin Children's Center had just the right approach that would work for he and Avery. From their website he easily learned about the children in need of adoption. See below.

Children of all ages, ethnicities and backgrounds need loving adoptive families, specifically:

- Children 2-17 years old
- Sibling groups

- Members of an ethnic minority group
- Children facing physical, mental or emotional challenges because of past abuse or neglect

Mark made a phone call and met with an adoption counselor to obtain additional information.

If you are interested in adoption, please consider DePelchin.

Depelchin Children's Center

Main Campus:
4950 Memorial Drive Houston, Texas 77007
Houston: (713) 730-2335
Toll Free Outside of Houston: (888) 730-2335
www.delpechin.org

~Back to story, page 130~

Christmas by Candlelight

Why Gracie Was Special

I wrote "Christmas by Candlelight" in anticipation of my own personal search for Gracie. Actually, the dog I hoped to adopt after retiring was the inspiration for the story. In writing the story, the human characters came after the dog.

I retired from my day job at the beginning of 2014. In addition to being able to write full-time and see my grandchildren more, I had told myself that I would adopt a dog once I'd be at home all day. It had been fifteen years since I'd had a dog so I was really looking forward to it. I knew I wanted a female less than fifteen pounds so she'd fit through the doggy door to my back yard.

I Googled "small dog rescue in Sugar Land" and away I went. I found my Gracie, a Chihuahua mix with soulful brown eyes, through Bandade Animal Rescue (www.bandade.org) and had to wait three weeks before she could come home due to final shots and spaying.

The day she arrived was just like a six-month-old baby coming home. I was nervous: Would she like me? Would she like her food? Could I housetrain her? Did I buy the right toys for her? Would she be happy at my house? Would the "real" Gracie be close to the "fictional" Gracie?

Obviously, she was just as happy being in a forever home as I was in adopting her. She had the best personality—affectionate towards me, gutsy, and so playful. I lost her after three short months due to a freak accident. I was heartbroken. Losing Gracie was awful. It's taken months for me to be able to talk about her without tears. RIP my sweet Gracie. I miss you.

~Back to story, page 139~

Jingle Paws
(Bacon-Cheese Dog Biscuits)

<u>Ingredients</u>

2 cups rolled oats
1/2 cup unbleached flour
2 teaspoons baking powder
1/2 cup natural cheddar cheese, finely grated
2 tablespoons parmesan or romano cheese, freshly grated
2 pieces bacon, cooked and crumbled
2 tablespoons canola oil
1/4 cup water

<u>Directions</u>

Preheat the oven to 325°F.

Combine oats, flour, and baking powder in a mixing bowl. Add cheeses and bacon, and stir until well mixed. Make a well in the flour, and add canola oil. Mix by hand or with a mixer until crumbly. Add the water all at once and mix until dough forms, and the ingredients are combined.

Turn the dough out onto a slightly floured surface and gently knead until smooth and soft. Spoon out the dough in pieces and roll into 1-inch balls.

Place the balls on a parchment-lined cookie sheet and press down with a fork. Bake 12–15 minutes until dry and firm to the touch. Turn the oven off and leave the biscuits in another 20–30 minutes. Remove from the oven, cool on a baking rack, and store the biscuits in a plastic container.

Makes 30 dog biscuits

~Back to story, page 157~

Love Drops
(Shortbread-Pecan People Cookies)

Ingredients

2 sticks salted butter, softened
3/4 cup Imperial confectioners' sugar
2 cups sifted all-purpose flour
1 teaspoon good quality vanilla
1 cup pecans, finely chopped

Directions

Preheat the oven to 325ºF.

Beat butter until fluffy and gradually add confectioners' sugar, flour, and vanilla. Mix well and blend in pecans.

Shape dough into 1-inch balls. Place on ungreased cookie sheets about an inch apart. Bake for 25 minutes or until pale golden-brown.

Roll cookies in additional confectioners' sugar while still warm. Roll in sugar again. Cool.

Makes 4 dozen cookies

~Back to story, page 167~

Houston Humane Society

After I lost Gracie, I couldn't imagine myself with another dog. How could any dog top my sweet Gracie? Well, life does have a way of getting on and going forward. I debated with myself about waiting months to adopt again or to get right back to it.

One Saturday I had intended to go shopping at Whole Foods in Sugar Land at the corner of Highway 6 and the Southwest Freeway. Instead of turning into the parking lot, I turned the corner and headed north on the freeway and eventually exited south on the Beltway. Yep, I was headed to the Houston Human Society. I had researched their dogs online but wasn't sure if I was ready to check them out in person. Guess I was.

Anyway, as I drove I worked on names, just in case I found The Dog. I decided on Sally for a female and Dexter for a male. I didn't put a lot of thought into the name as I'd done with Gracie. I had the thought in the back of my mind that it wasn't wise to go too deep this time in selecting a name. I had made of list of dogs at the shelter, primarily female with a couple of males. I knew I wouldn't consider dogs that looked like Gracie.

I was nervous looking for a new dog. I prayed I wouldn't cry explaining why I wanted a dog. I took a deep breath and walked in the door. The Houston Humane Society has a wonderful facility and I was at ease the minute I entered. I submitted the application I'd already completed and immediately began a search for the dogs on my list.

Although I had wanted another female, the dog I focused on was a little white male with funny front legs. With a volunteer we took him to a grassy play area. He was so excited to be free and ignored me completely. Yep, I found my dog. We went through the adoption process in record time and were soon headed home. He cried as we drove and I prayed he'd soon become comfortable with me.

Dogs are adaptable creatures and by evening, Dexter was on his way to being content in my home. He is a very sweet dog, loyal, and an excellent companion. It took him a while to realize the dog toys are for playing and that the whole back yard is his. He is now king of his castle. He and Gracie would have been great friends.

Houston Humane Society
4700 Almeda Road
Houston, TX 77053
(713) 433-6421
http://www.houstonhumane.org

Note: The original name for Jake's dog was Ernie, short for Ernestine. After adopting Dexter, I decided to change the name and make the dog a male. This story will always be a favorite of mine because of the dogs. I'm sure all the pet owners will understand.

~Back to story, page 194~

Rockin' Jingle Bells

Sugar Land's Special Coffee

Stir together in a coffee mug:
1 tablespoon chocolate syrup
2 tablespoons half-and-half
1/4 teaspoon ground cinnamon
1 teaspoon granulated sugar or 1 packet substitute, to taste

Heat in microwave for fifteen seconds
Add one cup of strong coffee
Stir and enjoy!!

For Iced Coffee:
Pour mixture into your favorite "blending" appliance
Add 4 ice cubes and set on blend
Pour into a tall glass, additional ice cubes may be added if desired

For Adult Beverage:
Add to the hot or iced coffee your favorite alcohol additive
Sara suggests: vanilla vodka, Irish cream liquor, and almond-flavored liquor

~Back to story, page 204~

Inspiration for The Coffee Café

The space in Sugar Land's Town Center that I used for Joan and Sara's imaginary venue, The Coffee Café, was determined strictly based on location. I wanted the space to have a good view of the Marriott Hotel and the plaza in front of the Sugar Land City Hall. Obviously, the location is real and has a business that is not a coffee shop.

And of course, there is a personal connection. A prior resident of the space was an Italian eatery. I took my daughter and my oldest grandson to lunch there for his second birthday. His was such a big boy that day and ordered spaghetti and meat sauce. I'll never forget him digging into the bowl with his hands and the sauce spread across his face like clown's makeup. He was so cute. Still is by the way!

I also wanted The Coffee Café to be a place I would personally enjoy frequenting. I love the idea of fantastic specialty coffee served alongside daily menu specials for breakfast and lunch that are both healthy and tasty. Believe me, I would be a regular at such a café.

This picture shows the fictional location of The Coffee Café relative to the plaza. On the day it was taken workers were starting to string twinkly lights on the trees.

~Back to story, page 212~

Sara's Double Chocolate Pie

<u>Pie Crust</u>

Mix 1-1/4 cups of chocolate wafer cookie crumbs with 3 tablespoons Imperial granulated sugar and 5 tablespoons of melted unsalted butter. Once the mixture is well combined, with the back of a spoon, press evenly on the bottom and sides of a nine-inch pie plate. Bake at 350 degrees for 5 to 10 minutes, time is based on how much crunch of the shell is desired.

<u>Pie Filling Ingredients</u>

1/3 cup all-purpose flour
3/4 cup Imperial granulated sugar
1/4 teaspoon salt

2 cups milk

3 egg yolks, slightly beaten

2 tablespoons butter

1 teaspoon vanilla

2 one-ounce squares unsweetened chocolate

Pie Filling Directions

In a medium saucepan, combine the sugar, flour, and salt; gradually stir in milk.

Cook and stir over medium heat until mixture is bubbly.

Once bubbly, cook and stir 2 minutes more.

Remove saucepan from heat.

Stir a small amount of hot mixture into yolks; immediately return to hot mixture.

Cook another 2 minutes, stirring constantly.

Remove from heat.

Add butter and vanilla.

Pour into the cooled cookie shell.

Place a sheet of wax paper over the filling and refrigerate for at least four hours.

Remove the wax paper and top with whipping cream and shaved chocolate.

Note: Sara will also add raspberries with the shaved chocolate when she's trying to be healthy.

~Back to story, page 246~

Sara's Song
Lyrics by Kyle Scott

We were so very young,
I left town in one direction,
You left in the other,
Sara opened her schoolbooks,
I played at diners and dives,
Books and bars are worlds apart.

This is Sara's song,
Oh, I miss you so,
It's been much too long,
Since I saw you go,
Oh Sara, where are you now?

We are older, wiser now,
Living life as best we can.
Just going day to day,
Playing too hard at living,
When all I need to do,
Is stop and listen for you.

This is Sara's song,
Oh, I miss you so,
It's been much too long,
Since I saw you go,
Oh Sara, where are you now?

I've been thinking a lot lately,
That it's time for a change.
I'm gonna pack my bags,

And hit the road again,
To find that place I'm longing for.

This is Sara's song,
Oh, I miss you so,
It's been much too long,
Since I saw you go,
Oh Sara, where are you now?

~Back to story, page 259~

Thank you and Happy Holidays !

NOTES

NOTES

www.ingramcontent.com/pod-product-compliance
Lightning Source LLC
Chambersburg PA
CBHW022141170626
46807CB00005B/2029